The Pension Plan

The Pension Plan

Josiah Vencel

The Pension Plan

ISBN: 978-0-578-23585-1

Fiction / Mystery

Mav Press
Bakersfield, CA
www.mavpress.com

To my own Gram. You were the best of us.

<< 1 >>

Marigold awoke as she had every morning for the past five years—despondent, widowed, empty—like a shriveled flower not yet dead. Her eyelids had betrayed her yet again, answering the call of a new day that held little worthy of anticipation or pleasure.

She rolled onto her side, away from the flickers of dawn's rose-red fingers tracing their way up her bedroom wall. That room once held the pillars of her life: a caring husband of fifty-seven years and a cross gathering dust high above her headboard. Now they were fading memories of another era, a time when life bubbled with happiness and relationships. All that Marigold cherished now was the daily hope of not waking, thereby ending the relentless heartache. Eight decades into life, she felt ready to leave it. But her religious impulse, or what remained of it, stung her conscience at the thought of usurping the Almighty's divine timing. Even the old woman, burdened by the great sorrows she carried, knew

1

she must wait to die. Resigned once more to that unhappy thought, she slid her weathered feet to the floor and began another wearisome day.

The irony of her current state was not lost on her as she shuffled mindlessly from one barren room to another each gray morning. In fact, it deepened her misery. Long-ago friends used to call her "Mary Canary" for her light heart and innate felicity. Since the passing of her husband and their only child shortly after, the canary had departed, leaving just the coal mine. Memories of better days, once a comfort after the untimely deaths, had since turned against her. That was why framed photos of smiling faces lay face down on shelves or buried deep within forgotten boxes in ignored closets.

Marigold's thin slippers moved slowly along a well-worn path on her linoleum floors. She no longer noticed the layers of dust gathered beyond the trodden passageway; she did not care to notice. Not much bothered Marigold anymore. Her breakfasts were bland, her coffee was cheap, and her curtains were drawn most of the day. After eating a paltry meal of toast and canned soup, she moved to her usual place of daily repose: a soft chair facing its twin, where her beloved partner used to sit contentedly. Nobody had burdened that recliner since his passing, and in her mind, nobody ever would. Like a moth to flame, however, she watched it every day, as if hoping he would suddenly materialize and the sadness would finally end. Every day was another disappointment.

As she sat rocking, the unfamiliar sounds of a car door shutting and steps on her front porch echoed into the dim room. Curious, she rose slowly and shuffled to a window, where she pulled back the edge of a curtain to peer outside. The strange sensation of new daylight stunned her weak eyes, but she made a sustained effort to see who might have come to visit. Nobody was there. *Of course not. How ridiculous a thought.*

Her unpracticed reasoning skills notwithstanding, Marigold was quite right. Nobody would visit her. Hardly a shadow—and rarely even her own—had darkened her doorstep in many months. The old widow was alone in every conceivable way. That realization, by far her most frequent companion, troubled her as she trod a less-familiar path back to her chair. Marigold had already begun to brood on lost friendships when a nearby thought interrupted the regret-filled world she was formulating—she knew she had heard a car door and steps.

Setting aside her ruminations, Marigold walked anxiously to the front door and squinted through the peephole. Again, nothing. Nobody. She stood looking a few more seconds and then placed her hand on the cool handle, which creaked from disuse as she turned it clockwise. The ancient door clicked and slowly opened. A calm breeze rolled down the hillside and kissed Marigold's pale, forgotten face. She instinctively inhaled. The breath enlivened her momentarily, and she performed the act a second time. Again, life! Peace seemed to float on the air. The rising rays of sun, heretofore an intruder upon her subterranean existence, held her gaze like a cherished lover returning from a lengthy journey. In these delicate moments, Marigold recognized something distant, yet dear, in the recesses of her memory, though she had no words for it. Was this experience what she used to know as living? As beauty? It beckoned to her. Unthinking, she loosed her grip on the doorknob and stepped into the morning.

Then, as unexpectedly as it had come, the moment passed. She stood upon her threshold, between two worlds—one full of darkness, the other of light—and wondered what to do next. For the first time in years, Marigold felt uncomfortable returning to shadow. She asked herself if, perhaps, she remained in that place long enough, might she breathe life once more? The thought brought a moment of happiness to her frail frame and weary heart. Marigold imbibed a last breath and receded into her house, feeling more than thinking.

What had just happened? Something felt different: something deep and wordless, something unfamiliar and yet intimately familiar, something rich and divine. She paused in the middle of the living room and gave utterance to the feeling that stirred below the layers of darkness within.

"I want to live."

In that instant, her chest began to tingle. The sensation moved to her arms and then to her legs. The feeling turned to fire, as if her heart began pumping acid through her veins. Pain coursed through her body like a flood, sweeping away all sentience and replacing it with guttural cries. She writhed in anguish as her organs failed one by one, culminating in a final breath, a final beat, a long-awaited demise.

The canary, reborn, was dead.

« 2 »

The trouble with socialism is that eventually you run out of other people's money," the old woman began. "I read a book about it."

Owen stood on the other side of the room and rolled his eyes. He moved to leave but, checking himself, repositioned his body against the wall and sighed.

"Okay, Gram, today's your day, so I will entertain the subject. But just this once. What's your beef with socialism?"

"Well, I suppose it might work in theory," she began. "But there has to be an endless supply of money to give to people who want it. And who doesn't want free money?"

"I wouldn't mind a little extra," the young man replied, feeling his thin wallet. "Seriously, if this is your case against socialism, you're not winning."

Ruthie ignored the tease and wasted no time springing the trap she had set.

"That's the catch!" she blurted cheerfully. "Everyone wants *someone else's* money. They won't take it themselves, of course. But they won't ask questions if the government does it for them."

"Does what for them?"

"Take money from person A and give it to person B. That's where socialism fails. There must always be enough person A's to provide for person B's."

The lecture ended abruptly with the sound of Owen's head hitting the wall, following by snoring that filled the kitchen where Ruthie was knitting the corners of a pie crust.

"Alright, I'll stop boring you. I know economics isn't your thing."

"No, no, Gram, this is fascinating," he replied before placing his head against the wall again and closing his eyes. A grin crept across his face; he opened one eye. Standing in front of him with a spoonful of cherry filling was his grandma, who, at barely five feet tall, towered with life, love and opinions.

"Open up, sweetie." She slid a dollop of filling into his mouth. "A spoonful of sugar ..."

"Helps the medicine go down," Owen recited compliantly after swallowing.

Something solid caught in his throat, and he immediately realized the ruse. He squinted at her like a parent watching a wayward child caught in the act.

"Did you just feed me one of your meds again?"

Ruthie turned quietly and attended to her pie as he stared at her from across the room.

"Oh, dear, I believe I did. It's just that you've been stressed at the office lately, and I was worried about your health. Your father had high blood pressure. It's called the silent killer, you know."

"I *don't* have high blood pressure."

"Well, *now* you don't," she said matter-of-factly. "I just gave you some medicine for it."

"Gram, if today wasn't your birthday, I'd teach you a thing or two about respecting me as a man. Which reminds me, ..."

"Oh, you're not a man yet," she interrupted with a laugh. "You need a family to support and a yard to mow. Being responsible for someone else makes you a man. I read a ..."

"Let me guess. You read a book about it."

She nodded and smiled.

Owen realized the conversation was drifting in a direction he did not like. He walked across the kitchen and kissed her wrinkled forehead.

"I think you're wrong," he whispered, "but I love you anyway."

She rewarded his gracious response with another spoonful of cherries just as the doorbell rang.

"Huh, the guests aren't due for another twenty minutes," she said. "My hands are covered in flour. Would you let them in, please?"

Owen walked through her living room to the entryway. Several partygoers stood outside with presents and balloons. He opened the door and invited the strangers in.

"Oh my, look at him," an old woman said. "What a handsome young man. You must be Ruthie's grandson."

He tried to reply, but she kept talking as a train of guests streamed inside.

"It's been such a nice day," she continued. "I've never regretted moving to this town, not for a moment. And we've been here almost fifty years now. Is that right, Harold?" She

7

turned to her husband, who had promptly left her side. "Fifty years?" she called to him without waiting for an answer. "Yes, I believe that's right. Let's see, I started working after the children went to school. I was twenty-eight then." Her fingers moved as if typing on a ten-key pad, and then she looked up at Owen. "That's when I met your grandma. We worked together for nearly thirty years. Can you believe it—thirty years for one employer? That's when loyalty meant something."

Owen sensed another lecture coming. Did every old lady carry a soapbox with her?

"Excuse me," he said, stepping backward. "I'll let her know you've arrived."

Owen had little patience for people who used too many words to convey too few facts. He hurried away while a few more elderly guests helped themselves through the front door. In a short time, the living room could have been confused for social hour at a retirement home.

Owen arrived at the kitchen just as Ruthie emerged, arms open wide. The scent of baking pie followed her into the room.

"Welcome everyone!" she hollered above the ruckus. "You are all so ... early."

"We're old and have nothing better to do," replied the verbose lady who had cornered Owen. "Besides, it's not every day that you turn seventy-nine."

The gathering of partygoers, approaching a dozen people now, stopped talking and smiled at Ruthie, who blushed at the attention. Owen, standing like a wall flower, watched as she joined the group of gossipy women and their husbands. The young man was surrounded by guests whose average age was more than three times his own; he felt out of place.

"If it wasn't your birthday, Gram," he muttered under his breath.

Indeed, if it were not her birthday and if she were not his only living relative, he would be sitting in his apartment with a glass of wine in one hand and the *Los Angeles Times* in the other. As Ruthie got older, though, Owen knew he could not miss a moment; longevity did not run in his genes. Family pictures staring at him from around the room told his story of loss. His father had died of heart disease several years earlier. High blood pressure was partly to blame, which is why Owen did not really mind Ruthie slipping medicine into his food. His widowed mother succumbed to cancer shortly after, leaving Owen in the care of his grandma. As a widow herself, she sacrificed her time and treasure to help him through college. When he failed to secure a job for a few months after graduating, she was there to house and feed him. "Don't you worry, sweetheart," she would say when he worried about money, "I have enough to share."

Owen made his way around the milling guests to the fireplace mantle, where family photos stood in old frames, testaments to Ruthie's continued love for those who had left the world too soon. But one of the pictures was recent. It was of her holding up the local newspaper, wearing the widest smile Owen had seen on her face in years.

"I was so proud of you that day," he heard the familiar voice say. Owen turned to see Ruthie's happy eyes staring at the photo. "Not everyone gets to see her grandson's name on the front page of the paper."

"One day it would be nice to have the news written about *me* rather than me writing about *it*. Besides, it's not a very big paper. You can save a cat in a tree and get an above-the-fold placement."

"Now listen to me," she countered with a rising finger that foreshadowed a sermon. "You are a good reporter who asks good questions. That article is one of many you will write. Work hard and be patient. One day, people will buy a paper just to read what *you* have to say."

Owen shook his head. "If and when that happens, newspapers will be a thing of the past. At least ours will be. This town can barely support the one it has." He looked at the sea of gray heads around him. "In fact, I suspect most of its subscribers are in this room."

"That's a sign of the times," interjected a frail gentleman eavesdropping on their conversation. He wore a simple, black hat with "Army Veteran" embroidered on the front. It stood on his head too high and slightly off center, an asymmetry that immediately bothered Owen.

"When I was a kid," the old man continued, "we viewed our country as a city on a hill, the envy of the world. We learned that lesson in our schools and *even* our newspapers." He leaned back to look up at Owen. "They've lost their way, though," he whispered. "Now they're far too liberal." The man's eyes widened as he stared earnestly. "You're not a liberal, are you, son?"

Owen made no attempt to respond; he just smiled. The veteran shrugged his shoulders and turned around. "Far too liberal," he repeated, this time to himself.

Owen edged away from the group for the solace of a safe space, free of soapboxes. Although his job required him to write about competing viewpoints, he felt uncomfortable sorting through them in real life—a quality he certainly did not inherit from his parents. Before passing away, his father had been a successful union negotiator who relished conflict, and his mother was a high school teacher who felt at home in a picket line. Owen grew up in a liberal family with intelligent parents. In his mind, those two things were inseparable: intelligence and liberalism. He preferred the term *progressive*, however, because it better captured the essence of his political philosophy: progress toward true equality using whatever means necessary. That was the message he heard at dinnertime, in classrooms, in the media, and just about everywhere—except at Ruthie's house.

This was difficult for Owen to reconcile because his liberal-equals-intelligent formula did not fit his grandma. Her old-fashioned conservatism irritated him, as it did his parents when they were alive. But she was no mindless hack. His daily exposure to her kindness and wisdom over the preceding years forced him to entertain the possibility that not everyone on his political right was a knuckle-dragging imbecile. At least Ruthie was not. But Owen was not so sure about her party guests. The smarter ones had bee-lined to the few available seats in the living room while the rest waited for some to spontaneously appear. Owen went to the dining room and returned with a few more chairs.

"What a sweet man," crooned a well-dressed woman who donned a gallery of gold jewelry. "Is he single?"

The group giggled. Ruthie did not.

"Yes, he is. But the way you go through husbands, Doris, I don't think it would be wise to introduce you to my grandson."

This comment sent the room into fits of laughter. The old divorcee blushed terribly but recovered sufficiently to reply, "It was just a tease, you see. Nothing more than that. A tease."

The room quieted down, but Owen could tell the old cougar was disappointed. Ruthie walked to his side and gave a proper introduction to those who did not already know him. Many of the wrinkled faces smiled at his handsome youthfulness and inquisitive eyes. For years, Ruthie had indulged her friends with stories of his boyhood, parental loss, college years and failed relationships. The old ladies probably knew more about Owen than he knew about himself. Such is the way with grandparents.

"How's work?" asked someone. "You still a reporter?"

The crowd turned to hear Owen's answer.

"Yes, I'm a low-level beat reporter at the *Sunset Times*," he said with undisguised discontent. "I mainly talk to people in town and write things. Nothing very important."

"Oh, dear, have you ever been hurt?" asked a concerned-looking lady.

Owen eyed her incredulously. Repressing his sarcastic urge, he replied slowly, "No, ma'am. A beat reporter is someone who is assigned to cover a particular area of the community. My assignment is local business. Once in a while, I help the guy who covers politics."

As he described his work, several faces looked on in admiration, which made him even more uncomfortable.

"Don't be impressed. It's not a flashy job by any means. Some days I scramble for something to write about. Honestly, I thought graduating with a journalism degree would land me a gig at a big-city paper, but sometimes you just take what you can get."

The old folks nodded sympathetically, but Ruthie would not allow the conversation to end on that sour note. She told everyone about Owen's work at the college weekly, his internship at the *L.A. Times* and his recent success at getting an article published on the front page of the local paper. Although Owen and his smitten grandma did not have much in common, they did share one distinct quality: They blushed like schoolgirls.

"Now look what you've done, Ruth," said a guest attuned to Owen's plight. "The poor boy has turned red as a summer beet."

Owen waved off the embarrassment but promptly excused himself to the kitchen to, supposedly, retrieve a cherry pie. Safely out of sight, he took a few deep breaths. Having regained his normal coloring, he grabbed the pie and returned to the living room, where a serious discussion was underway among the women. Those in the group not paying attention to the conversation eyed the contents of Owen's hands. They left their chairs and shuffled toward it. Owen placed it on a table and, hoping to protect the dessert from oncoming traffic, stood in front of it. He used hand movements to get his grandma's attention, but she was too engrossed in conversation to notice. Owen tried in vain to keep the hungry visitors at bay. Finally, in desperation, he began singing "happy birthday" loudly. The crowd turned and joined in, as did the hungry herd.

Ruthie rose to her feet.

"I'd like to thank you all for coming to my birthday party. I turn seventy-nine today. In all honesty, I feel my age and not a day younger. My bones ache when I wake up, my knees are stiff, and I've forgotten most of your names."

Her listeners gasped.

"Ha!" she chuckled. "No, I still know your names. But getting older, I am reminded that life is short and precious." She turned to Owen. "The gals and I were just chatting about two former co-workers who passed away recently. One worked in my department and the other in the tax collector's office. I lunched with these two ladies every week. We'd catch up on family news and so on."

"What happened to them?" Owen inquired.

"We don't know exactly," volunteered someone. "They died a few weeks apart. Something sudden, I was told, but I don't have any details."

"How terribly sad," Ruthie said quietly, capturing the sentiment of the group. A long moment passed in silence. "I'm sorry, everyone. This is supposed to be a happy occasion." She turned to her guests and offered an encouraging smile. "But *we* have today, thankfully. So, let's eat, drink and be merry."

"Hear, hear!" several guests intoned in unison.

"For tomorrow we die," replied an elderly man in the corner who had not spoken a word since arriving. The crowd looked at him and collectively groaned. "The quotation goes, 'Let us eat, drink and be merry, *for tomorrow we die*,'" he insisted.

The old gentleman's comment cast another pall over the event. And yet, it would not be a true gathering of retirees without conversations about grandchildren, arthritis and impending death.

Ruthie resumed her speech: "As I was saying, it's time for pie and ice cream. Put in your dentures, everyone!"

The rest of the party proceeded festively. Ruthie remained in good spirits, surrounded by long-time friends and the grandchild she loved. He loved her, too, and was graced with a kiss on his cheek when the guests had departed.

"It's a pity we all don't see each other more often," she lamented as she peered out the window toward the street. "They are such a feisty crew."

Owen nodded. "Yeah, they seem nice. But I don't think I could hang out with them too often, especially the old lady who wanted to marry me. And that curmudgeon who expected to die tomorrow."

"Well, that's just how Ted is. He was a close friend of one of the ladies who passed away and is understandably shaken. Even when you are as old as I am, it is unsettling to hear that one of your peers has passed away. You begin to think it could happen to you, too."

The comment bothered Owen, for he could not imagine the world without Ruthie in it.

"Don't worry, Gram," he reassured. "You are only seventy-nine and have a lot of life ahead of you."

She smiled at him tenderly before turning away in thought. Owen slipped his arm around her shoulder.

"What's on your mind?" he asked.

"It's just that—I can't stop thinking about my two friends. They were only a year older than me, and both seemed in good health. One even had a long trip planned this summer. And dying weeks apart! It's odd, don't you think?"

Owen shrugged. "Nah, a pair of old people dying in a town full of them is far from headline news."

« 3 »

O wen sat in his office cubicle on Monday morning and stared at a blank computer screen. He hated this moment of the day more than any other because it meant a story must be researched and written before he could go home. He did not mind writing, of course. He was a writer by skill as well as by trade—and quite a gifted one. Like many reporters, Owen could look at a situation that appeared benign and see in it a spark of intrigue.

"There is a story behind every story," his favorite college professor used to tell him. "Your job as a journalist is to pull back the superficial layer of everyday events and expose to your reader their significance to the community."

"What if there is no significance?" Owen once asked. "What if the events are boring?"

"Then *you* decide what makes them newsworthy. Remember, newspaper subscriptions don't always renew themselves. You need to give people a reason to pick up the paper every day—a *hook* that makes them feel like they are getting their money's worth."

"I see," Owen replied thoughtfully. "So, if a daily paper costs a buck, and I give my two cents in the form of a hook, where do the other ninety-eight cents go? If it's to a cigar-smoking executive who earns ten times more than I do, then I'm switching majors." His teacher and classmates laughed, and Owen knew he had succeeded in making his point.

Challenging corporatism in support of the "little guy" was a skill Owen learned from his parents and professors alike. He put it to good use during his college internship at the *L.A. Times*, where he was assigned to research leads for the paper's political and community reporters. Every week, Owen would contact activist groups throughout the metropolis for examples of capitalistic oppression of the poor and notable acts of discrimination. These kinds of stories resonated with the paper's readership and, more importantly, accomplished the ultimate goal of modern journalism: to shape public opinion.

"Anyone can use words to tell a story, even an idiot," his professor liked to say. "But a journalist uses words to advance an agenda. Long after the facts in your article are forgotten by readers, the assumptions and emotions you infuse into your writing will stick in their subconscious minds. Do this often enough, and you will grow a populace that thinks like you do."

It was a beautiful philosophy of journalism, Owen believed. Sitting in his reporter's chair, typing words that would be read by thousands of people, he fancied himself an influencer of minds, a shaper of culture. With this power at his fingertips, he would do his part for social justice and the many other causes his generation loved to protest about. But unlike them, *he* would walk the talk. *He* would make a difference in the world. *He* would be a writer worthy of the title *journalist*.

The sound of an empty mug hitting his desk jarred Owen out of his utopia.

"Kid, get me some coffee and come to my office—stat," barked a voice above him.

Owen looked at the old cup in which his boss' bean juice had dried the night before. It was a reminder that he, as the youngest reporter at the *Sunset Times*, sat on the bottom rung of the newsroom latter. He carefully grabbed the unsanitary vessel, performed the requested duty and headed to the corner office.

"Daniels, we have an issue," the gruff voice began before stopping to point at a brown-stained corner of his desk. "Put it there."

Owen carefully set the coffee mug in front of the plump, middle-age man. Like a pig to his slop, he raised it to his face and imbibed breakfast. Al Thomas would be considered by most fair-minded people to be an unattractive human being, both physically and socially. His breath stunk, he lacked basic interpersonal skills, he excelled at rudeness, and he could only focus on one thing at a time. It was this last quality that made him a good editor-in-chief. When reading an article submitted by one of his writers, he could black out the world while evaluating the quality and propriety of every word on the page. Al was uncouth, to be sure, but he edited words with the deftness of a surgeon holding a scalpel. Owen believed this was the only plausible explanation for Al still having a job.

With his coffee fix momentarily satisfied, Al started again. "We have an issue at the politics desk. Edgar just called to say he needed time off to deal with family stuff. Something about his marriage and kids. I said no, of course, because we don't have anyone to fill in. But he insisted."

Owen saw immediately where this conversation was headed.

"How about Dave?" he suggested preemptively.

"No. I've got him on community life and sports."

"How about Ginny? She already discusses politics in her column. Last week, she admitted to having a crush on a city councilman whom she renamed Hunky Harry."

"I don't care about Ginny's love interests," Al shot back. "Then again," he murmured, descending into thought. Owen held his breath, hoping to dodge the approaching bullet. That hope ended when the editor shook his head. "No, that could be a liability. I don't want the paper being accused of bias any more than it already is."

He seemed satisfied with this logic and chugged more breakfast. Owen's countenance fell as he watched his unhurried days pass before his eyes.

"That leaves you, junior," the boss declared with as much of a smile as his pear-shaped face could muster. "Congratulations on your promotion to the world of politics. You'll manage fine."

"This is a promotion? Do I get a raise?"

Owen's expression lightened at the thought. He needed extra cash to pay off his school loans.

Al's jowls jiggled back and forth. "Eh, not quite. I meant 'promotion' in the metaphorical sense. You remember metaphors, right? It's just a figure of speech, not something you can take to the bank—literally!"

The unintended pun amused Al, but not Owen. The young man could abide all manner of stupidity, but he despised

20

sarcasm at his expense. He collected his thoughts and replied evenly, "Look, I'm going to do you a favor and agree to this promotion, as you call it. But let's be clear about one thing. If I do this for you, I'd like something in return."

The editor leaned forward and narrowed his gaze. "What did you have in mind?"

"I don't want to be tied to this office. I've got a lot to write about, and I'll be doing offsite interviews and traveling around town. I need my space. That means you need to trust me to get my work done, even if I'm not sitting at my desk."

Owen tried not to blink while his proposal hung in the air. Al considered the request for a long moment and did what he later referred to as his good deed for the month.

"Tell you what. I'll make you a deal. If you can get the work done—and it better be *good* work, mind you—if you can get it done and to me by deadline, you can have your freedom."

Owen resisted the urge to smile, but he let a modest grin creep across his otherwise poker face. The key to negotiating, he learned from his dad, was to state your offer as a foregone conclusion and then try not to screw it up by smiling.

"Don't make me regret it, kid. No one else is getting this sweetheart deal."

"No one else is covering two major beats without a raise! It seems to me that the *paper* is the one getting the deal."

"*I* will be the judge of that. Now get to work! The paper doesn't write itself."

In spite of his hourly wage effectively getting halved because of his double workload, Owen felt rather satisfied with the outcome of his exchange with Al. In truth, he relished the chance to build his resume and reputation in the community, because one day he would leave the uneventful town of

Sunset Hills and land a job at a large paper. Dues needed to be paid, though, and here was his opportunity to make a name for himself.

He sat in his office chair and again stared at a blank screen. "The paper doesn't write itself," he repeated mockingly.

"It sure would be nice if it did. Then again, I suppose we'd all be out of jobs."

Startled, Owen turned to see the editorial assistant, Darcie, standing next to his cubicle with a cart of mail. She was one of the few staffers younger than him, and her presence made him feel more important than he actually was, for even the bottom rung of a latter looks down at something. For all her endearing qualities—her simple-mindedness, innocence and esoteric interests—Owen could not fathom why she insisted on dressing for a funeral every day. She must have owned enough black clothes, piercings and makeup to fill a Halloween store. He suspected it was her deathly attire that earned her the task of processing the newspaper's obituaries.

Darcie handed him an envelope. "It's from your grandma," she said. "Don't you have a home address where she can send mail?"

Owen nodded as he reached for a letter opener. "It's probably a thank-you card. I helped her throw a birthday party this weekend."

Darcie's eyes widened with delight. "Really? I suppose there were old people there. I love talking to old people. They have such interesting stories. And they're good at putting life and death into perspective."

The unusual comment interrupted Owen's reading. He set down the card and gave his full attention to the pale, earnest face.

"Put what in perspective?"

"Everything. Their time is running out and they know it. So, they invest—well, the wise ones do—in things that matter, things that last. You can sometimes figure out what motivated them in life by reading their obituaries. In fact, on Fridays I eat lunch in the archives room and read obits from past years. It's fascinating. You should join me sometime."

She watched his eyes for a hint of interest.

"Uh, as fun as that sounds, I've got my hands full with some extra duties. Maybe another time."

"Oh, come on! Here, let me show you how fun it can be."

She reached for the weekend paper in her stack of mail and opened it directly to the obituaries page before Owen could object.

"Here's one. James McDowell, moved here from the East Coast in 1960 to marry Catherine and raise a family, will be missed by all at the Lodge, survived by his wife, three children and seven grandchildren." Darcie shrugged. "Kinda boring, if you ask me. Not enough existential meaning. Let's try another."

"No, really, you don't have to do that," Owen pleaded. He was ready to move on to topics that involved the living.

"Oh, here's a good one," she continued. "Samuel James—I love two first names, don't you?—Samuel grew up in the Sierra Nevada mountains on a goat farm. After high school, he joined the military to see the world. While stationed in Asia, he met his future wife, Anna, who was vacationing there with her family. They fell in love, but his tour of duty kept them apart. They corresponded for two years before he moved to Sunset Hills, California. He got a job at an auto repair shop, but he wanted something with more career stability to please Anna's parents. So, he got a job with the county's fleet service, married his sweetheart and lived happily ever after. Died at eighty, surrounded by loving friends and family."

"Happily ever after—really?"

Darcie grinned. "No, I added that part. But isn't the story beautiful? The distance, the sacrifice, the love—it's a real-life fairytale," she added dreamily.

Owen would never have pinned someone gothic as a hopeless romantic, yet there she was, savoring the same satisfaction one feels after finishing a Jane Austen novel.

A thorn stuck in his mind, though. But he could not name the irritation. What was it? The dead man's military service? *No.* Meeting his future wife in a foreign land? *No.* Moving to town? *No.* Owen hated the feeling of knowing something to which he could not put words. His brow furrowed pensively. Darcie took the hint.

"You look like you're really into this. Awesome. Let's have another! Marigold Canaday (aka Mary Canary), age eighty, wife and mother, no surviving relatives, civil servant, friend of strangers …"

"Stop!" Owen interrupted. "Say that again."

"Friend of strangers?"

"No, before that."

"Civil servant?"

"Yeah, that's it. Does it say where she worked?"

Darcie scanned the write-up while Owen waited expectantly.

"Here it is. Ms. Canaday worked a stint for the city and several years for the county before retiring." She looked up at Owen. "As far as obits go, this one is pretty bland. If you want a good one …"

"No, no, that's enough. Do you mind if I borrow that for

a while? And could you get me a few weeks' worth of these, please?"

Darcie handed him the paper, grinning from one pierced ear to the other. He thanked her, spun around in his chair and turned on his computer. He read and reread the obituaries she had found: two civil servants, two people dead, both at age eighty. Normally that would be a coincidence worth dismissing, but by including the pair Ruthie had known, there were four men and women who died at the same age, in the same town and just weeks apart. The thought tantalized Owen, less for the sake of the unfortunate retirees and more for what he stood to gain from the discovery—a potential story.

« 4 »

The basic task of a journalist is to discover the truth and to report it. This requires a considerable amount of independent research, including interviews with experts and eyewitnesses who provide quotes, context and, ideally, drama to the story. Journalists tell these stories through the written word; the good ones do it with literary flair. They put flesh on facts. They elicit feelings in their readers. But before their stories can be told, they must be approved by an editor, who stands like an executioner above his guillotine, able to grant life or end it.

As promising as Owen's idea seemed to him, a story about old people dying in a town full of them was as newsworthy as a dog crossing the street. He could imagine pitching the mundane idea to Al and being scorned out of his office with expletives, sarcasm or, most likely, a soul-crushing combination of both. Owen knew he could only scratch his journalistic itch by approaching the subject indirectly, so he set to work developing a pitch.

As a youth, Owen learned from his father how to read people. "In a negotiation, understanding personalities is invaluable," he once said, "because each person has varying degrees of emotion, motivation, even morals that affect their willingness to accept a deal."

"Do you know all about a person before you negotiate against him?" young Owen asked.

"First of all, I don't negotiate *against* someone. I negotiate *with* him or her to reach a deal we both can live with. Second, I usually don't know much about the person on the other side of the table. I do my research beforehand, of course, but most of the time I must draw conclusions before we start arguing about the deal."

"How do you do that?"

"Well, I have to be like Sherlock Holmes and read the person quickly: their appearance, mannerisms, word choice, ego and so on. I like to start by asking simple questions that give me clues. From there I have to reach the best conclusions I can in a short amount of time. Hopefully my guesses pay off in a deal that pleases the union members."

Owen considered his dad's answers. "It sounds like you both want to do a good job for someone else. The other guy wants to save money so he can please his boss, and you want to get more benefits for your members to keep them happy. I think it would also help if you knew who the *other* person was trying to please and how to keep *them* happy."

"Right you are, son. Right you are."

The memory of his dad's proud smile warmed him again, just as it had many years earlier.

Owen finished the outline of his pitch to Al, confident it would work. When he had rehearsed the conversation in his mind a few times, he took his notepad and walked to the corner office where he had been promoted an hour earlier. He knocked on the closed door.

"What?!"

"Mr. Thomas, I'd like to discuss a story idea with you."

"Fine, but make it quick."

Owen took a deep breath and entered. Al's eyes remained on his computer screen. His paw reached for his coffee mug, which, amazingly, had managed to be refilled without the help of a servant. Resisting the urge to comment on that phenomenon, Owen began his pitch.

"I've got two ideas for a politics series while Edgar is on leave. I think one is stronger than the other, but you'd be a better judge of that than me."

Having his vanity stroked, Al's attention left his screen and moved to Owen.

"The first is based on a press release we received last week," Owen said blandly. "The city council is considering changes to various zoning policies, starting with commercial land use."

The wrinkles on Al's forehead deepened before he smacked a pudgy hand against them. "Seriously? C'mon, you can do better than that."

"I agree. That was definitely the weaker of the two ideas." Having given the editor an easy kill, he restarted, this time with more energy. "The second option combines the public sector with human interest. If you think about our town from a citizen's perspective, it seems to run on its own. Potholes get filled. Elections are held. Restaurants stay up to code. But these things don't just happen. There's an army of city and county employees that show up for work every day, do their time and go home to their families. They are just like us.

Without their tireless work, Sunset Hills would grind to a halt."

Owen paused to let the significance of that statement sink in.

"I think public employees are the unsung heroes of our community. This town has been in existence for, what, a hundred and forty years? Have we ever honored those who work to make it a great place to live? Maybe it's time the newspaper recognized the civil servants of the past and present. They are the unseen force that keeps the lights on while we are busy with our lives." Owen took a step forward. "I really want to write this series. What do you say?"

Then he shut his mouth and waited, wiping any semblance of insecurity from his face. The young reporter's insides trembled as the editorial executioner weighed the merits of the pitch in silence. Finally, Al spoke.

"What your series has going for it is that everybody in this town knows at least one public employee. That ensures broad appeal. And, I don't think we've covered something like this before. On the other hand, there will be a segment of readers who complain about their taxes being spent on exorbitant public employee benefits."

Al paused again in thought. "The story idea is solid," he said, more to himself than Owen, "but I don't want the paper to be criticized for fanning flames that have singed other cities over this issue. The last thing I need is for the publisher to accuse me of bad judgment." With that, Al looked up and let the guillotine fall. "I think it would be a good series, but I see too big of a risk. I don't want to put a political spotlight on the government workers who subscribe to the paper."

Owen had expected pushback and was ready with a quick response.

"You're right about not wanting to call out public employees. That's why I wouldn't call them 'public employees.' I would always refer to them as 'public servants' or 'civil servants.' The emphasis is on *serving* the community, not taking advantage of it."

When rehearsing his pitch, Owen had only planned his words up to this point, expecting the bait to have been taken by now. So, when the editor leaned back and strummed his fingers on his round belly, Owen's palms began to sweat. In that anxious moment, he remembered what he had told his father years earlier about everybody having someone to please. Nervously, he began his impromptu closing argument.

"I realize you're concerned about catching heat from your boss because a small percentage of readers might not like public employees or think the paper is supporting them over taxpayers. But I think we can avoid that by ... by ..."

Owen's mind suddenly went blank. He searched for something, anything, to say.

"By ..."

He glanced around the office for inspiration. His eyes fell on a newspaper on Al's desk, and then the answer came on him.

"By involving readers. We can ask readers to nominate deserving public servants they know. They can be retired or current employees. That way, readers are more engaged, they are buying papers featuring people they know, and public servants feel respected. Everyone wins."

"One thing in life is certain," Al corrected. "Everyone does *not* win." He stared at Owen and squinted. "But the idea has promise. I think I can support it under the conditions you just stated."

Owen abandoned his poker face, which gave way to a broad smile of relief. He thanked the editor profusely and promised to bring all reader nominations to him for pre-approval. Al instructed him to not screw up the series and to get back to work. Owen closed the door and, feeling full of himself, skipped down the hall toward his desk. Darcie was waiting there, holding a box of newspapers. Her midnight hair was now pulled back into a bun, revealing even more ear and eyebrow piercings. It would have been obvious to any woman in the newsroom that she had tidied up her appearance in anticipation of seeing someone important. Not Owen. He was oblivious to her efforts as he continued to savor the satisfaction of outwitting Al. He slid into his chair, set down his notepad and spun around to see Darcie's wide eyes.

"I brought you the last four weeks of obituaries," she said hastily.

"That's great!" He lifted the box from her and set it beside him. "I'll let you know if I need anything else. Thanks, Darcie!"

The girl grinned and floated away. Owen failed to notice; he was just glad to have more obituaries to read. Delving into the papers, he quickly found three more county retiree death notices from the preceding month. To track his research, which had grown too extensive to remember, he created a spreadsheet listing the information most pertinent to his inquiry: decedent names, dates of birth and death, and contact information for nearest of kin. The list already contained seven people: two from his grandma, two from Darcie and three he just found. To his amateur investigative mind, that many retiree deaths within two months certainly seemed to be a trend.

He grabbed his notepad and went to the archives room, a

massive storehouse in the basement that housed original issues of the newspaper back to 1945. He found the current year's editions and began pulling them week by week. He sat on the cold, concrete floor surrounded by stacks of papers, one hand thumbing through pages in search of obituaries while the other recorded key information on his notepad. Reading thousands and thousands of words in pursuit of just a few required considerable time and focus. Yet Owen's interest in the subject goaded him forward with no worry about time. With each new name he recorded, his adrenaline surged, his curiosity piqued. *Why had no one noticed these deaths? They were hiding in plain sight.*

Three hours later, his stomach growled for sustenance and his body hurt from sitting on the unforgiving slab. He tried to stand, but his neck and back were horrifically sore from hunching over papers for so long. The rest of his joints were likewise too wooden to heed his will. *This is what being old must feel like*, he concluded, thinking of his grandma. He decided to deal with his stiffness all at once rather than an arm here, a leg there. He winced at the thought of the agony he was about to force on himself. He carefully unrolled his curled frame onto the hard floor, took a deep breath and stretched every sinew in his body like a cat waking from a nap. He grunted in anguish, the sound filling the cavernous cellar and echoing back to his tingling head. He exhaled and felt young again.

"What are you doing down there?" came a concerned voice from the corridor. "Are you okay?"

Owen did not even bother turning his head. "Just relaxing," he replied as he savored the final moments of euphoria dancing along his spinal cord. There he lay, splayed on the ground like a fallen star, facing a row of ceiling lights in a dimly lit basement, flanked by a year's worth of obituaries, and holding in his hand the names of forty-four retirees who died at precisely age eighty.

« 5 »

O wen returned to the newsroom believing that the pages of his notebook contained a story worth telling, although he had no idea how significant a story it actually was—one that would send shockwaves through California and even the nation. Had the subject matter not involved the deaths of so many people, he might have called a friend to brag about his good fortune in stumbling upon the significant find. Instead, he kept the news to himself until he decided how to play his hand.

Owen mused at how many people, including Darcie, had overlooked the pattern in these numerous deaths. But not Owen, whose mind could not help but trip over such oddities. Yet, the circumstances leading to his discovery aligned so orderly that, in a way, he viewed them as predestined. *It's a gift from Fate*, he told himself, for he refused to use the term "God," except for the occasional outburst when he stubbed his toe. He considered the notion of God as a holdover from unenlightened times. Even his political ideology, he believed, demanded that he hold tradition and religion in contempt, that he embrace atheism or at least the softer ground of agnosticism. But to his mind, being an atheist was more principled. It was an emphatic declaration that no supernatural being existed in the universe; it was all just matter, energy and a lot of dumb luck. And so, naturally, it was the will of blind Fate that he should uncover dozens of age-specific deaths involving retirees in his town. This knowledge, with all its terrible consequences, was his burden to bear—and possibly leverage to advance his career.

As he passed Al's office, he glanced inside and saw a constipated face looking back. The editor impatiently tapped on his watch as a not-so-subtle reminder that Owen owed him an article in a few hours. With a slight cringe, the reporter recalled his double duty and made a mental note that research excursions, as interesting as they were, must take a backseat to his primary task of cranking out content for the newspaper. He sat in his chair and began typing the headline for his series: "Public Servants of Sunset Hills: A Force for Good." It was simple, catchy and positive. He knew Al would like it.

Unfortunately, the hours he devoted to the morning's obituary project were time he should have spent interviewing someone for the kick-off article in the series. Because he lacked the time to conduct proper research, he decided to start with someone he knew well: his grandma. Ruthie had invested more than twenty years in public service with the county. Owen remembered enough stories about her life and career to piece together a respectable first draft. An hour later, he called her for help in filling a few timeline gaps. She loved the series idea and poured compliments on him for creating it.

"Didn't I say that things would turn around for you! And how splendid that *you* get to write them! But no pictures of me, okay? I've put on a few pounds since retiring."

"Not to worry, Gram, I only paint pictures using words."

They talked at length about what led her to government work, how her career blossomed and why she stayed with the county for so long. Listening to Ruthie reminisce gave Owen a great deal of insight into her heart and nature. She told him a story of when a new employee had joined her department and contracted a serious illness that hospitalized him, she donated a week's worth of vacation hours to the stranger so his family could be fed. Another story Owen liked—because he could relate to it—was when Ruthie stepped into another position when a few co-workers had been laid off. She juggled two jobs for months until her boss finally promoted her to the higher position. Even though county policy entitled her to extra pay for the extra work, she refused it because, in her words, "It was a small sacrifice for the greater good."

Having grown up in a cynical, modern world, Owen listened in awe as Ruthie recounted highlights of her career. She did not brag. In fact, she talked more about others than herself. Through her tales, a picture of the old woman's character became clearer in his mind. He struggled to find the best word to fully capture that rare, irresistibly endearing quality about her. The only one that came close was *wholesome*.

With the facts of the article gathered, Owen turned to the topic that had consumed his attention all morning.

"Gram, I was hoping you could tell me more about the two women who recently died. You mentioned them at the party. Do you remember?"

"Oh, sure. How could I forget? They were my lunch pals

for many years. Sweet ladies. We had a delightful time to-gether. It's such a shame they are gone." Her voice trailed off.

Owen knew the subject troubled her, so he determined to keep his questions brief.

"I had hoped you could tell me if they had anything special in common. For example, did they work in the same department?"

"No, different departments on different floors."

"How about management," he continued. "Were they supervisors?"

"No, one was a clerk like me."

"Were they union members?

"Just Betty."

"Did they share the same politics?"

"Well, sort of. One was a JFK Democrat, which by to-day's standards is quite conservative. The other lady was a Republican."

The JFK comparison unnerved Owen, who could not imagine the Camelot president as anything but a liberal icon. But now was not the time for political hairsplitting. What was the link between the deceased co-workers? Growing frustrated, he began shooting wildly in the dark.

"How about their friends? Their enemies? Career goals? Personalities? Did the women have anything in common besides a lunch table?"

"Owen, what's this about? These are strange questions."

He shook his head on the other end of the phone. "I don't know. I had thought that, maybe, there was a connection between their deaths. It is odd, don't you think, that they died at the same age?"

"That is a tad unusual." She paused. "Really, they did not

have much in common besides work. We all just enjoyed talking about our lives and kids and grandkids. You know how we old women are."

Owen could hear a smile in her voice. He thanked her for her time and promised to write a great article about her career. Before hanging up, Ruthie again lavished praise on her grandson and invited him over for dinner soon. He accepted immediately, because what underpaid bachelor living alone would not want a free, home-cooked meal?

He spent the rest of the afternoon typing, proofing and editing. Although his article would not earn him a Pulitzer, he thought it was quite good. More importantly, it would attract the attention of readers and hopefully increase engagement without offending an entire segment of the community. At least, those were the stated goals of Al, who read the write-up and forced an approving nod in Owen's direction.

Another workday had ended, but Owen's mind found no peace. He wanted a connection of any sort that would explain the deaths of so many people. The missing link troubled him on the drive home. And at dinner. And throughout the evening news. And as he climbed into bed. He was stumped, and he knew it.

"If I was an eighty-year-old in Sunset Hills, why would I die?" he asked his ceiling.

No answer. Closing his eyes, he hoped sleep would come quickly.

For some people, dreams reveal solutions to problems that plagued their minds during the conscious hours of the day. One might doze off fretting about a particular crisis, but by morning, the answer would be obvious. Not so with Owen. When he awoke at seven o'clock, he was in the same miserable state as when he had fallen asleep. He rubbed his face and stared at the ceiling. Still no answer.

"I need help," he mumbled sleepily.

Lacking sufficient facts to draw reasonable conclusions might not stop an editorialist from making sensational claims in an opinion column, but a reporter had a higher standard of proof to meet. As he rolled out of bed, Owen decided he needed to recruit help from law enforcement. The trouble was, he knew no police officers.

He shuffled to the bathroom and repeated groggily, "Need a cop ... need a cop," until the cold shower water jolted him out of stupor. As his blood flow increased, his thoughts regained their normal precision. He knew he needed to have a confidential conversation with a police officer, probably an investigator, who had access to information about deaths in Sunset Hills over the past year. At the same time, he did not want to draw attention to his own investigation because if the facts became public, he would lose his scoop. And for a media man, protecting a scoop was essential—particularly for someone who needed to land a big story that would be seen by big papers in big cities. That was his one-way ticket out of lackluster suburbia. But finding a source who would feed him information without demanding much in return would be a very tough sell, and Owen knew it.

The drive from his apartment to his downtown newsroom usually took fifteen minutes. Most days, he would listen to talk radio or, if he sought a respite from real life, a favorite band. Silence was rarely an option because being alone with his thoughts felt uncomfortable. But today was different. Owen turned off the radio when he entered his car. For the first time in a long while, he had something intriguing to kick around in his mind. Certain questions needed answers: What other connection was he not seeing between the untimely deaths? Were they actually untimely? If so, what caused them? When did they begin? Why? Too many questions. Too few answers.

Lost in thought, Owen stopped at a red light near downtown, home to several banks, law offices, medical clinics and government agencies. The *Sunset Times'* building stood a block ahead, across the street from City Hall and the county's massive administrative campus. It was rumored that the newspaper's founder constructed the formidable brick building opposite these two epicenters of political power to remind the town's elected leaders that they would be watched and held accountable. Owen, like other reporters at the paper, found satisfaction in his workplace's symbolism. But, sitting at the stop light, he knew he would not obtain answers to his questions within that familiar edifice. They were more likely to be found down the street behind a badge and a gun.

« 6 »

Owen pulled into the police station's parking lot and realized that he was extremely unprepared. Having not
planned this detour in advance, he lacked his notebook and,
more importantly, a clear reason to even be there. He did,
however, have a knack for quick thinking, like the time he
talked his way out of a speeding ticket by asking the cute
officer for her phone number. Or the time he convinced a
restaurant manager to give him free meals for a week as part
of a "trendsetter marketing campaign," a term he made up
after realizing he left his wallet at home. Certainly he could
improvise here, too, and get the facts he needed to further his
investigation, all without drawing undue attention to himself.
Having sufficiently inflated his ego, he entered the headquarters lobby, walked to the receptionist and asked to speak with
an investigator.

"Sure," she replied. "Which one?"

"Uh, I don't know. I guess anyone will do."

This was red flag number one.

"I see. And what does your matter concern?" she asked while watching his suddenly nervous countenance. This question stumped Owen. He had hoped he could speak with a policeman directly and skip the middleman. He had to say something fast.

"Well," he began with less confidence, "I suppose death. Lots of death."

Red flag number two.

"Are you *reporting* a death … or turning yourself in?"

She inched backward in her seat as her hand felt for the panic button under her desk.

"No, no, no. I just want to speak with an investigator about the death of an old person. Old people." He leaned forward and lowered his voice. "It's kind of personal."

The receptionist watched his eyes for another moment before paging someone over the office intercom. Owen felt relieved, but he started to question the wisdom of this ad-hoc excursion. Before he could even take a seat to gather his thoughts, a young officer wearing a dress shirt and tie opened a side door and invited Owen to a nearby meeting room. The man introduced himself as an investigative aide. After stating a few formalities about keeping the conversation confidential, the aide asked Owen how he might be of service.

The reporter weighed his options. He could relate his findings from the day before and ask for help in finding the missing link between the deaths. This would likely require turning over his valuable notes and losing control of the story, which would risk the news going public and jeopardizing his scoop. Such an outcome was unacceptable. Another option, more appetizing, was to leave police headquarters empty handed.

Owen sat in his car, embarrassed, listening to NPR. The workday had begun, and he owed Al two articles in less than nine hours. If he exited the parking lot now, he could be at his newsroom computer within five minutes. But, if he left, he would probably never return. His single-mindedness in solving problems was a tremendous asset, but he knew from experience that once he flipped off that switch, it was nearly impossible to turn it on again. Given what he knew—what he *assumed* he knew—about the mysterious deaths, he was not willing to lay it to rest. Not yet. He swallowed his wounded pride and opened the car door.

The receptionist watched Owen carefully as he approached the counter a second time.

"Hi again," he smiled. "I'd like to speak with an investigator about some deaths."

"Again? Are you sure?" The receptionist eyed him cautiously as she delicately fingered the panic button.

"Yes, it's very important."

Owen's genuine expression disarmed the apprehension on her face. Even so, after agreeing to his request, she closely watched his movements until he took a seat in the corner of the lobby and picked up a magazine.

"Paging Officer Little. Officer Little to the front desk," her voice sounded over the intercom.

Owen watched the door from which the first policeman had emerged so promptly, but no one appeared. An unexpected frenzy of voices burst through the lobby doors as a few officers brought in two handcuffed hooligans. From their facial tattoos, Owen knew they were gang members. How people managed to get arrested first thing in the morning confounded him. *Why not sleep in?* he wondered. His eyes returned to the magazine when a shadow suddenly crept onto its pages. He leaned to one side and then the other, but no-where seemed to offer sufficient light for him to read. Annoyed, he put away the magazine, looked up and discovered the source of the considerably large shadow staring down at him.

In view of his six-foot, six-inch, broad-shouldered frame, Officer Little was ironically named—there was nothing little about him. Owen's wide eyes followed the man's stature, which continued up, up, up toward the ceiling. He could not tell whether the immense figure before him wore a bullet-proof vest or if the bulges beneath his uniform were just chest muscles. Though the officer's belt held a medley of badges, radios and weapons, all seemed superfluous. Any criminal with half a brain would dare not resist this awe-inspiring specimen of strength. The reporter sat speechless.

"I'm Officer J.R. Little," resounded the voice in a full octave lower than Owen's. "Can I help you with something, sir?"

Owen recovered his mind and stood up quickly, hand extended in respect and, truth be told, utter submission. As the two shook hands, Owen realized for the first time how pathetically skinny he was, particularly when compared to the dark-skinned beast of a man before him.

"I'd like to talk with you about a private matter involving some local deaths," he said quietly.

"Certainly. Follow me."

He escorted Owen to a meeting room with a surveillance camera in the ceiling corner. The reporter eyed it nervously, not wanting his secret to be exposed to any more people than was necessary. The officer observed this concern and assured him that the camera only recorded video, not audio.

"Now," he said, "What's on your mind?"

Owen swallowed hard and leaned forward, as if to share a secret.

"I'm a reporter for the local paper."

Officer Little immediately pushed away from the table separating them and glanced at the door.

"Don't worry," Owen said. "I don't want a quote. I need help with something I'm researching."

"Let's start with your name," the investigator replied. He took a pad from his pocket to take notes.

"Owen Daniels. I cover politics and business for the *Sunset Times*. Actually, I was just assigned to the politics desk yesterday."

Officer Little put his pen down and cocked his head to one side, as if trying to place the young face across the table.

"Daniels?" he repeated. Owen felt a wave of anxiety shoot through his body. The giant man leaned in again and asked, "Was your old man Robbie Daniels, the union negotiator?"

"Uh, yeah. That was him."

"No foolin'," the officer bellowed with a broad smile. "That man's famous around here. He negotiated some great contracts for us. In fact, it was his idea to get us annual sick leave payouts. That paid for my Caribbean vacation a few years ago and a wedding ring before that—or as my wife calls it, 'the rock.'"

His sudden laughter set Owen at ease.

"I'll be honest with you, kid. When Robbie died, a lot of us around here took it real hard. I considered him a friend, and it really bothered me that I couldn't go to his funeral. I was on assignment that day. I'm sorry."

"Don't worry about it. My dad really loved what he did. I'm sure he would have been happy about your vacation. And

47

your wife's rock. Happy wife, happy life, right?"

"No doubt, no doubt," he chuckled.

The pair chatted for some time about the elder Daniels and his respected reputation throughout the safety community. Owen had not realized during his youth how much of an impact his father had on so many careers and lives. It was his dad's tough negotiating skills that secured additional pay items and other perks from the city manager and county supervisors for police officers, sheriff deputies and firefighters. Those benefits improved the personal finances and job retention of thousands of people in town. To hear Officer Little brag about the deeds of Mr. Daniels was to Owen like listening to old hero stories around a campfire. He felt proud.

"Now, what brings you here today?" asked the officer.

"Well, it's something that I will tell you about, but I need you to promise that you won't mention it to anyone else—for now."

He paused and waited for a response. The officer's brow furrowed a bit.

"If a crime has been committed, I need to say something, you understand?" he offered, almost apologetically.

"That's just the thing. I don't know if a crime was committed. That is what I need help investigating."

"Okay. Keep talking."

Owen sat back in his chair and began relaying the events that led him to this point. He told about his grandma and the deaths of her two friends, about how he dismissed it as a coincidence until a co-worker read about the deaths of other eighty-year-olds, and about how he spent hours uncovering dozens more age-specific deaths over the past year.

"That *is* odd," agreed Officer Little. "But is that all you have to go on? Did these people have any other similarity, like an enemy or a disease?"

"I think they were all public servants, although I would need to do more research to verify that. But, no, there was no other connection I'm aware of. That's why I came to see you. I was hoping," he said with his best salesman-like smile, "that you could tell me something about their deaths. Maybe the link is not in their lives but in their deaths. Is that something you could look in to?"

The investigator appeared intrigued. "I have access to autopsy records, so I could ..."

He stopped short and spent a long moment considering something. Owen watched him with keen interest. In spite of his bear-like size, Officer Little was no meathead. It was obvious to Owen, even after their short conversation, that the man before him possessed a strength of will and character as impressive as his physical stature. The fact that he had not made an immediate commitment to helping Owen with his investigation meant that the officer also possessed self-control. Owen instinctively trusted him.

Officer Little took out a business card, wrote something on the reverse side and placed it back in his pocket. He stood up, shook his head side to side without saying anything and motioned for his guest to leave the room. Owen was flummoxed. One moment he was on the cusp of recruiting the exact person he needed to help crack the mystery; the next moment the policeman was playing charades. What just happened?

In the hallway, the two started walking toward the lobby when Owen felt a massive hand on his shoulder directing him through a side door into an empty stairwell.

"Sorry about that," the officer said in a low voice when the door had shut behind them. "That room has surveillance on it. If I am asked about you later, I needed it to appear that I denied your request." He handed Owen his card. "On the back is my cell number. When you are ready, call me with a few names to look up. I have access to a database of autopsies through the coroner's office."

"Perfect. Thank you so much, Officer Little."

"Let's skip the formalities going forward. Just call me J.R."

He reached out his immense hand to meet Owen's. Though separated by a half-foot in height, twenty years of life and vastly different backgrounds, Owen and J.R. had struck a friendship, the foundation of which was laid years earlier by the late Robbie Daniels.

Back in the newsroom, it took Owen but a moment to pick the first few names from his notebook and call the officer. To his surprise, J.R. offered to look them up on the spot. Owen held the line while his new partner typed the names of the three decedents one by one.

"Nothing's showing up. That means no autopsies were performed. When did they die?"

Owen rechecked his list. "Oh, my fault. I gave you the names of people who recently died. Let me find an older one." Owen flipped to the last page of his notes. "How about this one: Gladys Day. She passed away almost a year ago."

J.R. typed the name. With each keystroke Owen heard on the other line, his anticipation grew. He desperately wanted this to be the day when everything made sense, when a clear line was drawn through the dots on the page, revealing a grand picture of intrigue that would make him famous and bring the *L.A. Times* begging to hire him.

"Well, it's not much," J.R. began. "I see an autopsy here, but the results were inconclusive. The official cause of death was cardiopulmonary arrest. That's a fancy way of saying she stopped breathing."

"I hear that's common when someone dies," Owen said casually before freezing in embarrassment. He just made a death joke to a policeman. He held his breath and waited for J.R.'s response.

"Yeah, it's very common from what I hear, too," he snickered. "Well, there's not much to work with here. You need more data."

Owen scanned his notes again and, in the interest of time, offered to email the full list of names. J.R. consented but said he could not process the list for several days. That schedule suited the reporter, who had a lot of his own work to complete. The pair exchanged salutations and agreed to chat again when either had more news to share.

In the interim, Owen continued writing his series on public servants. The first article about his grandma was received well, garnering much interest and positive comments online. At the end of Ruthie's article, he asked readers to submit nominations for deserving government workers who had made the community a better place to live. Owen received more than a dozen that week and several more over the weekend. With so many options to choose from, he and Al prioritized the nomination list and decided to alternate features between retired and current workers.

Working with Al each day, albeit briefly, did not repel Owen as he had anticipated. Despite the editor's coarseness and repugnant scent, the young reporter acknowledged that his boss brought a helpful perspective to the project, borne from years of editorial decision-making and some political savvy. But that was the extent of their interactions. In keeping with their agreement, Owen came and went at his leisure and emailed his articles at the end of each day. One evening, Owen missed a deadline by a few minutes because a source failed to return his call on time. To his surprise, Al did not verbally berate him as happened to other reporters who submitted late material. Owen could not decide whether to chalk up his luck to Al having a good medication day or perhaps something more promising: a growing affinity for a protégé? Owen opted for the medication theory.

Three weeks passed without a word from J.R. until Owen's office phone rang one Friday afternoon.

"I went through your list and found a few things you should see," the deep voice said quietly. "Can we meet tonight?"

Owen's heart raced, tempered only by the recollection of Ruthie encouraging him to keep his blood pressure in check. He spoke in a lower tone to mask the excitement in his voice. After they had agreed on a rendezvous location and time—an old bar a few blocks away at eight o'clock—Owen hung up the phone.

"Yes!" he exclaimed.

A few heads in the newsroom turned his direction, but he was happily unaware of their glances. He put the finishing touches on his final article of the week, emailed it to Al and grabbed his notebook in preparation for his first surreptitious meeting with an informant. Owen strode out of the newspaper office full of life, in love with his work, and tantalized at the prospect of what mysteries the evening would reveal.

« 7 »

From early in his career, J.R. made a habit of sitting in seats that faced doors. This position allowed him to see everyone entering the room, thereby giving him a moment's advantage if a criminal barged in. He would be the first person to draw a gun or, if deterrence was preferred, the first person to stand against an intruder. Such was his role in life. As the largest person among his family and friends, J.R. was the designated protector. This title was awarded to him by his single mother after a robber attempted to burglarize their home when he was fifteen years old. The young man, who already stood six-feet tall, selflessly threw himself against the thief and pinned him to the floor while his mother beat the criminal's head with a lamp. From then on, J.R.'s rough neighborhood viewed him as its protector. Somewhere deep within his being, he felt an instinct, a visceral compulsion, to stand against all who would harm someone he loved. Over time, those he sought to defend included not just loved ones but also strangers in need and the community as a whole. When he left for college, he determined to enter the field of criminal justice so that he could protect others with deadly force, whether that be with a firearm or his own massive arms.

◊ ◊ ◊

Owen entered the tavern and stood in the doorway, peering into a darkness that slowly cleared as his eyes adjusted to the poorly lit room. J.R.'s dark suit and complexion blended in with his surroundings, almost too well to be seen. Perhaps that was the point. Owen moved toward the corner table where the officer sat next to something he intentionally kept out of view. His arms were folded atop his burly chest, and he sat erect in a seat that was clearly too small for someone his size. Before Owen could say anything of substance, the officer hushed him.

"Just a moment," he whispered. They waited in silence until a man rose from a nearby table and walked to the bar to order another drink.

J.R. picked up three thin folders and placed them unopened on the table. He laid his hand on top and looked at Owen soberly.

"You are not authorized to see these autopsy reports. We disclose these sorts of records only on a need-to-know basis or under subpoena. In this instance, you don't *need* to know anything, and you didn't come with a subpoena."

"Then why ask to meet if you can't show me anything?" Owen asked with confusion and a touch of annoyance.

"I didn't say I wouldn't show you. I only said there are rules about who gets to see these. I want you to understand that I am bending policy because I think you are on to something. The chief could reprimand me for this. You follow?"

The officer ended his comments as they began—serious, almost pleading, as if to say, "I'm going out on a limb for you. Don't make me regret it."

Owen nodded respectfully. "I understand what you're doing. I swear to keep the matter confidential."

The officer looked down and opened a folder. "I researched the forty-four deaths in our coroner's database. There was nothing unusual about them—no blunt-force injuries, no gunshot wounds, no unusual bleeding. They looked like normal, age-related deaths—*all* of them. However, there were post-mortem notes on three of the deceased victims."

"Victims?" Owen repeated. "Why use that term?"

"Well, it's an inference based on the circumstances of their deaths."

J.R. pointed to the first report. "The notes here say this lady was found, barely breathing, by her husband. He thought she was taking a nap, but he couldn't wake her. He called 9-1-1, but she had passed by the time the ambulance arrived."

J.R. closed that folder and replaced it with another. "Same story with this guy, whose daughter found him lying in his garden. She thought it was a heart attack and called the ambulance. Again, too late. The last case is more interesting."

He placed the third folder on top of the others and opened it. "This is an autopsy for Gladys Day, who died a year ago," he began, turning the page around for Owen to look at a picture taken at the scene of her death. "She was eating dinner by herself, cooked by a home health nurse who was in another room, when the old woman's face fell smack into the food."

J.R. propped his forearm on the table and used a whistling sound to simulate her fall.

"It looks like the impact was softened by her meatloaf," Owen commented with an irreverent laugh. "Sorry, that wasn't respectful," he added, still smirking.

"It's alright. I was thinking the same thing."

They looked at one another and snorted laughter, drawing a glance from the bartender. So much for being discreet. When they had settled themselves, J.R. continued.

"The nurse called 9-1-1. She was questioned by police and, pursuant to policy, investigated. They needed to rule out homicide, specifically food poisoning. So, they took blood samples. That's when they found a trace amount of a drug in Ms. Day's bloodstream—*not* one of her normal prescription meds. The inconsistency led to a partial autopsy."

"What drug did they find?"

J.R. shook his head. "The report didn't say. It just referenced an 'unknown trace substance.'"

"Well, whatever the drug was, apparently a trace amount wasn't enough to kill her, right?"

"Right. At least, that's what the report implies. It *is* possible that the unknown substance contributed to her death in some way but that the pathologist performing the autopsy did not identify it correctly."

"Is it possible they missed something?"

J.R. leaned in. "Not just possible," he replied. "I confirmed it."

"You confirmed what?"

"No disrespect to Sunset Hills, but we don't have the best pathologists," he said with a grimace. "They are good enough to get the work done, but when it comes to the high-end stuff, they ... uh ..." J.R. struggled to find the right word to describe his colleagues. "They get by. Let's leave it at that. When they know they lack the tools or knowledge to render a good diagnosis, they consult an outside specialist in San Francisco."

"I assume they didn't do that with Ms. Day?"

"No, we handled that one in-house—unfortunately. But, I sent her blood sample on file to our consultant and asked for his opinion, off the books. That's what took me so long to get back to you." J.R. opened his jacket pocket and pulled out a folded piece of paper. "This is what he emailed to me:

It's not an unknown drug ... just new to the CA market. It is a phenobarbital / chloral hydrate / morphine sulfate mix (barbiturate), better known as an assisted-suicide drug. Stops pulmonary and cardiac activity within minutes. Abnormal finding: drug should have appeared in much higher concentration in patient's blood, so it's uncertain if this was the primary cause of death. Would need further analysis to verify."

"So, let's assume this lady died from a barbiturate," Owen speculated, "even though your consultant thinks there wasn't enough of it in her blood. No offense, but that proves nothing." He looked down at the first pair of files. "What does she have to do with these two?"

"I wondered the same thing," J.R. replied. "These two seemed to die natural deaths, so there was no crime for us to investigate. But the relatives of the deceased thought something was odd. Why would their folks, out of nowhere, drop dead? It's a reasonable question. That's probably why they requested autopsies."

Owen perked up. "And what did *they* find?"

J.R. opened the two files again and pointed to the coroner's notes. "Look for yourself."

Owen scanned the scribbled text, full of medical terminology that meant nothing to him. But when he came upon the words "unknown trace substance in blood," he looked across the table, intrigue in his eyes.

"You're reading it right," J.R. assured. "That's the same thing written in Gladys Day's notes. It's a good thing I reviewed her autopsy first, because after that I knew what language to look for. All three of these eighty-year-olds had an 'unknown trace substance' in their blood that, in my opinion, killed them. *How* that happened—I have no idea."

"Out of the forty-four names I gave you, just these three had autopsies performed?"

His question was tinged with disappointment, having expected J.R. to have uncovered the link between *all* of the deaths—and, more importantly—something to provide the basis for a feature article. Owen could imagine Al's eye-rolling reaction when he saw the headline for his big scoop: "Three Old People Dead, Not Sure Why."

"You look troubled," J.R. observed. "Remember, real-life investigations are rarely quick and easy like the TV shows would have you believe. They take time. Don't give up yet."

This was Owen's first lesson as an investigative journalist: Truth that is deliberately cloaked in darkness does not find you; you must find it through diligence and much patience. In this moment, though, sitting across from J.R., Owen did not fully appreciate the instruction; he only felt frustrated.

"Forget about the forty-four names for now," J.R. continued. "Just focus on these three. What do we know? What are the possible explanations?"

Shaking off his melancholy, Owen attended to the question. "Well, if it was an assisted-suicide drug in their blood, like your consultant suggested, it's possible they killed themselves. But that's not likely. Or they could have been killed by someone else. But there is no proof of that. Or," he shrugged, "they just died of natural causes."

"I think we both agree the last option is the least likely, particularly in light of the many others who died at the same age. We don't have any leads to justify pursuing this as homicide, which leaves us with suicide. Is that something you could look in to?"

"Sure. But it's a dead end—no pun intended."

The pair discussed some final details and shook hands. "I'm sure you've had more important things to do lately, so I really appreciate your time," Owen said. "Again, I promise not to say a word about your involvement in any of this."

"Or *write* a word," J.R. reminded. "Now, just to play it safe, let's have you leave first."

Owen stepped away while J.R. finished his drink and checked his phone. A few minutes later, the officer stepped from the bar into the evening shadows.

◊ ◊ ◊

The following week, between writing projects, Owen set to work calling every phone number listed on the obituaries he compiled. Some numbers were out of service, but many rang to the person who handled the burial of their loved one. Owen disguised his true intention by referencing the newspaper's new series featuring public servants, which had already become well-known in the community. He introduced himself as a reporter and asked to speak with someone who knew the deceased retiree.

"I am very sorry for your loss," he would begin. "If you are willing, I had hoped to collect some information about so-and-so as additional background for the series I'm writing. My belief is that we can honor people like so-and-so in life and in death. Do you have a few minutes to talk?"

Most people gladly obliged his request. "Oh, what a nice idea," was a common refrain he heard at the onset of a conversation. "He or she would have liked that recognition." All proceeded to plan until Owen transitioned to the crux of his call: uncovering the emotional and psychological state of the retiree just before dying. He knew people did not commit suicide unless they were depressed or hopeless. But how to uncover that critical information without offending callers proved more difficult than he had anticipated.

"No, my mother was not depressed. What kind of question is that?" Hang up.

"No, my husband never talked about killing himself. How rude." Hang up.

"Mind your own business, you sadistic jerk!" Hang up.

Clearly, Owen needed a new strategy. On the next call, when it was time for his transition, he tried a more indirect approach: "In the final years of life, what did your loved one live for?" It was a broad question, and responses ran the gamut. With very few exceptions, they painted pictures of individuals who embraced retired life and its many joys. These were *not* the profiles of people longing for death.

Owen felt ambivalent about these stories. On the one hand, they convinced him that forty-four retirees did not kill themselves with a cocktail of lethal drugs. He believed this fact intuitively from the start; now he felt certain of it. On the other hand, this conclusion thrust him back into the conundrum where he found himself at the start: seeing a pattern of apparently connected deaths with no reason for the pattern. He saw the threads but not the tapestry. He was stumped once again.

To distract his frustrated mind, he began researching his next business article for the paper. The topic was the promotion of a corporate executive who had risen through the ranks of leadership in his firm for two decades. The firm's governing board recently appointed him to the top spot. The prior executive, an old gentleman, had served the company for many years and was to be honored at a "transition celebration" later in the week at an upscale restaurant. As the newspaper's business reporter, Owen received an invitation to the ceremony. He decided to attend for the free food.

As he started drafting the article, his thoughts drifted back to his investigative plight, the bane of his existence. Sure, he could analyze a stack of obituaries all day, but no new information would be found. The people were dead, and unfortunately for him, dead people did not speak. They could not say if they were depressed, because they were dead. They could not say what they held in common with former coworkers, because they were dead. They could not reveal anything at all, because they were dead. What Owen needed was a new source of facts. He needed dialogue. Actually, what he really needed was to interview the dead people.

Owen stopped typing, pushed away from his computer and tried to recall the idea that had just flitted through his subconscious while his conscious mind focused on writing. What was it? His mind slowly retraced his last thoughts until he believed he found it: He needed to interview dead people before they died. No, that was not it. He needed to interview *living* people before they died. That was it! He needed to interview seventy-nine-year-olds who were *going* to die.

« 8 »

It is one thing to call the relative of a deceased person and ask questions about the psychological state of their loved one pre-mortem. It is an entirely different matter to call a *living* person and ask the same questions. Owen imagined the conversation playing out like this: "Hi, I am a newspaper reporter. Don't ask me how I know this, but I think you're about to die. Could we chat about your emotional stability and any enemies who might want you dead?"

Owen quickly dismissed this plan, returning his attention to finishing his writing assignment. After he had sent it to Al, he walked to the break room for a snack. Owen had interviewed enough government employees to know that working in the private sector afforded him certain advantages, one of which was his employer stocking the kitchen with lots of junk food. Public employees were not so lucky; they had to provide their own snacks because they were prohibited from receiving "gifts of public funds," even a candy bar purchased at taxpayer expense. One interviewee likened it to a school teacher having to bring her own paperclips to work. Owen scoffed at the restrictive policy, but then again, how could someone who hardly paid any taxes empathize with taxpayer complaints?

Chocolate in hand, Owen turned to leave the break room when Darcie walked in. She met his eyes and immediately looked at the ground. He found the behavior unusual, as she rarely lacked an abundance of words for any occasion, particularly with him. That day, however, the young woman dodged his attention.

"Girls can be so odd sometimes," he thought.

Confused, but not enough to unravel her oddities, Owen kept moving. Darcie looked surprised and blurted from the other end of the room, "How are the obits coming? Do you need more?" She faced him now, blinking nervously.

Owen turned toward her and, for the first time, noticed color on her face. Darcie had replaced the shades of black that normally covered her lips with a dark-red hue. The rest of her appearance maintained its usual gothic display, which distinctly contrasted with her lips. Owen stared for a long moment, not because he found her exceedingly attractive but because he realized, at last, that she had lips—and they looked nice. With some effort, he forced his thoughts from this realization to the content of her question, which was …?

"I'm sorry, what about obituaries?"

"Uh, nothing." Darcie blushed and turned to face the wall.

Owen stared at the back of her unmoving head for an awkward moment before quietly stepping out of the room. He spent the return trip to his desk trying to understand what had just happened. Finding no satisfying answers, he resumed his earlier consideration of how to broach the topic of untimely death with strangers. His chair squeaked as he sat down and scanned his cubicle for inspiration. In the corner sat the notes he had collected for the next installment in his public-servant series.

"I've got a couple dozen nominees here," he said to himself. "Let's see who wants to talk."

He opened his spreadsheet, sorted it by age and focused on the two oldest. He picked up the phone and called the first, a seventy-five-year-old curmudgeon whose prompt reply to Owen's friendly introduction was, "That sorry excuse for a paper couldn't write the news to save its life. You're not getting another dime from me!"

"Sir, I don't want your dime, just ..."

"Not a red cent! Now go away before I call the police!"

Hang up.

"That didn't go so well. Here's hoping the next retiree will be nicer."

◊ ◊ ◊

Mary Lou Rogers heard the phone ringing from her front patio, where she and her husband sat drinking tea and reading their respective books. Theirs was a simple life filled with simple pleasures: long morning walks, a garden full of vegetables, a library of classics and the enduring friendship of a lifelong spouse. Mr. and Mrs. Rogers were fortunate, some would say, because they retired earlier than most people—in their mid-fifties. But they would say that they only wanted more time to do the things they loved most with the people they loved most. The tradeoff for their early retirements was having to live on less income than their longer-career counterparts. But in keeping with their philosophy of simplicity, they gladly accepted the exchange.

Owen's call rang four times without being picked up. He grew worried that he had hit another roadblock in his investigation. He waited a few minutes and tried again. This time, Mary Lou answered with a pleasant, "Hello, Rogers residence. It's a beautiful day, isn't it?"

The unexpected greeting disrupted Owen's flow of thought. Wasn't *he* the one supposed to be asking the questions?

"I—I guess so. Actually, I haven't been outside much today."

"Oh, you're missing the most delightful breeze. At my house, it is whistling down the hillside and through my chimes. Just a marvelous day. Where do you live?"

Again, wasn't this Owen's interview? He said roughly where he lived—she was a stranger, after all—before introducing himself and his wish to interview her for a possible article about her public service.

"Well, isn't that nice! A real reporter calling *me* of all people! My husband, Jim, was just teasing about sending in my name to the paper. I told him, 'Don't you dare.' I would not have a clue what to say about myself. I just worked like everyone else."

"That's what I'm looking for," Owen encouraged. "Stories just like that, about people like you who invested years in government to make the community a better place to live. Someone obviously thought you were deserving of a nomination. That's how I got your phone number."

"Oh, that Jim! He's such a sweetheart. Young man, you make my job sound so glamorous. It really wasn't. I don't think I would be a good person for your article. I'm sorry."

"No, you are the *exact* person I need!" Owen countered, increasingly nervous about losing his one remaining old-person lead. That was not an option. He had to make the sale as easy as possible. "I don't even have to write anything if you don't want me to. I would just like to chat for a while."

"Hmm. Please wait."

He heard voices on the other side of the phone having an entire conversation in whispers. Owen listened carefully but could not make out anything with clarity.

"Okay, sir," she agreed with a touch of excitement, "but only under one condition."

"Name it."

"We'd like you to interview me here, in my house, over a cup of tea."

Owen accepted the offer, even though he despised tea, which he believed to be little more than flavored grass. The following afternoon, he drove thirty minutes west of downtown toward the rolling hills for which the town was named. There was nothing to draw him to this deserted area—no good stores or restaurants—so he had never visited. The long roads wrapped around hilly bends, and tall pines rose into the clear blue sky like a battalion of soldiers. Despite its absence of modernity, the peaceful scenery charmed Owen. The paved road became a dusty one, leading down an embankment to a little cottage nestled on a hillside overlooking a valley of farmland. He parked in the Rogers' driveway and spent a minute beholding the lovely scene.

The Rogers sat in rocking chairs on their wood-paneled deck when they heard Owen's car door shut. Mary Lou smiled at Jim, and together they went to meet the young man.

"Welcome, welcome," she said. "You must be Mr. Daniels."

They shook hands and exchanged greetings. After she had introduced her husband, she began walking around her house toward the backyard.

"Aren't we meeting inside?" Owen asked.

"Heavens, no. The best talking is done on a walk. Follow me."

"No, really," he objected, "I'm not dressed for a hike."

"Oh, you'll be fine," she laughed. Mary Lou took a few more steps and then turned to look at him. "Actually, you'd better hide the red on your shirt. It might upset the bull in the valley." She winked and began her descent down the gentle hill with Jim by her side.

The trio walked quite a distance over the next half-hour and discussed many topics unrelated to work. Owen continually drew the conversation back to his main interest: Mary Lou's twenty-year career as a county librarian. He asked several probing questions about the working relationships she developed, challenging emotional experiences during her career, reasons for retiring so young and friendships she maintained into retirement. Owen paid careful attention to Mary Lou's psychological state before and after retiring, hoping by chance to uncover a secretly depressed woman on the verge of committing suicide. Alas, the old woman was as healthy and emotionally stable as ever—and just two years before turning eighty.

By the time the three entered the cottage, they felt winded but alive. Even Owen, who found little enjoyment in purposeful physical exertion, enjoyed the feeling of a stronger heartbeat and flushed cheeks. As he sat in the Rogers' tiny living room, his grandma came to mind. Not only would she be proud that he had just exercised, she would like it here. The home and the land felt wholesome, like her. Owen glanced around Mary Lou's modest abode. There was a worn-out couch, a recliner, a makeshift library that once served as a TV nook and family photos on every shelf.

While heating a pot of water for tea, she observed Owen's watchful eyes.

"It's not much," she admitted, "but it's perfect for us— our little piece of heaven."

Her reference to the supernatural bothered Owen, but he managed to swallow his intellectual judgment.

"So, Mary Lou, how long have you lived here?"

"More than two decades. We built it shortly before I retired. Jim stopped working a year before I did so he could oversee its construction. For a while, money was tight. But between my county salary and his modest 401(k), we scrapped enough together to pay the bills."

The subject of finances had not been discussed during their hike, so Owen opened his notepad and asked a few more questions to round out his profile of Mrs. Rogers.

"I won't ask about your salary as a public servant," he began, "but I'd like to know if it's true what they say about government workers earning less than people in the private sector. What do you think?"

"Well, it's true that we didn't earn much—at least we thought so at the time. Salaries are *much* higher now than back then. But we had an understanding with county management that we would accept lower pay in exchange for reliable retirement benefits."

Owen admitted to not knowing anything about her retirement plan and asked how it worked.

"I'm a bit fuzzy on the particulars," she confessed. "However, I *do* know I will receive a monthly pension for the rest of my life, kind of like Social Security. I had the nice people at the retirement office explain that to me twice just to make sure I understood."

Jim walked into the room, set Owen's mug of tea on the end table and dropped into his old recliner. He pointed at Mary Lou impishly. "And if she kicks the bucket, I'll get a hundred percent of her pension for the rest of *my* life! How's that for a good deal?"

"Oh, you wouldn't know what to do without me," she retorted pleasantly. "Who would wash your clothes and cook your dinners and …"

Her voice trailed off in Owen's mind, which fixated on Jim's comment. If his wife passed away, would he *really* receive her full pension until *he* died? What if he lived to be ninety? Or a hundred! Certainly there was a limit on how long payments would continue, right? Owen began doing math on his notepad. If Mary Lou earned, say, $1,000 per month from her pension, and she retired at age fifty-five, and now she's seventy-eight, that's $12,000 a year times twenty-three years. He scribbled the equation and came up with $276,000—more than a quarter of a million dollars! That number seemed too high, so he checked his math. Sure enough, it was correct. He sat stunned as he considered that figure. Then, he added another ten years of payments, assuming Mary Lou died next year and Jim lived a decade more. That increased the payouts by another $120,000. Owen tallied the pension payments, totaling $400,000 from the start of Mary Lou's retirement to Jim's death.

"Wow," he crowed.

His exclamation interrupted the couple's playful banter. Their eyes met his in confusion, and his met theirs in embarrassment.

"I—I am sorry," he stuttered. "I was talking to myself."

He glanced down at his calculations again and decided to ask another question to break the awkward silence. "If I might ask, Mary Lou, about how much is your pension?"

"I don't mind," she replied. "Just don't put it in the paper. I earn about $2,000 a month now. They also add two percent every year for inflation."

Owen tried not to let his jaw drop. He knew his original estimate needed to be much higher because it did not take into account annual cost-of-living increases. That could easily put the total beyond $600,000—even higher if Jim outlived her by more than ten years.

"Were you one of the higher-paid employees in your department?" he asked.

"Oh my, not even close," she giggled. "I was somewhere in the middle. At the end of my career, when I was a supervisor, I made a decent wage. But it's nothing compared to what they earn now. I heard salaries have more than doubled since I retired."

Again, Mary Lou's voice trailed off while Owen worked out calculations based on current salaries. He laid his pen down and took a sip of tea. Not bad for liquid grass. This revelation, however, did not obscure what he had just learned from the Rogers. It did not trouble Owen that Mary Lou's monthly pension or the total benefits paid to her and Jim were unreasonably high. What surprised him was the realization that she was just one of thousands of retirees receiving such benefits. Even with his imperfect math skills, Owen knew that would get very expensive very quickly.

He finished his drink and thanked the couple for their hospitality. He genuinely had had a nice time, gaining a new appreciation for the simplicity of country living. Even so, he relished the idea of reentering the city, full of the sights, sounds and conveniences of modern life. As he drove down the dirt road, his mind returned to the huge sums of money being spent by Mary Lou's pension plan: thousands of people each being paid thousands of dollars every month, totaling untold millions. The numbers became too large for Owen to figure in his head. Distracted, he did not see a family of skunks crossing the road. He hit the brakes, but it was too late. His first impulse was to go directly to a carwash, but he decided to pull over to assess the damage.

Owen stepped out of the car to check his paint and tires. No noticeable damage. Satisfied, he headed back to his door when his eyes fell on the animals lying dead, one after another like a line of corpses in a morgue. As repulsive as roadkill was to behold, he looked on with a small measure of satisfaction.

"I wonder if they would give *me* a pension for that act of public service," he quipped. "But they couldn't pay me enough to touch one of ..."

Then a thought arose. Something he had not considered until that moment. A question that tingled along his neck, down his back and to his feet. What if the connection between the forty-four dead retirees had nothing to do with their jobs, emotional states or co-workers? What if the common denominator was that they all retired from the same pension plan?

The workday had ended, but Owen's question lit in him a fire to confirm the speculation as soon as possible. His mind would not find rest until he knew for certain. He sped toward downtown as the sun dipped behind the hills. Most of the lights in the newspaper building were out, except for a few upstairs. Owen entered the back door and hurried down the hallway toward his office. His rushed movement startled Al, who cursed and accused Owen of trying to give him a heart attack.

"That would require a heart," Owen muttered under his breath.

At his desk, he rifled through his notes on the decedents. Ages, dates, departments, family members—but nothing about pensions. He tapped his finger on the papers in frustration. He knew he was close, but once again, he lacked information. Unfortunately, J.R. would not be able to help this time. The only way to confirm whether the listed names were retirees of the county pension plan was to go directly to the retirement office. Determined to make that his top priority the following day, Owen turned off his desk lamp and headed home.

« 9 »

The young woman stood in front of the conference room, her long, dirty-blonde hair pulled back into a ponytail, revealing a single dimple on her right cheek. She wore a classy, fitted top with sleeves rolled up to her elbows and a knee-length skirt that accented her attractive figure. Her black high heels matched the rims of her reading glasses, which she fingered carelessly while watching stragglers find their seats. She glanced at the clock, waiting for it to strike nine o'clock. The room neared capacity, full of middle-age men and women with eager expressions on their faces. It would be impossible to discern from appearances alone why such a diverse group of individuals would be sitting together—some professionals, some blue-collar workers, a few uniformed officers. But the woman facing them knew.

"Good morning, everyone," she said in a pleasant voice. "My name is Lily Allen, and I'd like to welcome you to this month's pre-retirement seminar. Today, we will cover a variety of topics that will provide all the information you need to retire successfully from the public agency where you work. My role here is to guide you through the retirement process, which, I confess in advance, may seem complex. But I promise you that it will make perfect sense by the time you leave."

Her smile was returned by grateful faces in the front row. Lily continued her introduction flawlessly, as if reading from a script. She had given this hour-long speech dozens of times over the past several years and had most of it memorized. This experience, coupled with a natural aptitude for public speaking, made her a valuable resource to the pension plan, which had entrusted to her its communications and member outreach program.

She was a few minutes into her presentation when a hand shot up in the crowd.

"Yes, sir?" she asked with a nod in his direction.

"I'm still a few years out from retiring," said a sheriff's deputy.

"Well, I'd hope so," Lily teased. "You don't look much older than me!"

She smiled at him in good humor as the attendees giggled. It did seem odd that someone so relatively young would be preparing to retire. "Go on," she encouraged.

"I've got twenty-one years of service as a sheriff's deputy, and I'm forty-five years old. I wanted to know when I will be able to retire, if I decide to do that."

Lily pushed a button on her laptop and a slide appeared on the screen behind her.

"That is a great segue to discussing eligibility for retirement," she said. "From the badge on your vest and the gun on your hip, I'm guessing you are a safety member, right?"

The man nodded.

"Safety members are eligible to retire when they have ten years of service credit and are age fifty. But, the law also allows safety guys like you to retire before fifty if they have twenty years of service."

"You're saying I could retire *now*?"

"Yes," Lily answered. "But with every additional year you work, your age will also be higher, as will your service credit. That translates to a higher pension for you at retirement." She lowered her voice and leaned toward the audience. "In fact, I know of a few safety members who worked 34 years and retired with a pension that equaled their final salaries! Could you imagine that: earning six figures every year for the rest of your life?"

Lily enjoyed watching the expressions of people after hearing this anecdote for the first time. Their responses were always the same: wide eyes and disbelieving head shakes. The deputy also fell silent.

"Is that good news for you?" she inquired of him.

"Uh-huh. I didn't realize what a lucrative career I chose."

Lily clicked to the next slide and began discussing her next topic when the side door swung opened. A man in his twenties, apparently lost, entered the room and took a seat at the back table. Some of the attendees looked at the new arrival, glanced at the clock and rolled their eyes.

"This is a pre-retirement seminar provided by the county pension plan," Lily said to the young man. "You look to have arrived about, oh, thirty years too early."

This comment incited scattered laughter in the room, causing the late arrival to redden with embarrassment. He squirmed, but Lily promptly apologized for the jest and advised him to stay afterward to discuss the earlier content he had missed. He forced a tolerant grin in her direction and opened his notepad.

◊ ◊ ◊

The hour passed quickly as Lily covered the presentation material, answered the group's questions and dismissed them promptly at ten o'clock. The young man waited until the older attendees had exited the room before flipping his notebook closed and approaching Lily. She stood behind her lectern, organizing her papers. For the last hour, the grudge he held against her prevented him from viewing her objectively. But now, standing just a few feet apart, he was struck silent by the loveliness of her appearance.

"Hi again," she said warmly. "Glad to see I didn't scare you off."

Recovering his attention, he extended his hand.

"My name is Owen Daniels. I'm the political reporter at the *Sunset Times*. Do you have a few minutes to chat?"

Her warm smile descended into a horrified expression and open mouth. Owen, taking pleasure in her discomfort, continued poker-faced while she stood, flushed, blinking at him. He placed his index finger under her chin and lifted slowly to close her gaping mouth. Lily snapped from her shock and shook his hand before gushing multiple apologies for her earlier remark.

"My indiscretion in no way reflects the views of the pension plan toward its stakeholders, the public and certainly not the media. I am very, very sorry if I embarrassed you, Mr. Daniels. So very sorry."

Owen remained quiet and steady, enjoying the poetic justice on display. Lily commenced a second round of apologies. This was entertainment at its best. Just this once, Owen decided to indulge himself by fanning the flames of shame.

"I admit, it certainly wasn't the kind of thing I would expect to experience at this reputable organization, Miss ...?" He squinted at her ID badge and read slowly: "Lily Allen, Communications and Outreach Manager." He stood to his full height, several inches above her head. "You claim this isn't how your stakeholders are treated, but now ... well, to be frank, I'm not convinced."

From her distraught face, it became immediately clear to Owen that she knew she had lost. If he wanted to embarrass her before her boss or quote her in an article, she could not stop him. She lowered her gaze and uttered words that instantly made Owen regret his joke.

"I am truly sorry," she said earnestly. "Will you please forgive me?"

Forgiveness? Owen was not sure what to make of that. In his twenty-five years of life, nobody had ever asked him that question. An off-handed "I'm sorry," to be sure. But this seemed different, though he did not know why. Moments passed as he considered what to say.

"Sure, all is forgiven," he replied in a kind, albeit awkward, manner.

Lily lifted her gaze, her edifice of professionalism suspended for the moment, and met Owen's gentle look. Whatever just transpired with his statement of absolution put her at peace. It put *them* at peace. Sensing that, Owen moved to speak but was preempted by Lily remarking that she had not formally introduced herself. They shook hands a second time and, as it were, began afresh. She motioned to the front row of seats, and they sat for a while discussing their respective jobs. Lily explained that she began working for the pension plan straight out of college and for the last six years served as its only communications person. She wrote the marketing material, gave the presentations and met with the media; she was the go-to person for all things related to communications.

"No disrespect intended," he interjected, "but why wouldn't someone more knowledgeable about finance give presentations to members? Pensions deal with money, don't they?"

"Valid question. Having written and spoken about the plan for so many years, I've become sort of an in-house expert. I know I am relatively young, but the director has entrusted all of our agency's outreach activities to me. I never violate her trust, particularly with the media."

Having recounted her short career, Owen summarized his own, including recent events that thrust him into the arena of local government. With each passing sentence, Lily grew more at ease knowing that he had not arrived that morning to grill her about the high cost of pensions or other common criticisms of her industry.

"Working in a field that is regularly under the microscope of concerned citizens and reporters has sensitized me to the opinions of media outlets," she explained. "Don't get the wrong idea. I never cower before them, but I never entrust myself to them, either. No offense to you, Owen—and this is definitely off the record—but I view the media as vultures, ready to descend at the sight of blood and to pick at a story until nothing remains but a putrid carcass. I've seen it happen here and in other cities. It's not pretty." She paused and squinted a half-smile at him. "You don't look like a vulture, so what brings you here today?"

Owen resisted the urge to continue staring at her faultless appearance. He fought to disprove the accusation that men cannot pay attention to the words of a beautiful woman for more than a few seconds, but it had already happened twice during their short conversation. The battle raged in his mind, but alas, he succumbed to his inborn weakness. Apologetically, he asked Lily to repeat her question.

"Why are you here?" she said slowly.

He looked at his notepad and fidgeted awkwardly. "I—I wanted to ask a favor."

"Sorry, we don't do favors here," she replied immediately.

Owen looked at her face, flat with seriousness—another dead end that drained any remaining hope from him. But then her expression brightened and the dimple in her cheek reappeared.

"I'm just kidding. I specialize in good deeds. What do you need?"

Owen grinned, partly because he found her funny and partly because she had played his favorite game—and scored a point. He opened his notepad and showed Lily the list of forty-four individuals who, he believed, previously worked for the county. She perused it, commented on Owen's atrocious handwriting and asked if this would be a formal public records request.

"A what?"

"A public records request. Anyone can make a records request of a government entity under California's Public Records Act, and the agency has ten days to respond. Here at the pension plan, we call them PRAs. They come in waves and are typically from the usual suspects."

"Who are the usual suspects?"

"The local taxpayers' association, which likes to keep tabs on the amount of tax dollars being spent on county employees. And Transparent California, the group that publishes a list of every governmental retiree in the state who makes more than $100,000 per year."

"That's probably not a long list."

"You would be surprised. Our county has many people making big bucks in retirement. But you didn't hear that from me!" she quickly added. "Anyhow, will yours be a PRA request?"

Owen considered his options and, in the interest of time, replied in the negative. Although he could wait ten more days to satisfy his curiosity, he was impatient for an answer.

"No, I'd prefer not going the formal route, if that's okay with you. But I will take you up on that good deed."

Lily looked at his notepad, then at him, then toward the open door in the room, and then back to Owen. His pleading eyes met her uncertain expression. She bit her lip.

"Okay, I'll help you out. But this time only—and on one condition."

Lily could have asked for the moon, and he would have agreed.

"I'm listening," he replied evenly.

She cast a flirtatious smile his direction. "You must not mention my earlier *faux pas* to anyone, especially my boss."

That was an easy deal to make, so Owen agreed. However, he refused to part with his notepad when she asked for it. He only allowed her to make photocopies of the pages containing the list, which she handed to a clerk in the office to research.

"It should only take thirty minutes," she told him.

To pass the time, Lily suggested that he meet the executive director, who, she explained, would be upset to know that a reporter was on site without her knowledge. Slipping back into her communications role, Lily warned, "One thing you need to know about my boss is that she has a strong aversion to conflict. The best news to her is no news—and I tend to agree. Having the pension industry shot at in the newspapers so often makes a person gun shy."

They walked through a series of hallways, past several cubicles and to the boss' office. Lily lightly knocked on the door and walked in with Owen by her side. The first thing he noticed upon entering the executive suite was its immensity. He estimated the length of one wall to be thirty feet with the ceiling towering to at least twelve. Cherry wood cabinets full of binders, books and reports lined another wall, where a large television screen hung. Four waist-to-ceiling windows permitted an abundance of natural light to fill the room, although an advanced shading feature automatically filtered out ultraviolet rays that entered on bright summer afternoons. The only thing cheap Owen noticed in the impressive office was his pair of jeans. He felt out of place, but he reminded himself that his greatest asset was his title, which apparently struck fear into the hearts of government officials everywhere.

"Alexis, this is Owen Daniels," Lily began. "He is the new political reporter at the *Sunset Times*. He just dropped by to introduce himself."

Owen took Lily's impromptu cue without hesitation. "I just wanted to let you know that my predecessor at the paper is on leave for a while, and I will be filling in."

The executive stood hastily and congratulated Owen on his promotion.

"I've read your articles about retired public employees," she said. "I knew one of the men you wrote about. We worked together at the district attorney's office when I was new to county government. It was unusual seeing his name in the paper so many years later."

"Maybe I'll feature *you* one day," Owen replied with a faint smirk. He wanted to test Lily's description of her boss as gun shy.

At this, the color drained from Alexis' face. She shook her head and hands involuntarily, as if to say, "Not a chance." Clearly, Owen had touched a nerve.

"Or maybe not," he suggested after a few uncomfortable moments. "I always interview the person before writing a word. The basis of a good article is good research, you know."

Alexis' demeanor warmed at Owen's afterthought, but his last statement seemed to trouble her anew.

"So," she inquired tentatively, "are you here to do research on the pension plan? Because, if so, we would need to block out some time. I've got …." She looked at her desk calendar, furrowed her brow and turned to face Owen again. "I don't have time today."

These final words were spoken matter-of-factly. Alexis closed her lips and watched Owen's response. He recognized the sales tactic. He had used it when pitching an idea to Al that he knew was a long shot: the throw-it-out-there-then-shut-up technique. Whether or not he had misread her intent, Owen decided to take her words at face value.

"No, not today. I'm just passing through."

"Well, in that case," the executive said. "Lily, why don't you show Mr. Daniels around the office, introduce him to management staff and finish up in the lobby."

Owen and Alexis exchanged departing pleasantries and shook hands. It was a brief interaction but enough for the reporter to form an impression of the administrator as a guarded, nervous sort of person. She selected her words carefully, a characteristic that Owen appreciated, and conducted herself with the professionalism expected of someone in that position. Yet something about the short conversation left him uncertain. About what, though? Perhaps her aversion to bad press? Maybe she was having an off day? As he exited her office, he felt a cool breeze on the palm of his right hand, but the perspiration was not his own.

Their next stop was not really a stop at all. Lily entered the pension plan attorney's doorway to make the requested introduction. But the attorney, with one hand holding a phone and the other thumbing through a stack of legal documents, mouthed, "Sorry," toward the waiting pair. They backed out slowly and closed the door.

"Most days, she posts a sign on her door that says, 'Do not disturb,'" Lily explained.

"That's a tad unfriendly, don't you think?"

"Not if you saw her to-do list. Alexis runs almost every decision by legal counsel. I don't know if it's because of her insecurity in making hard decisions or if she just wants the attorney to earn her keep." Lily grinned. "I suspect it's the former. Even though Alexis is the boss, I sometimes wonder if our attorney is the grand puppet master."

She contorted her hands over Owen's head like a puppeteer, and the pair laughed as they approached the office of the new chief investment officer, Peter, a clean-shaven gentleman in his late 40s who donned a pricey, pin-striped suit. Lily introduced Owen as a local reporter, a fact that intrigued the investment pro and set him on a rant about the public's need for a better understanding of economics.

"The greatest threat we face today is not inflation," Peter began. "It's deflation. It's the devaluation of products and services that sets in motion a self-reinforcing cycle of lower prices and monetary fragility, like an economy hell bent on digging its own grave. That's what happened in 1929, and it started to happen in 2008. The U.S. equities markets stood on the edge of a knife both times."

Owen understood about half of what Peter said and felt like drowning in so many new concepts. He had expected a quick "hi and goodbye," not an economics class. But something amid the flood of words hooked his attention—a comment about how people view investment losses incorrectly. He asked the investment officer to elaborate.

"Most folks think that a ten percent loss can be recovered by a ten percent gain. That seems intuitive, right? But if our pension plan loses ten, we don't need another ten to get back to even. We need eleven percent."

Owen shook his head. "Sorry, I'm not following."

"Don't feel bad. You're not alone. An example might help. If you had invested one dollar in 1929 when the Great Depression began, you would have lost about eighty-nine percent by 1932. Of the original dollar, what would you have left?"

"Eleven cents."

"Right. So, how much would you need to earn to return to one dollar?" he asked rhetorically. "Eighty-nine cents. Your remaining eleven cents would have to earn an astonishing nine hundred percent to get you back to one dollar!"

"Wow, I see what you mean. Wouldn't that take a long time?"

"Oh yeah. If you invested one dollar in the index in 1929, you would not have a buck again until 1954. Well, 1957 if you adjust for inflation. The takeaway point is that we—the pension plan, as an institutional investor—are just as

86

concerned with *not* losing money as we are with *making* money. Losses hurt us as much as gains help us—maybe more. That's why the threat of a new recession keeps me awake at night."

The impromptu lecture came to a close. What Owen had hoped to be a brief conversation became something altogether different: a crash course in investment strategy that he never knew existed. One of the delusions of his youth was believing he possessed a lot of knowledge when in fact he knew quite little. In the last ten minutes, Owen's bubble of delusion had deflated somewhat. Later, he reflected on that conversation and blushed at his intellectual cockiness.

For the time being, though, he remained an overconfident fool strolling through the hallways of a pension plan office that held the key to unlocking a mystery plaguing his inquisitive mind. After a few more introductions, Lily led her guest to the clerk tasked with researching his list of deceased public employees. She glanced over the pages before passing them to Owen. His eyes widened as he scrolled line by line, name by name, his cheeks flushing with color until he reached the last page. He caught his breath, folded the papers carefully and inserted them into his notepad.

"It's been a pleasure," he said, "but I should get back to my office."

As he turned to leave, Lily reached out and touched his arm. Her soft fingers against his skin halted his progress. They both looked at her hand and then at each other. She withdrew it quickly.

"I'm sorry. I … uh."

They were stuck in another moment of awkwardness, broken only by Lily removing a business card from her pocket and extending it formally.

"Mr. Daniels, it was nice meeting you. If you need any more information about pensions, don't hesitate to contact me or Alexis."

Forcing his own recovery from the strangely pleasant moment, Owen thanked her for the tour and introductions. "And especially your hospitality," he added with a wink.

Lily reddened and glanced modestly at the clerk, who was transfixed by the drama unfolding outside his cubicle.

"Oh, don't stop on my account," he told her. "This is quality entertainment."

Owen failed to hear the comment as he walked away, his thoughts consumed by what he had just seen: a list of his dead retirees, *all* of whom were receiving lifetime pensions from the same retirement system. The possibility of coincidence had just been obliterated. The only valid explanation remaining was a conspiracy to commit murder—very targeted murder. But why? And how? He needed time to evaluate this development and to plan his next move. He spent the drive to his office in silence, mulling over the situation, raising questions without answers, deciding who to entrust with his news. At work, he slid into his office chair and fired up the computer just as his phone rang.

"Sunset Times. This is Owen."

"Hi, it's Lily at the county retirement department. I was just calling to thank you again for stopping by and, um, to ask if you are planning to write an article about the pension plan. Alexis wanted to know so we can be prepared."

Write about the pension plan? The thought had not dawned on him. Of course he would not write anything. There was nothing to write about. Or was there? Maybe he *did* have a story to tell, though not about the pension plan. But the deceased pensioners—*that* was very newsworthy.

The thought intrigued Owen. It seemed counterintuitive to publicize the fact that dozens of county retirees had died at the exact same age over the past year. After all, that was the crux of his scoop. Then again, perhaps that was the best way to peel back the next layer of the mystery and uncover the fuller truth.

"Owen, are you there?"

"Sorry, I was just thinking. You can tell your boss that I don't plan on writing an article *about* the pension plan. But something else is coming."

« 10 »

What does it feel like to be a superhero, a mysterious nobody who descends into a dire situation to right a wrong perpetrated by evildoers colluding under the cloak of secrecy? The average person may never know such a feeling. But, insofar as it was possible for mere humans to experience the heroic impulse and its rewards, Owen Daniels was that superhero. Well, he thought so. To the rest of the world, he remained a nobody who had accomplished nothing.

Had he taken a step back to consider his discovery from the perspective of what was actually known, he might have arrived at a very different conclusion about his situation and himself. Were a fair assessment to be made, Owen might have realized that, though he identified what the deceased retirees held in common—they had all received pensions from the same retirement agency—he remained in the dark about motive, method and, most importantly, the identity of the murderer. All told, Owen knew very little. But to his credit, he had followed a lead that revealed something previously hidden in plain sight. It was this revelation that swelled the young reporter's pride, such that the corridors of his newsroom strained against his sense of professional prowess.

Owen devoted the remainder of his workday to completing a business write-up and researching another article due the next day. He was ahead of schedule and, to reward himself, decided to leave the office early. On his way out, he even smiled at Al, who cocked his head sideways like an agitated bird but squawked nothing in protest. Feeling too chipper to spend an evening alone, the young man drove to a sports bar to watch a football game. There, surrounded by dozens of strangers with whom he could share a few exciting hours without the hassle of interpersonal commitment, he felt happy. It was not a lasting happiness, he knew, but a fleeting one that would surely succumb to the wearisome gravity of real life. Tonight was like cotton candy for Owen's soul—if he had believed in souls.

Later that evening, he retreated to the porch of his apartment building, wine bottle in hand, to consider his next steps. Who could he trust with the story? How much should he disclose? What should he investigate next? An hour and an empty bottle later, his plan was set. Tomorrow would be another great day, he determined.

"What the …!" shouted the surly editor after Owen burst uninvited into his office the following morning.

"I've got something good, boss! You're going to want to hear this."

Al, with fingers still grasping his unwashed coffee mug, uneasily set down the swashing liquid that had been jolted en route to his unshaven face.

"No one except the publisher enters my office like that.

This better be good."

"I promise not to disappoint."

Owen began by revealing the string of deaths he had uncovered while researching his article series, conveniently omitting the fact that it had been an intentional pretext for his side project. He walked through the events as they happened, starting with his grandma's birthday party and continuing through his meetings with J.R., Mrs. Rogers and the pension plan staff. Although Owen had initially considered not sharing these details with Al, he eventually opted for full disclosure because, if his plans were to succeed, he needed his boss' buy-in. And if things went sideways, his support. By bringing Al into his confidence, Owen had tied his journalistic fortunes to a man he was learning to trust. From the risings and fallings of his listener's eyebrows, he knew his story had achieved its intended objective: to recruit an advocate.

"So, what do you think?"

Al reclined in his chair and pensively rubbed the scruff under his sagging chin.

"That's not half bad, kid. Before talking about what to do with your story, you need to get one thing straight as a reporter. Before you walk into a meeting, you need to know where you are going with your interview. It was stupid of you to show up at the police station without a list of questions. Come prepared or don't come at all. Got it?"

Owen nodded. Strangely, he did not feel angry about the brief dressing down. It felt less like the old-lady lectures he was accustomed to receiving and more like a coaching session: short and to the point. Owen could deal with that kind of instruction, even from Al. The editor resumed rubbing his jowls. Then he leaned forward on his desk and looked at Owen intently.

"What do you want to do with this story?"

"I'd like to publish a teaser in tomorrow's paper, announcing a full-length article to come out in the big Sunday edition. That will give me a few days to tie up loose ends in my research and write a masterpiece for you."

"I like that approach," agreed Al. "You don't blow it all at once. You set up a fat pitch for the weekend when readership is high. Yeah, that's good. Get to it. I want to see your notice in an hour."

Owen shot from his seat and hurried to his cubicle to begin writing. Thirty minutes later, he emailed the following to Al:

While researching the series on public servants, the Sunset Times stumbled upon an unsettling connection between dozens of county pensioners who passed away in the last year. The commonality: each died at exactly the same age. The Times will publish an article in Sunday's paper devoted to this deadly mystery.

Al tweaked the wording slightly and forwarded it to the newspaper's layout editor with a demand for good placement. The rest of the day dragged on for both men, anxious to learn how the public would receive the notice. Such is the plight of writers who invest themselves, often immoderately, in their work. But Owen knew the true test of its merit would not be known until Sunday at the earliest. Tomorrow's public response would be a foretaste of things to come.

The following day, Owen awoke earlier than usual so he could go to a coffee shop around the corner where new issues of the *Times* awaited sunrise customers. Of course, he could have driven to his office to read a free copy, but his excitement prevented him from delaying a minute longer than was necessary. He entered the store and grabbed the first paper from the newsstand, flipping through each section of the Wednesday edition until he found his glorious words atop the popular Local section—and above the fold! There it was, his baby, for all to see. He promptly bought the paper and drove to his grandma's house a few blocks away.

Ruthie, in the midst of her morning routine, sat at her little table with a cup of tea and buttered toast when Owen bounded through the front door.

"Look at this!" he exclaimed, shaking the paper back and forth with every step.

"Oh, dear! You're going to give me a heart attack."

"Not today, Gram. Check out the Local section." He set the paper on the table, kissed her cheek and turned back toward the door. "Running late, gotta go. Call me later and tell me what you think."

She started to reply, but Owen was already out of earshot. His car door shut, and she heard him drive away.

"That boy will be the death of me," she said, reaching for the stack of papers. "And he drives too fast."

It was past eight o'clock, and most of rush hour traffic had dissipated downtown. Owen circled the parking lot next to the newspaper office and found a choice spot. In its heyday many years ago, when the paper's advertising revenue and subscription base supported a full staff, the lot had brimmed with vehicles. Life was good for a newspaperman in that era. But in recent years, as residents gravitated to online news sites, the paper's income suffered, as did its staffing levels and morale. No longer was it difficult to find a good parking spot in the mornings, even for late arrivals. Despite all this, the hallways of the office buzzed with life as Owen entered.

"Good morning, Mr. Daniels," said the receptionist, who had never used his surname before.

"Uh, hi," he returned.

"Hey, buddy, how's it going?" said a man passing on the staircase that Owen barely knew.

All this overt friendliness perplexed him until he turned a corner and ran into Darcie, literally. She bounced back a step and reflexively apologized. But when she saw it was Owen, her face immediately brightened.

"Oh, I had no idea you were working on that lead. I'm so impressed. I thought you were genuinely interested in the obituary stories, but in reality, you must have seen something I didn't. Of course you did because you're smart like that. And I think you did a great job, by the way. I really look forward to reading your article on Sunday. Seriously, you're awesome! Bye."

With that torrent of words released, she grinned broadly at him and moved along.

Owen stood motionless, trying to piece together what had suddenly happened to his co-workers. He walked slowly toward his desk, looking around at other writers, whose heads popped above their cubicles and computers to see him pass by. Some smiled. Some just glanced and returned to their tasks.

"Did this have anything to do with my teaser?" he wondered as he sat down to check his phone messages. All doubt ended when a sharp-dressed man exited the distant elevator and meandered through the cubicle maze toward Owen.

"Are you Daniel?" he asked.

"No, but my last name is Daniels. Owen Daniels. You look familiar. Aren't you …?"

"Steven, the assistant publisher. The boss asked me to

congratulate you on your upcoming story. If this plays well with readers, he thinks it could be a boon for the company."

"How so?" asked Owen, unsure how his scoop would benefit anyone else.

The executive leaned in and lowered his voice.

"No offense to the rest of the writing staff, but we're not exactly well known for our vigorous journalism here. Your article could be a step in a different direction for the paper in terms of branding, market share, revenue, etc. And, depending on how this plays out, *you* might benefit."

He winked at Owen, turned on his shiny black heels and strode away.

Owen sat dumbfounded. While he did not place much stock in the implied promise of Steven, the fact that the publisher sent an emissary to convey a personal message to him—the youngest reporter on staff—meant a lot. It soon became apparent that the optimism and anticipation he felt were shared by his fellow reporters, many of whom offered their congratulations and expressed hope for uncovering their own scoop one day. Whether due to jealousy or a genuine desire for professional excellence, Owen's outperformance had somehow incited a desire in others for the same success. On that notable Wednesday, the entire newspaper office, particularly the newsroom staff, tasted of the glory days that once were common at the *Sunset Times*. Years later, Owen recalled that day as one of the best and worst of his career.

He received several more contacts that morning, each of a different character. The first came from the news director at the local television station, who asked to interview the young sleuth for the nightly news segment. Owen graciously declined the offer, for what reporter in his right mind would share a valuable scoop with another media outlet? In spite of the ridiculous request, his sense of self-importance swelled. The second contact was a text from J.R.: "Just saw your write-up! Good job finding the connection. Working on something interesting with forensics. Will be in touch. Btw, watch out for cockroaches … they don't like the light."

The more Owen thought about it, the more he relished the idea of shining the light of truth on criminal cockroaches and their misdeeds, just as his journalistic predecessors had done. He fancied himself as serving the public good in his own small way, of being a modern-day Woodward. Darcie interrupted Owen's momentary self-obsession by dropping a stack of newspaper clippings on his desk. She stood next to it, her fingers fidgeting by her sides, expectation on her face. She diverted her gaze from him to the papers and then back to him.

"Hi, Darcie," he said hesitantly. "What's all this?"

"Oh, these are more obituaries," she answered in her usual gunfire cadence. "I don't know if you've seen the recent ones since we worked on this several weeks ago. If not, here they are. There are about a hundred and twenty-three in total. I might have counted them for you. In fact, I did."

Owen blinked. Clearly, he was not understanding her meaning. She began again using different and far more words, two characteristics of speech he did not value.

She needed a distraction.

"Uh, thank you very much," he interrupted gently. "I'm going to have my hands full with other duties, so how do you feel about helping me track death notices of retired county employees? It could be our shared project. What do you say?"

"I'd say I died and went to obituary heaven!"

At that, words failed the young woman; her face glowed with elation. Owen also liked his proposal, but his motivation was more practical than hers. She could supply him with additional drama for his story, which, as he envisioned it, could stretch for as long as was required to bring the murderer to justice. He did not invent the axiom, "If it bleeds, it leads," yet he would apply it unapologetically. The logic was cold, no doubt, but more deaths meant more for him to write about. And Darcie was a means to that end, one that would bring him the notoriety he craved.

"I couldn't have found this without you," he said truthfully. "I'm confident you will continue to be an asset to me."

"I'm just glad to be invited for the ride. I won't let you down, I swear. I'm in this to the end."

Owen's final contact before lunchtime came from his grandma, who said she read his teaser notice in the paper multiple times.

"It worries me, Owen. It worries me a lot. If there is someone out there killing retirees, they might ... they might ..." She could not bring herself to complete the sentence. "I've already spoken to a few of my friends," she quivered. "It's— it's like a death sentence."

"What do you mean?"

"My eightieth birthday is next summer," she replied in a broken whisper.

In his excitement and single-minded focus over the preceding weeks, this fact had been lost on the normally conscientious young man. He flinched as if in pain and sat silent, holding the phone against his ear for a long moment.

"You are sure?" he asked stupidly.

Neither spoke. Owen heard Ruthie's soft whimpers on the other line. His heart broke for her. He ached in parts of his being unfelt since the passing of his parents. His own eyes blinked away tears.

"I'll figure this out, Gram. Please don't worry. I will fix this, and you and I will celebrate your next birthday together, I promise. I promise you."

But, really, what could he do? Reporting the news is far different than solving a crime. He desperately hoped Ruthie would not know his promise rang hollow. Owen gently laid the phone in its place and then his face in his hands. He felt responsible for his grandma's suffering. Responsibility for the murders—if indeed they *were* murders—was not his to bear, and yet his notice in the paper was the source of her pain. *His* notice. The news that brought him praise that morning was the same that would bring him a lifetime of regret if Ruthie were to die. For this cruel irony, he suffered silently at his desk. His trusted Fate was unavailable to accuse of injustice. For this day only, he desired the existence of a God to believe in and hate. Yet his worldview afforded no such satisfaction; his universe proved to be unfeeling and unfair.

The dark clouds continued to gather with the late arrival of Al, an employee known to the *Sunset Times* as much for his consistent attendance as for his distasteful appearance. He typically arrived before the rest of staff and stayed until they had departed. And yet, on this celebrated day for the newspaper, he was noticeably absent all morning. As he proceeded down the hallway toward his office, too briskly for his weak knees, his skin looked thicker and pastier than usual. Beads of sweat dotted his worn, wrinkled brow. The man who carried the editorial weight of the paper on his shoulders seemed to carry a different, greater burden. He hurried into his office and shut the door with a thud that drew the attention of the entire newsroom. The noise jolted Owen from his woeful thoughts to Al, whose unpracticed fingers worked feverishly to close his street-facing window blinds. Through the vertical pane of glass by Al's door, Owen observed his boss sitting in the same helpless posture he had held a minute earlier: a flushed face buried in quivering hands. What to make of this odd sight, Owen did not know, nor did he care to ask. Not now.

For the remainder of that bittersweet day, Owen performed his work soberly, as someone who bore a load unknown and unshared by his cheerful well-wishers. He continued to thank them when they dropped by to compliment his work, but sadness tempered his pride. Off and on, he poked his head over cubicle walls to glance into Al's office. There was no movement within, which worried Owen because, regardless of personal problems, the daily paper had to be published. It was a steam engine without brakes, barreling toward an immutable deadline every evening. The reporter finished writing his pieces and emailed them to his editor. More to satisfy his curiosity than out of compassion, Owen knocked on Al's door and waited.

"C'min," was the barely audible reply.

"Hey, I just sent you my articles. I'm heading out."

Owen took the opportunity to look around Al's office for explanations of his strange behavior. Nothing seemed out of place, although his coffee mug sat near the edge of his desk—empty and dry.

"Fine, go," he said without looking up.

Owen moved to leave when he heard Al mutter something else. He turned to face the typically outspoken man, whose gaze flitted from his computer screen to the visitor and back again. His lips moved as if trying to verbalize an unspoken thought, but no sound emerged. Owen could see he was deeply troubled, as if torn on whether or not to say more.

"Go already!" he thundered.

Owen surmised that Al had decided against opening up. It was just as well, for he needed to leave the building for a place, any place, that did not remind him of his grandma's call. He picked up fast food on the way home and spent the evening with his music and musings. Before succumbing to sleep, he called Ruthie.

"My article will come out on Sunday," he said softly, "and I'm hoping someone who knows something will come forward to help us. Before getting too worried, let's see what comes of that."

"Thank you, sweetheart. You are my knight in shining armor. Why don't you come over this weekend? It would be good for me to see you."

Both grandma and grandson drifted to sleep wishing the distance between them was just a bedroom wall, not miles.

Determined to write a great article for the Sunday edition, Owen set to work the next day organizing his facts and sketching an outline. He pulled information from numerous interviews conducted over the past two months, strategically using his "public servant" series as a contextual springboard to the present subject. He began his piece the same way he began his series—with a story about Ruthie, a feature that personalized it immediately for him and, he believed, would pull on the heartstrings of readers. He wrote for hours, deliberating over every word, every sentence, to construct a compelling narrative that would both inform and persuade. He ended with a personal appeal to his readers:

If you have any facts that could help unravel this local mystery and save the lives of innocent retirees, including my widowed grandmother, please contact me immediately. On behalf of our town, thank you in advance for your help.

Owen reread the two thousand-word piece and nodded approvingly. He spun around toward Al's office but did not see him there. Without a second thought, he emailed the article and left for lunch. For the first time in twenty-four hours, Owen felt optimistic about Ruthie's prospects. The article would expose the issue publicly, creating widespread awareness of the criminal activity that he hoped would, at least temporarily, end the deaths. Only a fool would dare continue his lawless activity under the watchful eye of an informed citizenry—or so he believed.

When Owen returned, he passed by Al's office and heard low voices inside. Before he arrived at his cubicle, the door opened and a voice bellowed, "Daniels, get in here." The editor sat behind his desk, arms crossed, eyes diverted. Next to him stood Steven, who stepped forward to close the door after Owen had entered.

"Have a seat, kid," Al instructed.

Owen complied and quickly surveyed the faces of the men, both of whom looked downward, almost ashamed. Steven fidgeted with his watch while Al bit into his bottom lip.

"What's this about? Is something wrong?"

Steven spoke first. "Uh, Mr. Daniels." He paused to collect another breath. "A situation has arisen that prevents us from publishing your article on Sunday. The reason has nothing to do with you."

Owen's blood boiled.

"What?!" he burst. "This is *my* article, *my* story! People are expecting to read it. We've already announced it."

Steven and Al nodded sympathetically.

"We know," said Al. "But ... but ..." The editor's hand trembled involuntarily. "But there are other considerations now. Things that are outside of my control. And, uh ..." Al shook his head. "We just can't let it go out."

"Al, people's lives are at stake!" Owen protested.

"I know!" Al fired back, his eyes meeting Owen's for the first time. He exhaled and looked away again. "I know."

"Look, we understand you have questions about our decision," Steven added, "but we are not at liberty to share them right now. It's probably a lot of ask of you, but please don't ask. I'm sure you will find out eventually. For the time being, your project needs to end, effective immediately. No more writing, no more inquiries."

"I can't even research?" Owen shouted. "Why are you pulling this story? Everything was cool yesterday. You said it yourself. What happened?"

Steven rocked his head back and forth like a boat at sea. Following a long moment of having words stick in his mouth like cotton, he simply replied, "I'm sorry, I can't say."

With that unsatisfying answer, Al dismissed the indignant young man, who slammed the door behind him. Having gained a piece of the world and its commendation just a day ago, Owen had suddenly lost it. His fortunes and hopes had come crashing down in an unexpected, blindsided instant. His star had fallen to earth and left in its wake a trail of anger, sorrow and, more poignantly, fear for his grandma's safety. Helpless, Owen retreated to the archives cellar and fumed.

Had he been at his desk where his phone lay charging, he would have heard it ring. He would have answered it and spoken to J.R. He would have learned that the officer had identified the manufacturer of the assisted-suicide drug found in the blood of autopsied eighty-year-olds. And he would have received contact information for a scientist at the pharmaceutical company who clinically tested the drug. Whether it was the work of Fate or someone else, the result was the same: Owen missed the call that mournful afternoon. He would have to wait until the next day to learn these facts—sufficient time for the young man to face his grief, harness his anger and defy his boss.

« 11 »

Livid. That was how Owen felt before dozing off on his couch, surrounded by half-empty bottles of various inebriating beverages. A restless, dream-filled sleep did not improve his bitter condition through the night. But by the time daylight had broken through his windows and he had slept off his vitriol, the word that most accurately captured his state of mind was *determined*. Determined to use whatever resources necessary to forestall or prevent the inevitable. Owen was not a bare-knuckled fighter. Like his father, he was a strategist. Faced with a challenge, his mind would survey it like a map and chart a course within seconds. His capacity to crank out to-do lists had benefited him on many occasions, but it was his ability to work through those lists efficiently that won him praise.

For now, the only item on his to-do list was swallowing something to quell the pounding in his head. As he slumbered toward the bathroom, he tripped over clothes he had apparently left there last evening, landing him face down on his backpack. A bee-like sound and bluish glow emanated from one of the unzipped pockets beneath him. He startled in fear and pushed the bag across the tile floor, watching it blurry-eyed until the light and sound vanished. Crawling forward, he fumbled for the pocket and put his hand in.

"Idiot, it's your phone," he grunted.

He left it there and resumed his to-do list. A warm shower and cup of coffee later, Owen emerged a changed man, relatively speaking. He picked up his phone and checked messages: one from Ruthie, asking about dinner; one from J.R., requesting a call back; and one from Al, asking if he was okay. The last one surprised him. He never viewed his boss as the caring type, but it was not entirely compassion Owen perceived in the gruff voice; something else haunted it. Dismissing the thought, Owen sat on the couch with his notepad and dialed J.R.

"Hey, sorry I missed your call. Yesterday was rough."

"I figured. I read the correction notice in this morning's paper."

"What correction?" Owen stammered.

"You haven't seen it? Hold on a sec. I'll read it to you: 'The *Sunset Times* will not publish an article on Sunday about deceased county retirees due to the absence of evidence.' Is that true—there's no evidence?"

"Well, if you don't count the confirmation I received from the pension plan—the one I handed to my boss—then, yeah, I suppose there is none," Owen said sarcastically. "Something is not right about this. My editor and publisher were completely on board with the story earlier this week, and then for whatever reason, it got pulled. That's not how we do things in our business."

"Sudden flip flops like this don't happen on their own," J.R. agreed. "In my experience, someone on the outside steps in and demands a change. It's typically people in power: those who have something to leverage or lose. Who could pull that kind of weight with your bosses?"

"I don't know. Maybe the families of the victims? Maybe the murderer? Maybe the pharmaceutical company?"

"I'd say no to all three, but each for its own reason. Out of curiosity, why did you say the pharmaceutical company?"

"Because it was *their* drug that killed the retirees—and I assume not in the way it was intended. If I were the drug maker, I wouldn't want my meds at the crime scene. Or in a front-page article."

"Funny you should say that because that's what I called you about yesterday. Our pathologist consultant identified the drug in the victims' bodies as a unique barbiturate cocktail that is only manufactured by one company: Hemlock Pharmaceuticals in San Francisco. I dug around and learned that the state assemblyman who pushed hardest to pass California's assisted-suicide bill *and* Hemlock's contract with the state represents the area where the drug company is located. Ironic, huh?"

"Crony capitalism at its best," Owen mocked. "I hate when politicians pick favorites."

"Huh, I would not have pegged you as a libertarian."

"I'm *not*. I'm a liberal."

J.R. hesitated. "Yeah, maybe. Regardless, I feel you on the corruption thing. So, you ready for the contact info?"

"The what?"

"I have phone numbers and addresses for the clinical director at Hemlock and the state assemblyman. Do you want them? I assumed you would want to follow up."

Pursuing J.R.'s leads was tantamount to resigning if his efforts were discovered. But refusing it might seal the fate of his grandma and perhaps dozens more people in his community. Since waking up that morning, between throbs in his head, Owen committed to making sacrifices—whatever the cost—to save Ruthie. Therefore, accepting this offer, even if it meant losing his job, was a simple decision. As J.R. relayed the relevant details, Owen scribbled them onto his notepad. The last item provided was a texted photo of a retiree's redacted autopsy report.

"The blood work is referenced in there. You might find it useful with the pharma lady."

Immediately after hanging up, Owen called Hemlock Pharmaceuticals to schedule an interview with Dr. Michele Kemp, the drug company's director of clinical research.

"What's the nature of the proposed meeting?" her secretary asked.

"Um." He hesitated. "I am a reporter looking for information and a few quotes about your new drug. It's for a project we're working on."

"What media outlet are you with?"

"The *Times*," he answered honestly. By the silence that filled the next few moments, Owen knew the secretary was deciding which *Times* he meant. If he was lucky, she would feel embarrassed and assume he meant the *Los Angeles Times*. But if she asked him to clarify, he dreaded having to lie outright. He had never been a good liar.

"The *Times*?" she asked.

Owen could not tell whether the uncertainty in her voice was from skepticism or insecurity. He swallowed hard.

"As in Los Angeles?"

He swallowed hard again. "We are actually located north

of Los Angeles. It's a little-known fact."

The *Sunset Times* indeed resided north of L.A., so his statement was factually true, albeit misleading. Though not a good liar, Owen excelled at dissembling.

"Okay. I've got you on Dr. Kemp's calendar for half an hour today at one o'clock. Will this be a phone or in-person interview?"

"Definitely in-person," he replied.

Buoyed by the success of his first call, Owen dialed the state assemblyman's headquarters in the heart of San Francisco. The receptionist, apparently accustomed to reporters' calls, did not sound impressed or intimidated by Owen's credentials, even his misleading one.

"Besides," she said, "Assemblyman Ramos has other appointments all afternoon before leaving for Sacramento this evening. I'm sorry, but he has no time to speak."

Owen contented himself knowing that at least one of the meetings would happen today. As he readied for his trip, it dawned on him that he was late for work. "Moron!" he said aloud. He called in a sick day and, to his surprise, Al agreed immediately and even told him to "take care."

It did not really matter to Owen, but his boss' odd behavior had become a point of curiosity rather than a cause for derision. Had the old buzzard grown some humanity this week? Had he discovered that other people had feelings, too? Regardless of where that rabbit hole led, the reporter's day was now free, and the only thing between him and the big city was another ibuprofen and cup of coffee. Before leaving, he called Ruthie to tell her where he was headed.

"I'm going, too," she announced. "I haven't been to the Bay Area in years. I'll just tag along while you work, okay?"

The request caught him off-guard. He muttered

something inaudible as he considered how to best say no.

"What's that, sweetie? If you're worried about me getting in the way, don't be. Just drop me off at the pier and I'll walk around. I'd like to see Alcatraz one last time."

Owen realized what was happening. If Ruthie believed this might be the final year of her life, she would want to spend it doing something that made her feel alive and happy. He could not resist the force of that logic.

"Yes, of course you can come, Gram. But only on the condition that you buy lunch."

"That goes without say, dearie."

He picked her up, and the two began their long drive to San Francisco. The beautiful farmland through California's rich-soiled central valley reminded Ruthie of distant memories. She told him stories of her poor Oklahoma family and their hopeful trek to the sunshine state when she was a little girl. An older boy in her high school eventually caught her eye and, having pledged their love to one another a year later, they eloped in secret.

"Only my sister knew," she confessed. "Your grandfather was a good man. He worked hard to provide for me and your dad—God rest his soul. Times were good then, and so were the people: simple, honest folks who just wanted to be free to pursue their dreams."

When the factory in Sunset Hills closed, she explained, her husband lost his job.

"That was when I started working for the county. My measly income sustained the family until a local farm hired your grandpa. He loved the work; he was made for it. But one day, when you were just a baby, he walked under a broken fertilizer sprayer and got soaked. His body absorbed the chemicals, and his liver could not handle it."

Ruthie's cheerful chatter paused as she recalled the memory. Owen left her to her thoughts. He waited a moment and then placed his hand on her wrinkled fingers and squeezed them gently. She glanced over and smiled at his handsome profile as he maneuvered the road ahead.

"You're a sweet boy. Have I told you that?"

"Often," he smiled back.

Three hours later, they crossed the magnificent Golden Gate Bridge and headed toward San Francisco's famous Pier 39, known for its clam chowder and hideously pierced squatters. Ruthie insisted on sampling both, by which she meant taking a photo with "one of those street freaks."

In spite of his concern for her safety and against his better judgment, he dropped her off near the pier.

"I'll be back after lunch. Keep your phone on. And don't talk to strangers!" he yelled into the cool ocean breeze.

She laughed. A strong gust tore through their conversation, making it difficult to understand one another's goodbyes. Before Ruthie turned to leave, he heard her shout, "Eat, drink and be merry!" Her red scarf flapped lustily in the wind as she marched off, a wild twinkle in her eye.

◊ ◊ ◊

Owen sped to Hemlock's corporate office for his appointment. Compared to other pharmaceutical behemoths, Hemlock occupied a relatively small space in the drug market, focusing primarily on specialty medications designed to manage chronic pain, block nerve function and, most recently, induce death. What the drug maker lacked in market share, however, it disguised behind a sprawling campus outside the city limits. The tall, glass panels lining the all-white administrative lobby reminded Owen of the afterlife: a

113

calming, luminescent nothingness. He walked through the entryway and gazed in awe at the crystalline paneling surrounding him, which brilliantly directed sunlight to various features in the ethereal room: original artwork, a hologram display, a two-story tank brimming with colorful fish and a staircase winding upward to an observation deck.

"Whoa," he said quietly, taking in his surroundings. He did not realize he was standing still until an "ahem" from behind caught his attention. A well-dressed somebody cut around him and walked past the lobby's welcome desk, where two guards sat monitoring screens and visitors. He made his way in their direction, and the guard who had been watching Owen since his arrival asked about his business there. Owen introduced himself as a reporter from the *Times* who had an appointment with Dr. Kemp. The guard verified the meeting on a checklist and asked to see identification. Owen showed his driver's license and received a guest badge without further inquiry. The guard provided directions to the scientist's office in an adjoining building.

Through one bright corridor and then another, the reporter came upon two imposing doors with "Clinical Research" displayed on the wall above. The entire aura of the facility—large, white and sterile—made him feel like a contaminating presence. A head-to-toe antibacterial scrubbing commencing as soon as he entered would not have surprised him. He walked to the receptionist, identified himself and sat in an alien-like chair that appeared to float. He estimated that the furniture in the seating area alone cost more than he earned in an entire year. For the first time, he doubted his decision to enter the field of journalism instead of science. One full minute of analyzing the inexplicable chair settled his internal debate about whether he had chosen the right career path. A pleasant voice interrupted his musings. A tall, slender figure in a lab coat stood opposite Owen, hand outstretched.

"Welcome," she said. "I am Dr. Michele Kemp. My office is on the next floor up. Please follow me."

As they walked to a nearby elevator, she surveyed him from the corner of her eye. He was young, not dressed particularly well, clean-shaven, holding a notepad and missing a media badge.

"Where is your media identification?" she asked sharply.

The unexpected question halted Owen's breathing. He stuck a hand into his trousers pocket, fumbled around and drew out a worn badge that had "Los Angeles Times" and his photo on it. He flashed the card just long enough for Dr. Kemp to see the newspaper's name and his picture. What skirted her notice was the issuance date, five years in the past, and the word "Intern" in bold, which Owen had carefully covered with his thumb.

"You've come a long way to talk to me," she said in the elevator. "I look forward to our discussion."

In her office, overlooking the beautiful campus acreage, Owen took a seat and flipped open his notepad to ask the first of several prepared questions. Despite his occupation and the respect it usually carried with people he met, he felt strangely insecure. Dr. Kemp had a superior intellect, Owen recognized, and therefore he needed to be particularly careful with his words. He read the first question to himself and opened his mouth to speak. But she beat him to the punch.

"So, Owen, on which subjects do you report: politics, science, pop culture, something else? I ask because—you need to know up front—my field is science. Politics does not interest me. Generally, people do not interest me. With that said, where are you planning to take this interview?"

One thing was certain: No one could accuse Dr. Kemp of being indirect. Her manner of speaking was fast-paced and methodical, as if she had rehearsed the conversation beforehand. But given what Owen had observed so far, he believed she was just that cerebral, that focused. He looked down at his questions, counting the ones that involved politics—far too many. Narrowing the focus would at least let him dig deeply into how the drug worked. That would be a win.

"I admit, I did have a few somewhat-political questions to ask, but I will respect your wishes about staying on point with what you actually do here."

She smiled at his concession and opened up about her job at Hemlock.

"It's an appropriate corporate name, actually," she said, "although it was called something else until about three years ago. Hemlock was the substance that Socrates ingested to end his life. Interesting, don't you think? When the FDA approved our most recent drug, Hemlox, my ..., I mean, our management team decided to update the corporate branding. *Why* they made the change at that time is a political question, so don't inquire," she reminded.

"How does Hemlox work in the body. What does it do?"

"The long answer will go over the heads of you and your readers," she warned. "Are you ready?"

He nodded naïvely. After a minute of ferocious note taking, Owen quit scribbling and let her finish her molecular-laced monologue.

"And now, the short answer," she chimed.

He picked up his pen again to record as much as possible. Dr. Kemp spoke slowly and carefully.

"Hemlox is a cocktail drug, meaning it consists of four different chemicals, each of which performs a unique role in the end-of-life process. One without the others will lead to paralysis, asphyxia or excruciating pain. They must be ingested together and in the full dosage for the intended effect to occur."

"Has it ever *not* worked?"

"By the end of our clinical trials, it worked every time. It's simple physiology, like a math problem: A plus B always results in C. Hemlox works the same way. The sodium thiopental anesthetizes the patient. The barbiturate puts them to sleep. The pancuronium paralyzes all voluntary muscles. And the potassium chloride serves as the immediate agent of death, causing cardiac arrest."

"How long does the process take?"

"Just a minute or two."

Owen fell silent. He felt ambivalent about the idea of people killing themselves with this drug. His liberal bent told him that a person should be completely free to do with their bodies as they pleased. But the part of him that was Ruthie's grandson told him that the life of a loved one was sacred. On her worst days of pain, when her arthritis flared and she felt lonely, the thought of her with Hemlox in her medicine cabinet frightened him. He held these two strong viewpoints in tension. At the moment, however, Owen the grandson felt more passionate than Owen the liberal.

Dr. Kemp noticed Owen's discomfort.

"Remember, this is a patient's decision, and he or she must follow a lengthy process of doctor approvals and waiting periods. Nothing will be forced on individuals who are not ready to die."

"Are you sure about that?" Owen pulled up the redacted autopsy report on his phone and handed it to Dr. Kemp. "Take a look at this blood work and tell me what you see."

She spent a long while examining the notes, line by line.

"Based on what I'm reading, it is definitely Hemlox. I would recognize that chemical profile a mile away." She tilted her head curiously and spent another minute rereading the report. "I'm—I'm confused by this. The serum levels of the drug are insufficient. It's barely enough to put the patient to sleep. But I don't see any unusual supplemental substances to augment the effect."

She mumbled something to herself, returned the device to Owen and looked at him quizzically.

"Who is this person?"

"I would be happy to answer your question, but first I'd like to ask one of my own. What role did Assemblyman Ramos play in making Hemlock Pharmaceuticals the single-source provider of assisted-suicide drugs for the entire California market?"

He let the words hang in the still, sterile air. As was his practice when dropping a bomb on a listener, he assumed a poker face and waited.

"My one condition for this interview was that we would not discuss politics," she replied. "Your question is unambiguously political."

Owen held her gaze and kept silent; he no longer felt insecure. She tapped her foot slowly and stared into his unblinking eyes. After several painfully long moments, she exhaled loudly.

"Many people collaborated on the bill. That's how it works in politics. You should know that."

"That was not my question. What role did *Ramos* play?"

Had Dr. Kemp not expressed interest in the blood work of the mystery patient, Owen realized the interview would have ended and he would have been escorted by security to the parking lot. Because she had not kicked him out yet, he knew he possessed a secret that intrigued her as much as her secret intrigued him. So, each waited for the other to crack. Owen sat stock still while the scientist checked her cuticles, read an email and cast unkind stares at her unmoving guest. He concluded that the prim, proper doctor was unaccustomed to delayed gratification. At last, the impatient scientist had had enough.

"Fine," she blurted. "Ramos made a deal to award the contract to us. That's all you are getting. Now, who is this person?"

Owen jotted a few notes and replied with a knowing grin.

"She was an eighty-year-old who did *not* want to die."

Dread-induced silence filled the room. Owen watched as the implications of his comment rushed through Dr. Kemp's intelligent mind: A world of potential liability had just arrived at her employer's doorstep. She stood, full of agitation.

"Out! Get out now!" she barked.

Owen's time at Hemlock Pharmaceuticals had ended abruptly, but he had anticipated this. He did not come to make friends but to pursue a lead. With his notepad firmly in his grasp, he retraced his steps down the corridors, through the afterlife-like lobby and into the crisp afternoon breeze.

He drove to Pier 39 and parked on one of the frighteningly sloped streets that terminate at a dock hugging the edge of the cold Pacific Ocean. He called Ruthie's cell phone to arrange a meeting location, but she did not pick up. He placed another call—also unanswered—followed by a worried text demanding to know her whereabouts. No reply came. Remembering her final words before they had departed—"Eat, drink and be merry"—he recited the rest of the foreboding saying: "for tomorrow we die." He began jogging down the steep hill, a pace that became a sprint with the unwelcomed aids of both gravity and momentum. As he approached the pier, his leg muscle cramped, causing him to lose control and nearly plow into one of the intricately pierced street freaks.

Though his stride just missed the squatting man, Owen bowled through the "$5 for photo" cardboard sign he held. "Watch it!" came the surly reply, but the weary sprinter was not listening. He focused only on finding his grandma amid a sea of heads, none of which looked remotely familiar. Even the bright scarf she wore was not visible from his current location. Thinking that perhaps she took a stroll, he trotted along the street, looking anxiously through the crowd of pedestrians and into each store along the pier. This continued for several minutes, leaving Owen breathless from both physical exertion and worry. He sat on a lonely bench facing the ocean, wondering if Ruthie had chosen to end her life on her own terms in a place she held fondly in her memory. Was the pain of knowing next year's fate too much for her sweet heart to bear? Could she really have left him without saying a final goodbye? The thought tortured him as he stared blankly out to sea.

A group of smiling tourists passed around him, chatting excitedly about Al Capone. Owen disregarded their conversation until he spied a red scarf flapping in their midst. He pushed his way into the crowd toward the fabric, only to realize it belonged to another woman. The group continued walking while Owen stood watching. He sulked back to his spot on the bench, not noticing a stranger moving a spoonful of steaming clam chowder in his direction.

"What you need, dearie, is some of this. It's sooo good!" He turned to see Ruthie at his side. "It really is good," she insisted. "Try it."

"Where have you been?" he chided. "I was worried sick!"

She took a bite of the chowder and exhaled a ring of steam as the heat from her mouth met the chilly air.

"Well, after you dropped me off, I took a photo with that nice man down there," pointing to the vagrant who had yelled at Owen, "and he recommended I go on the Alcatraz tour. That's where I've been for the last hour. I saw the Golden Gate Bridge, sea lions and of course the island prison. There is lot to do here, you know." She filled her mouth with another bite. "This is really good," she repeated.

"I'm just glad you're okay. I was worried you had—"

He could not bring himself to say the words. Ruthie did not appear to understand his reticence, so she fed him some chowder.

"This will cheer you up."

"Mmm, that is good. You didn't just slip me a beta-blocker, did you?"

"Not this time," she replied innocently. "Why, do you want one? I've got plenty to share."

"No thanks," he smiled. "Just seeing you is enough."

Back in the car, Owen asked her to call Assemblyman Ramos' office to recheck his afternoon schedule. He had hoped for a quick meeting with the politician, but his earlier conversation with the staffer gave him little hope. Ruthie, however, had better luck.

"Yes, dear," Owen heard her tell someone on the other line. "My grandson and I would like to speak to the assemblyman for a few minutes. We are in the area now. ... Uh huh. ... Oh, just something important on our minds. ... Certainly, we can do that. Okay, bye now."

"Phone drop," she said proudly as she dropped the cellular device in her lap. "Is that how you young people say it?"

"I think the term is *mic drop*, but you were close," he laughed. "Keep practicing."

The City by the Bay is one of the most expensive places in the United States to live and rent. And yet, Assemblyman Ramos enjoyed a charming office space off Market Street, a main thoroughfare that cut through the San Francisco Peninsula, just blocks from the offices of the influential U.S. congresswoman and U.S. senator. Much of the political power of the state and federal governments could be found in the small, densely populated area where Owen and Ruthie struggled to find a parking space.

"There are too many people and not enough parking garages," she said resolutely.

Owen believed in mass transit, but his current parking frustration put him in no position to disagree. Eventually, they found a place to park and paid a fortune in quarters for it. Ramos' office was a few blocks away, so they walked along the wind-swept streets, arm in arm, while Owen hid his notebook and *Times* badge inside his jacket pocket.

"Gram, I haven't told you exactly why I wanted to speak to Ramos. I had hoped to press him on his sponsorship of the recent assisted-suicide bill and his connection to Hemlock Pharmaceuticals. It might take me a little while to broach those sensitive topics, so I'll need to ask him some softball questions initially to get him comfortable with me. I need his trust first. You don't need to say anything unless he asks."

"I'll try to hold my tongue, but no promises," she winked.

Had Owen known how much his grandma disliked the assemblyman's politics, he would have been wise to extract a promise of silence from her. The two entered the office building, and Ruthie introduced herself as the earlier caller.

"You're in luck," the receptionist said. "Mr. Ramos has not left for the capitol yet. I'll see if he is still available." She dialed an extension, placed her hand over the receiver and quickly whispered to the guests, "What is this about?"

"Recent legislation," Owen replied.

While the lady spoke to a back-office worker about the visitors, Owen leaned toward Ruthie and explained the drug Hemlox and Ramos' alleged role in its legalization. Her eyes narrowed. A locked door buzzed, and the receptionist led them to a small conference room with large pictures of the assemblyman hanging on the walls. They sat down at a shiny, redwood table and absorbed their surroundings. Heeding his boss' earlier advice, Owen began rehearsing his planned conversation in his mind. A minute later, the door opened and in walked the politician, performing his well-worn grin-and-greet routine to his supposed constituents.

Owen wasted no time priming the pump. He immediately rose to his feet and walked toward Ramos with outstretched hand and stars in his eyes.

"It's such an honor to meet you, sir. I'm a big fan of your policies—always have been. No disrespect intended to our party, but seriously, it doesn't give you enough credit for your relentless support of the common worker. If the congresswoman in your district ever retires, you really need to run for her seat. You'd definitely have my vote!"

"I appreciate your support, young man. We shall see, we shall see," was his toothy reply. "And who is this?" he asked, facing Ruthie.

"Oh, just an old lady." She feigned a smile and sat down with her arms crossed. They joined her at the table.

"So, what brings you two here today?"

Owen had decided to not disclose his real name or occupation, believing it would put Ramos on guard and undermine his purpose there. Instead, he planned to play the part of a hapless constituent seeking counsel from someone in-the-know about physician-assisted suicide for his ailing grandmother: Was it legal? What was the process for obtaining the drug? Were there protections against improper use by non-patients? Somewhere in there, Owen hoped Ramos would open up about his role in pushing the suicide bill through the legislature and awarding a sole-source contract to Hemlock Pharmaceuticals to supply the key drug statewide. It was an ambitious agenda, but he needed to try. Owen's first question was on his lips when Ruthie, cheeks aflame, fired her own question at the politician.

"If I wanted to kill myself with Hemlox, how would I do that?"

The old woman's shot across the bow left both Ramos and Owen with wide eyes fixed on her angry expression. Ramos cleared his throat and adjusted himself in his seat.

"That's really a discussion you need to have with your doctor," he answered carefully. "There are several steps you would need to take before obtaining the drugs. It is all out there on the internet. I suggest you do some research."

Owen tried to take control of the discussion, but Ruthie interrupted again.

"Is it possible that if I had a bad day, or even a bad month, that I could make an emotional decision to take a drug that would kill me and steal me from my grandson forever?"

Ramos shifted in his chair but had no time to respond as Ruthie pushed on. "As I see it, you've put a drug on the market in the name of 'freedom' and 'personal choice,' but those are just smokescreens for what this actually is: self-murder.

Murder! Yes, it may be legal to murder myself, but it is not moral. Legalized killing is still killing, even if I am the one doing it."

With that deluge of opinion, Ruthie marched out of the room and back to the lobby, where she opened a magazine and began reading an article about San Francisco nightlife. Two paragraphs in, she shuttered and promptly closed the periodical.

In the conference room, Owen apologized profusely for his grandma's behavior. Ramos offered another toothy smile and dismissed it as the ravings of someone who clearly misunderstood the benefits of the law. As if to justify it, he told Owen why he sponsored the bill three years earlier and how he stood firm against "religious extremists" and others who opposed the idea.

"They were so vocal that we couldn't pass it during the normal legislative session, so we pushed it through in a special session by tying it to healthcare funding. It was a brilliant move," he boasted. "As leaders, we have to use every tool at our disposal to do what's best for California."

Something about the comment rubbed Owen the wrong way, even though he agreed with Ramos in principle. However, he still believed a bill should stand or fall on its own merit. If the people and their representatives wanted it to pass, it should pass the normal way—without any tricks that skirt the democratic process. He desperately wanted to argue the point, but it was more important to keep Ramos on track.

"Tell me more about how a person like my grandma would obtain the medication."

Ramos said the entire end-of-life process was well-regulated. Basically, it entailed getting two doctors to agree, at least fifteen days apart, that the patient met a long list of criteria—diagnosed with less than six months to live, no psychiatric issues, able to swallow independently, and so on—before the first physician would hand-deliver the prescription to a pharmacy, where the patient would sign for the drug and take it home.

"I'm told it is a beautiful experience," Ramos continued. "It allows a terminally ill person to end life in the time and place most fitting for him or her. Calling it 'physician-assisted suicide' or 'euthanasia' puts a stigma on something that I consider compassionate."

"How can you be sure the drug won't fall into the wrong hands and be used to hurt innocent people?"

"It's not possible. The drug company protects its assembly line and inventory with the greatest care. In fact, its contract with the state imposes stiff penalties for any security breach or even a change in its manufacturing process without the prior approval of regulators. And I am told that every batch of products released to pharmacies is bar-coded and carefully tracked. It's a tight process, young man. There's no need to worry."

"I read somewhere that Hemlock Pharmaceuticals was awarded a state contract to supply all of California with the drug. Did any other firms receive a contract?"

Ramos looked away momentarily and then at Owen. He grinned awkwardly.

"No, it just so happened that the FDA approved Hemlock's new drug about the time the state passed its law authorizing end-of-life planning. During early negotiations of the contract, the company president agreed to use some of his profits to support the community if the law passed. That made my decision even easier."

"What does 'support the community' mean?"

Ramos offered a delayed smile.

"Well, it means the company is giving back to the city and county through various programs that help the needy and through corporate income taxes that grow state coffers, which benefits us all. It's a win-win-win." He squinted at Owen. "You certainly ask a lot of questions. Where in the Bay Area do you call home?"

"Oh, a little south," he replied.

Owen knew it was time to leave. He thanked Assemblyman Ramos for the meeting, promised to vote for him if given the chance—which would never happen—and excused himself. Ruthie saw the lobby door open and Owen walk through it with an urgent stride. She followed him outdoors and down the sidewalk, where he wheeled around to face her.

"What got into you back there? You nearly scared him off!"

She smiled. "No, I didn't. I gave him a piece of my mind—yes, that's true. But I also played the bad cop, which made him nervous. When I left, you became the good cop. I bet he relaxed with you, didn't he?"

Owen nodded.

"Then my plan worked," Ruthie said.

He stood blinking at the little old woman who had outwitted a pair of intelligent men without either being the wiser.

"Wow, I didn't see that coming."

"Never mind that. Did he tell you what you wanted to know?"

"Sort of," Owen replied, still puzzled by his grandma's shrewdness. "He talked about Hemlock Pharmaceuticals supporting the community, but that's an odd thing to put in a 'deal,' as Dr. Kemp put it. Deals imply mutual benefit, so what did Ramos get in exchange for pushing the bill and later the contract? I doubt it's just poor folks benefiting."

They turned and began walking the busy streets.

"Another detail of the conversation troubled me. What are the chances that a small, relatively unknown drug company gets a lucrative state contract selling suicide pills at the *same* time that California legalizes suicide for residents? There is a place for coincidence, but really, at the same time?"

The two Daniels discussed the meeting on their ride home and pointed out other inconsistencies in Ramos' comments. Owen had never realized what a fascinating mind Ruthie hid underneath that sweet, unassuming demeanor. She could read people such as Ramos quickly and decisively. Like her skilled negotiator of a son, Ruthie seemed to intuitively understand human motivations and had an uncanny ability to influence them. Owen's dad employed this skill in union negotiations, whereas Ruthie employed it to instill wisdom in those willing to receive it. In this sense, her grandson was her crown jewel.

As the sun set, they pulled up to Ruthie's curb. Owen walked her to the front door and bent to kiss her forehead.

"I had a good day, Gram. Thanks for coming along."

"Me, too," she said with a squeeze of his hand. "You're so good to me. I feel safe with you."

Owen desperately wanted that to be true. Her confidence in him, as misplaced as it might be, gave him confidence. It compelled him to continue having uncomfortable conversations, as he did today, in pursuit of the truth that would free them both from fear. Ruthie disappeared behind the door. When Owen heard her deadbolt lock into place, he returned to his car and drove home.

« 12 »

The following weeks passed without incident. Owen continued his investigation under the radar, keenly aware that the slightest revelation of his side project could cost him his job and perhaps Ruthie's life. He took pleasure in filing his first Public Records Act request to obtain a list of Assemblyman Ramos' campaign contributors, hoping to confirm his suspicion that Hemlock Pharmaceuticals paid off its political debt each campaign season. One downside to the PRA submission was identifying himself and his employer, disclosures he hoped would not bite him one day. Also feeding his distrust of Ramos was an infuriating detail buried in an old newspaper article he found: The assemblyman sat on Hemlock Pharmaceuticals' board of directors until a year before the company launched its perfectly timed assisted-suicide drug.

Customary practice is to recuse oneself when a conflict of interest arises. Ramos' membership on the board posed an obvious political conflict, but in media interviews he argued, "My ties with Hemlock were severed over a year ago. I can be—and will be—unbiased when voting for any contract before the Assembly." When pressure mounted against him, largely from watchdog groups and competing drug companies that wanted a slice of California's market share, he agreed publicly to abstain from the vote. But when his party needed his support to approve the controversial sole-source agreement, he reneged on his abstention pledge. Owen knew this betrayal failed to prove any connection to the Sunset Hills deaths. If nothing else, it exposed Ramos as a typical politician.

The few remaining leads Owen pursued turned up little. As he struggled to find his footing in this new world of investigative journalism, he frequently relied on J.R.'s insight into criminal behavior. On one occasion, the investigator discussed one of the more interesting aspects of his job—evaluating crime scenes—about which Owen knew nothing.

"When I step on site, the basic questions I ask are who, what, where, when and how. The most difficult question to answer is *why*. Motive is not always obvious. Some people plan crimes way in advance; we call that the long game. Others jump into a crime blindly; we call that stupid. What the long-gamers and the stupids have in common is motivation. Every criminal has one, maybe two, impulses that drive his actions. It's tempting for detectives to assume we know why these fools break the law. But sometimes we're just guessing."

"Why not ask them?"

"Oh, I do. But they don't like telling me."

J.R. saw the reporter's quizzical expression and continued his tutorial.

"The *act* of crime can be committed without much feeling. But the *reason* for crime can be very personal, very close to the criminal's heart."

Owen shrugged. "I suppose motive doesn't really matter as long as they go to jail."

J.R. paused to consider Owen's words.

"You know, even if we figure out how the old folks are dying, we might never know why. These are not ordinary murders because this is not an original criminal. From what I've seen so far and from what you've told me, this is a sophisticated mastermind, a long-gamer, someone who won't be easy to find."

"Well, that's not particularly satisfying. I had hoped to turn the bowels of this mystery inside out for all to see on the front page of my paper—above the fold. But what you're telling me is, that's not realistic?"

"Not necessarily," J.R. replied. "Just don't get your hopes too high."

Owen was a realist. He knew his initial work had just scratched the surface and brought him no closer to identifying a suspect or motive. If state government was at all involved—and it appeared to be—he might never be able to peel back every putrid layer of corruption to find the wizard behind the curtain. And so, he was forced to wait for the next shoe to drop. It fell on a Monday morning when Darcie stopped by his cubicle with a new obituary of a county retiree. He noticed her disposition had changed distinctly after the unexpected retraction of his teaser notice.

"I feel just terrible about your situation, what they did to you," she lamented to him the day after it happened. "It was my project, too, sort of. *Our* project. It's just not right."

While Owen had an outlet for his frustration—further

investigation with a co-conspirator—Darcie had to chew on the unspoken injustice every hour of every workday. And unbeknownst to him, it affected her deeply. Even more oddly, her feelings seemed to parallel his. When he had a bad day at the office, her mood suffered. When he expressed excitement about a well-written article, her pale complexion colored. Owen, of course, remained oblivious to the emotional co-dependency that had developed in his co-worker. What he did notice—and had come to appreciate—were Darcie's frequent visits and interesting conversation. Her voluminous word count and rapid-fire speech had become tolerable, even enjoyable. So, when she brought the paper to his desk that morning, they spent a few friendly minutes discussing their weekends. Before leaving, she handed him the day's obituaries.

"I know you're not supposed to look into you-know-what anymore, but there's another eighty-year-old retiree, Bud Milhouse, who just died. Page twelve, if you are interested. But you didn't hear it from me!"

He looked at Bud's photo in the paper and instantly recoiled.

"If that picture is any indication of his disposition while alive, he must have been hideous to live with," Owen thought. "J.R. may want to know about this."

Over the years, funerals have evolved from being solemn remembrances to "celebration of life" services that afford people the opportunity to joyfully remember the life events of their departed loved one. Not so with Mr. Milhouse, whose best friends were those who hated him least. Even his widow, Betty, spurned the usual somber attire for the occasion in favor of jeans and a Harley Davidson jacket. It took Owen a while to identify her because no one there shed a tear. He overheard her tell another attendee that when the funeral ended, she was going directly to the nearest casino. The comment stunned the reporter, who could hardly contain the urge to interview her on the spot. After an unusually short graveside service, the widow freely spoke to him about the deceased.

"Bud was a complete arse. Wretched through and through. I might cry 'bout his death … just not today. Today I celebrate!"

The unabashed honesty proceeded from Betty with such unfiltered liberality that Owen wondered if her husband died of Hemlox or poisoned meatloaf.

"I see," he said slowly. "Actually, I am not interested in the kind of person he was as much as in his job—the job he retired from."

Betty squinted. "Why 'ya care about that?"

Owen explained his article series featuring county employees, past and present, who contributed to the betterment of the community. Betty laughed uncontrollably.

"Bud ain't what you'd call a model employee. He called in sick all the time, especially as he got closer to retirin'. I visited him at work once, and his boss told me to get 'em to retire quick 'cuz he wasn't doin' no good there anyways. Work and Bud didn't go together nice-like."

"How long did he work for the county?"

"Fifteen years or so." She got distracted by someone approaching in the distance. "Seriously, boy, you don't wanna write about Bud. That'd just hurt your paper's street cred."

When she had finished another disparaging story about her husband, she looked over Owen's shoulder and stepped backward.

"Uh, I should go now."

"Mrs. Milhouse," came a deep, familiar voice behind Owen. "My name is Officer Little. I'm with the police department. I am sorry about your loss. Before you leave, I'd like to ask you a few questions."

Owen turned to see J.R. standing next to another detective. Betty appeared anxious in the presence of the policemen, but whether her reason stemmed from negative run-ins in the past or an awareness of guilt in the present, Owen could only guess. He stepped aside and listened to J.R. question her about Bud's pre-retirement employment, co-worker relationships, circumstances surrounding his death and her plans for life without him. Her response to the last inquiry piqued Owen's interest.

"Bud got a nice pension from the retirement folks," Betty explained. "When he retired, I talked him into picking an option that'd give me his full benefit when he died. So, every month from now to when I die, I'll get paid what he got paid. When I'm done gamblin' tonight, I'm gonna take myself on one o' them pleasure cruises to Mexico. It might sound bad … but I'm glad the jerk is gone. The world's a better place now."

J.R. looked at Betty soberly. "Mrs. Milhouse, we have reason to believe that your husband's death involved foul play."

"I didn't do it! I swear to the sky. I was at my sister Colleen's trailer all day when it happened. Go ahead, call her and ask! Oh, I loved Bud. I won't be the same without that man, no, I won't. He was a good man."

"Calm down, ma'am. You are not a suspect. Please relax."

Betty wiped away crocodile tears and sniffed.

"But," J.R. continued, "we need to take a closer look at

your husband's body. Do you mind if we have our people examine it before the burial occurs?"

"Take whatever you want," she snorted. "Take the whole rottin' corpse."

If ever someone deserved to be questioned for murder, it was Betty, who not only hated her spouse but would receive his entire pension for the rest of her life. And yet, J.R. did not pursue the lead. Instead, he served her with a subpoena to claim the body and wished her luck with the slot machines. As the other detective walked to his patrol car, J.R. and Owen lingered at the gravesite.

"Are you just taking blood samples?" Owen asked.

"No way. I'm not going to squander the opportunity to run a full autopsy on this guy. We haven't had a comprehensive look at a body killed by Hemlox because we haven't known who to look for—until now. This is our first chance to see the effects of the drug on the inside of a body. I'm sort of excited."

"You're a sick man," Owen said as he jokingly elbowed the officer. J.R. returned the favor, nearly knocking his friend over Bud's headstone.

"Ow! If that's what your elbow can do, I'd hate to be on the receiving end of your fist."

The pair walked down the flower-lined path toward their vehicles, discussing the retiree deaths as they meandered along.

"You know," J.R. observed, "the differences between the victims are really just superficial in nature, probably irrelevant. The two main similarities, on the other hand, are striking. Number one is their common age at death; there is nothing new to learn about that. Number two is the retirement system that paid their monthly benefits. Even though I'm entitled to a pension one day for my city employment, honestly, I don't know how it works. Do you?"

"I'm not getting a pension at all, so I'm just as ignorant."

"I think it's time we paid a visit to the retirement office. Maybe they will have a clue why retirees are dying at eighty."

"Well, it can't hurt to ask. Just to warn you, the agency's executive director, Alexis, is weird about media attention. You should have seen her face when I suggested writing a piece on her. She's got issues."

"Then it's best I go alone. I don't want her clamming up even more after I walk in the room. I'm told I have that effect on people," J.R. said with a hint of pride.

"You? No way," Owen grinned. "Okay, you can have Alexis all to yourself. But promise me you will record the meeting."

"What for?"

"For me, of course."

◊ ◊ ◊

A few days later, J.R. arrived at the county's retirement office with a notepad, voice recorder and Bud's obituary in hand. Though Owen could not attend the meeting in person, he was there in a sense, having sent a list of questions with J.R. Anxious to stay close to the action, the reporter worked at a bench in a park a block away from the building. He could even see it from where he sat. He took pleasure, imagining the intimidated look on Alexis' face when the burly investigator walked in. How he wished to be a fly on that wall.

Alexis indeed looked overwhelmed by Officer Little's stature and commanding voice, but she had begun to perspire even before they had shaken hands. In keeping with her cautious disposition, the executive invited her legal counsel to attend the meeting. The pair sat opposite J.R. at a long conference table in her grand office. They exchanged niceties before he set the recorder between them and turned it on. Legal counsel shifted in her seat and moved to protest, but J.R. preempted her.

"The purpose of this meeting is to investigate the recent death of Mr. Milhouse. I just need background information about the man's retirement; the recorder will be used to supplement my note taking."

The ladies looked at each other and had a silent conversation using only facial expressions, a talent that impressed the observant investigator, whose eyes had never learned to speak.

"Okay, officer, what would you like to know?"

J.R. picked the first question on his notepad and readied his pen. "Let's start with an overview of the retirement agency and how a pension works."

"Our communications manager is best at answering such questions concisely, but I'll do my best to cover the basics. The retirement association is loosely tied to the county, but we are not accountable to the county's Board of Supervisors like other departments. Every employee in this building, including me, answers to the Board of Retirement, which consists of elected and appointed officials. Every retirement board in California has one primary directive: to ensure retirees get paid their promised benefits."

"What do you mean by *promised*?"

"Our agency does not *approve* benefits for public employees. We simply *administer* them. For example, many years ago, the Board of Supervisors passed a pair of resolutions that improved pension benefit formulas for all current and future employees. The biggest increases were approved in 2000 for safety members and 2005 for general members. It's important to remember that our retirement board did *not* vote for those benefit enhancements; the politicians did."

"Then I suppose they immediately retired, huh?"

"I know of one that did. But others kept getting reelected. The point is, we—the retirement agency—only administer benefits. We are independent, like an escrow company."

J.R. looked out the window, trying to recollect something. "A few years back, I recall hearing that anti-pension protesters stormed a board meeting, and we were called out to restore order. Was that you guys?"

Alexis rolled her eyes and nodded.

"But you are saying that those protesters were in the wrong board room because you guys don't actually grant the benefits?"

She nodded again. He scribbled a few notes.

"Okay, I get the gist of what you do here. Now tell me about pensions—how do they work?"

Legal counsel chimed in. "A pension is a monthly retirement allowance, payable for life, that is calculated according to a formula whose factors include benefit tier, years of service, age at retirement and final average compensation. As these data points change over the course of public employees' careers, so do their retirement benefits."

"Uh-huh," J.R. muttered in confusion. "Would you repeat that, please?"

"In other words," Alexis interjected, "a pension is a monthly payment—similar to an annuity you could buy from a financial company—that we issue to members of our system who are eligible to retire. With some exceptions, the retirement eligibility age is fifty. When we calculate a member's retirement benefit, we look at four factors: their age at retirement, their years of public service with the county, their highest annual pensionable earnings and their benefit tier. Generally speaking, the older they are and the longer they've worked and the more money they've earned, the higher their pension will be. That benefit is payable every month until the retiree dies."

"I once heard about a firefighter who was paid six figures in retirement—as much as he made during his career—and he retired in his early fifties! Is that really possible?"

Alexis' head wobbled side to side. "That's a question we have heard many times. Well, it is possible, but not common. The vast majority of our eight thousand retirees make far, far less. I think the average benefit payment is about $3,000 per month. But, yes, we do see those high-earners every now and then."

J.R. did the math. That number of retirees making that much on average meant the agency paid $290 million per year in benefits. Alexis watched him write out the figures, saying nothing about how retiree payroll increased with each passing year. She did not know Owen had already informed J.R. of the immense payroll, which had doubled in the past decade due to a wave of Baby Boomer retirements and larger average benefits. He underlined the tally on his notepad and circled it twice to be unmistakably obvious to his host. Then he looked at Alexis.

"Please continue."

Alexis swallowed. "If there is an eligible surviving spouse when the retiree dies, some or all of the benefit continues throughout the beneficiary's lifetime. So, we will pay the retiree until death and then the beneficiary—if there is one—until death." She looked at J.R. somewhat sheepishly.

"It's a very nice benefit we provide to our public employees."

Until now, the detective had not fully grasped the long-term nature of a pension. His wife would be thrilled because longevity ran in her genes. He thanked Alexis for the layman's explanations before confessing, "Everything you just said is new to me and, honestly, a tad complicated."

"And we just scratched the surface," she added.

"I think I understand the basics of how a pension works. Can you tell me how long your members usually live after retiring: ten years, twenty years?"

This answer required more deliberation between the pension executive and attorney. After a series of whispers beyond earshot of J.R., the executive finally answered, "That is a question best left to our actuary."

He shook his head. "I don't know what an actuary is."

"Retirement agencies like ours hire specialized statisticians called actuaries to evaluate the annual 'experience' of their thousands of plan members. From this data, actuaries make certain assumptions to help map the statistical probability of certain events occurring at certain times in the lives of those members. For example, our actuary expects the average general member to retire at age sixty and the average safety member to retire at age fifty-five. These are assumptions that can change over time, of course. We have assumptions about all sorts of things: the length of a career, having a spouse, age at retirement, age at death, investment returns, inflation ..."

"When does your actuary expect retirees to die?" J.R. interrupted. This was the moment he had been waiting for. He gripped his pen, ready to transcribe whatever Alexis said next.

She whispered a few words to her counsel and replied, "We don't know the exact mortality assumption. I think it is buried somewhere in an actuarial memo I saw last year. That's a great question for our actuary, though. He will be at next month's board meeting. I'm sure he will know."

J.R. set down his pen and bit his lip. He had thought the answer was at hand, the piece of the puzzle that he and Owen needed to keep the investigation moving. He knew his young friend would not be pleased. Alexis and her attorney again counseled quietly while J.R.'s mind churned, unsure where to take the interview because his follow-up inquiries depended on knowing the answer to the mortality age question.

"We can't tell you when retirees are expected to die because we don't have that number here," the executive restated. "But I can tell you what happens *after* they die from an actuarial perspective."

"Okay, let's go with that."

"At the end of the year, all of our retirees' dates of death and ages are provided to the actuary, who figures out when the deaths occurred in relation to our mortality assumption. If they died *early*—before they were expected to—we call it an 'actuarial gain' because the pension plan now has fewer bills to pay. If they died *late*—after they were expected to—it is called an 'actuarial loss' because the long-living retiree is costing the plan more money than was set aside for him or her. The 'gain' and 'loss' terminology refers to the death's financial impact on the pension plan."

J.R.'s conscience shuttered. Calling dead humans "gains and losses" disturbed a man who, after years of investigating horrid crimes, developed a hardness that he believed had immunized him against such things.

"Gains and losses?" he repeated. "That seems rather

dehumanizing. People are more than dollar signs."

"It's just industry language," Alexis quickly replied. "We see our retirees as people, each of them. But to actuaries, they are numbers on a spreadsheet. It is their job to be statistical, not personal. When it comes to the business of advising a public pension plan, actuaries wield an enormous amount of influence in making recommendations to the Board of Retirement, many of which increase costs for the county."

"How so?"

"When the fiscal year ends, the consultant performs a valuation that compares all of our actuarial assumptions against all of our plan experience: what our members actually did that year, how our investments performed, and so on. They quantify the difference for each experience-versus-assumption item and then add them up. You can think of that number as the bottom-line total of actuarial gains and losses. If the total is positive, there are more assets available for us to pay to retirees later. But if the total is negative, it's a debt that must be paid off later—we call that an 'unfunded liability.'"

"Like a mortgage?"

"Yes, in a way. Except, our pension plan gets a new 'mortgage' every year. In fact, we have several layers of unfunded liability that are slowly being paid off by the county."

J.R. scribbled feverishly, trying to write enough words to jog his memory when he met with Owen later. Writing quickly and legibly was not his forte. When a person is built like an NFL linebacker and has a natural inclination to protect others, note taking remains low on the list of skills to improve upon. J.R. jotted his final word and looked at the ladies, both of whom had leaned forward to see what he wrote. He pulled the paper closer and placed a giant hand on it. Glancing at his watch, he realized that the meeting was approaching its scheduled end. He scanned his list of questions and selected one he hoped would shed light on a possible motive in the retiree deaths.

"Who is harmed when your actuarial assumptions don't line up with reality? Uh, I mean your ..." He reviewed his scribbles. "Your *experience*?"

"Nobody," Alexis replied without hesitation.

Legal counsel whispered something to Alexis, who nodded and thanked her.

"Well, nobody, meaning not an *individual*. As an *entity*, however, the county is on the hook for *all* pension liabilities—for ensuring that the pension plan has sufficient assets to pay *every* retiree and *every* eligible spouse *every* dollar owed *every* month of their retired lives."

A light of recognition filled the officer's eyes.

"The county is funded by local taxes, so it's primarily taxpayer funds being sent to you, right?"

"Correct. And don't forget we earn money through investments, too—usually."

J.R. made a few more notes and leaned back in his chair, thinking about the various factors at play.

"Let me make sure I understand. Your agency pays lifetime pensions to county retirees and, when they die, to their spouse, if they have one."

Alexis nodded.

"The pension plan—your agency—makes assumptions about what will happen in the future as it relates to your members. When something different happens in real life, like retirees dying later than expected, that creates a liability—a debt—that will eventually be paid off."

Another nod.

"Good. And when you don't have money set aside for

those liabilities, the county has to make up the difference by sending more taxpayer funds to the pension plan. Is that right?"

Polite clapping sounded across the table.

"Not bad, officer."

"My handwriting might be below average, but my memory is decent."

He closed his notepad, grabbed the recorder and handed a business card to Alexis.

"Would you look into the mortality age before next month's board meeting, please?"

"Certainly."

Feeling very satisfied with the interview, J.R. exited the building with a head full of pension knowledge and a first-rate hand cramp.

◊ ◊ ◊

While the investigator conducted his interview at the retirement office, Owen drafted an article for the newspaper's weekend edition. He reclined casually on a park bench at the edge of a lake when J.R.'s patrol car pulled up unseen. The officer noticed his Zen-like colleague and blasted his siren in Owen's direction. The unsuspecting victim startled in fright and fell off his seat onto the grass.

"You're going to give me a stroke!" he shouted at J.R.'s amused face. With one hand over his heart, he grabbed his backpack and joined the cackling officer in his front seat.

"If I end up dying because of that, my grandma will find out, and she will hunt you down!"

J.R.'s face froze momentarily before roaring another round of laughter.

"Hunt you down," he repeated, this time with a smirk.

When the laughing subsided, they decided to take a walk through the park to discuss what J.R. had just learned. He reviewed his notes with Owen, intensifying the reporter's awe at the immense amount of money being spent on public pensions.

"According to their financial reports, they've got eight thousand retirees that cost the retirement agency nearly $300 million every year. I'd like to see the trajectory of pension payments over the next decade as more and more people retire. Are we talking half-a-billion a year? A billion? How long can the pension plan survive that kind of payroll growth?"

"It's not whether the pension plan can survive," J.R. corrected. "It's whether the *county* can survive. Alexis said the county is ultimately on the hook to fund the pensions."

Owen stepped through some scattered leaves on the lakeside path and kicked a few. One large leaf caught the wind and landed on the lap of a hooded man fiddling with something in his hands. Owen turned to apologize, but the man did not bother to reply.

"Well, sucks for the county," he observed.

J.R. shook his head. "It actually sucks for *us* because we are the ones paying taxes to fund their budget. At least my taxes help pay for my own pension from the city. You only get what you save, right?"

Owen grunted, knowing he did not earn enough to save a dime for retirement. He changed the subject: "What did you learn about retiree mortality?"

"Not as much as I would have liked. Alexis doesn't know the age at which retirees are expected to die. But she said she'd get back to me shortly. I'll text you when I hear something."

"That's disappointing. Did she have any ideas about who might benefit when they die?"

J.R. reread his notes about actuarial losses and gains and did his best to illustrate each scenario by describing retirees who die "early" versus "late" compared to the morality assumption—whatever age that happened to be. The young man bristled at the terminology, but a wry grin crept across this face.

"So, are you saying that if you fell in there and got eaten by a shark," pointing to the nearby lake, "I would pay fewer taxes?"

"I suppose, but I don't know of any great whites that swim in fresh water, do you?"

"Well, not in California."

"Uh, not anywhere," J.R. chuckled as they rounded a bend. "Now that you mention it, there is a group that would benefit from retirees dying sooner than expected."

"Taxpayers are all I've come up with," Owen offered. "I realize it's a wild speculation, but it's at least conceivable that local citizens might have a motive in seeing retirees die. Taxpayers have the most to gain financially from a pension actuary's perspective."

"It would be premature to rule out the possibility, but I've never known average Joes to take their tax bills *that* seriously. Besides, how would they know who to kill and when?" J.R. shook his head. "I just don't see that happening."

They continued wondering aloud about other groups or individuals who would have something to gain. J.R. suggested the county because of its gigantic liability, but Owen said his past research did not turn up a single negative, public comment from county leadership about making annual contribution payments to the retirement agency.

"Besides," Owen reasoned, "the county is spending *other people's* money, not its own—so it doesn't really have skin in the game."

The pair agreed that county leadership's involvement in the local deaths was doubtful at best. A silent minute passed as they rounded the far corner of the lake and turned back toward the parking lot. J.R. rubbed the sides of his shaved head.

"All the puzzle pieces are not on the table. We're not seeing a complete picture yet. Even knowing when the retirement agency expects retirees to die is not enough to find a suspect. We need better information."

Another few moments passed in silent thought. Owen focused on his steps while J.R. watched wildlife scurry along the path lining the expansive park they had hiked. Suddenly, the officer's gait noticeably slowed. Owen looked up but did not see anyone approaching.

"What's the matter?"

"We're being watched," came the calm reply. "The man in the hoody across the water is taking our picture. Don't look over ..."

His words came too late. Owen glanced toward the man and caught his gaze. The stranger lowered his camera and trotted away in the opposite direction.

"It's no use following him," J.R. said. "By the time I get over there, he'll have disappeared." He looked over at his friend with worried eyes. "This means you are on someone's radar—and not in a good way. Do you want an escort back to your office?"

"No," he said with some hesitation. "I think I'll be okay."

As Owen drove away, he made various attempts to

explain away what had just happened, not for the sake of objectivity but to settle his nerves. A half-dozen excuses ran through his troubled mind. Perhaps the stranger happened to leave at the same time they saw each other. Maybe he felt nervous about being seen by a cop. Any number of explanations could justify someone departing so quickly. But self-talk notwithstanding, the reporter could not shake the sick feeling buried in his gut. He decided to forego returning to the office and instead headed to the safety of his living room, where he would finish the day's assignments.

Shrouded behind darkening clouds, the afternoon sun waned overhead as Owen pulled into the lot nearest his apartment complex. He glanced around nervously, gathered his belongings and walked briskly toward the outdoor staircase. He felt for the keys in his pocket and jingled them on the way upstairs. When he stepped onto the second-floor landing, he turned toward his front door and saw it standing ajar. His movement halted as he caught his breath. Every inclination in his person cried out to reverse course and flee. He slowly and quietly retreated down the stairs, where he turned a corner and immediately dialed J.R. with quivering fingers. No answer. Again, he dialed. No answer. He waited there five minutes, cortisol coursing through his body. Still no reply from J.R.

"You can't stand here all day, you coward," he whispered to himself. "This is *your* apartment."

He narrowed his eyes, his anger and courage swelling. Glaring at the open door, he stormed up the stairs and through the door, yelling and flailing his arms wildly.

"Where are you?" he shouted. "Come out! Show yourself!"

Nothing stirred. Holding his breath and listening for the

slightest noise, he dropped his backpack quietly. His adrenaline rush began to subside, causing his body to shake. As he stepped to close the door, he noticed a manila envelope by his foot. He had overlooked it when barging into the room. Lifting it slowly, he placed it on the counter and opened its seal. Inside he found several photographs of Ruthie in her front yard. From the perspective of the photographer, Owen realized the photos were taken from the sidewalk just outside her home, a location where he had stood hundreds of times. Someone was watching *her*, too. Another wave of fear—this time for his grandma—shot through him like lightning. The hair on his neck bristled. He dropped the photos and instantly called her.

"Are you okay, Gram?" he blurted before she could say a word. "Where are you?"

"I'm here at home, and I'm fine. Is everything okay?"

"I—I think so," he said with short breaths. "Can I come over tonight?"

"Of course. You're welcome here anytime, sweetie. See you soon."

Owen hung up in emotional disarray. Not only was his apartment violated, but so was Ruthie's privacy. Both of them were being watched, but by whom? Where could they be safe? Should he tell her about the photos? No, she would be wrecked. He decided against it, but still, she needed to be warned somehow. What should he do? An unfamiliar sense of indecision plagued his unsteady mind.

Amid a flurry of disordered thoughts and feelings, he grabbed the photos and rushed to his car, making straightway to the newspaper office. He wheeled into the parking lot and passed several co-workers who were leaving the building as he entered, eyes aflame, heart racing. He burst into Al's office and slammed the door.

"Why did you pull my article last month? Tell me now, and drop the nonsense about it being a management decision. Why!"

Al's eyes grew hot, offended not only by the interruption but by the insolence of a young reporter demanding anything of him.

"Who do you think you are? Get out!"

"No!" he shot back. "Tell me the truth. Were you threatened? Did someone threaten you?"

Owen tossed his photos in front of Al, who looked at them with a strange, horrible familiarity. The color drained from his face as he leaned back in his chair and placed the corner of his fist into his mouth. He stared at the images and gave no answer for a long time. Owen waited patiently, his pupils fixed on his boss' every shutter, every twitch.

Between broken breaths and glances outside, Al whispered his secret. "They're watching."

« 13 »

Owen ate his dinner in silence, debating what to tell Ruthie about the day's disturbing events. To disclose the photos and break-in would impose another horrific burden on her already-afflicted mind. But to withhold them would rob her of the chance to escape those who watched in secret, who threatened from behind the veil. He had faced dilemmas in the past, though none as personal as this. Unwilling to place greater hardship on the person he loved most, he chose to bear the weight of the threats alone.

"Gram, let's leave California," he said suddenly. "Let's move to ... I don't know, how about Florida? There are a lot of old people there."

Ruthie laid down her fork.

"And why would I do that? All my remaining friends and family are here."

"We'll go together. If you sold your house, I bet you could buy another one for cash in a different state."

"Does this have anything to do with me turning eighty next summer?"

"Yes, of course it does. Gram, please consider it," he said with pleading eyes.

The genuine worry covering her grandson's face delayed what would have been an immediate refusal.

"Owen, my boy, I will not be scared out of the town I know and love. But I see you are quite troubled by this." She sighed. "Tell you what. I'll agree to think about it. But don't get your hopes up, okay?"

Feeling a touch of relief, Owen relaxed and forked a few green beans into his mouth.

"I got one bit of good news today."

"Really? What was it?"

"Remember how Al had made that arbitrary rule about me not researching retiree deaths? Well, he retracted it today, although I still can't write about the topic."

"Oh, that's encouraging. But don't forget to pursue your leads wisely. You don't want to draw attention to yourself," she said with a wink.

Owen flinched at her words as flashes of the sub-rosa photos resurrected from where he had buried them in his memory.

"I'll be careful," he promised, knowing that somehow he had already violated the oath and put both of their lives at risk. The knowledge of his carelessness haunted him through the wet, wintery weeks that followed, as if the skies wept empathetically over his burden. Yet, they cleared on occasion, shining some semblance of light into his life. Owen's relationship with his boss continued to improve, as both men had stared down their common demon and, in their own ways, chosen to live with fear as a companion. Though he rejected the religious aspect of Christmas, Owen bought Al a small placard inscribed with England's famous World War II adage, "Keep Calm and Carry On." It hung in the editor's office as a reminder and a challenge.

That week, a few interesting pieces of information arrived in quick succession. The first came from J.R., whose autopsy results on Mr. Milhouse revealed fatty liver disease, atherosclerosis and trace amounts of Hemlox in various bodily tissues, from his head to his feet.

"From the look of his clogged coronary artery and diseased gut, this guy could have died just as easily from a heart attack or liver failure than from the drug," he told Owen. "But my money is on the Hemlox. I also intend to interview his widow again for the sake of due diligence, but the coroner's declaration of a natural cause of death essentially closes the investigation."

The point of the autopsy, Owen knew, was not to bring a criminal charge against anyone. It served to confirm the death cocktail in Mr. Milhouse's bloodstream. And to that end, J.R.'s inquiry proved successful.

The next revelation was an official response to Owen's Public Records Act request for a list of Assemblyman Ramos' campaign donors and donations in the preceding four years. It was in this timeframe that the politician had resigned from the Hemlock board of directors, sponsored the assisted-suicide bill, and pushed the Hemlock Pharmaceuticals contract through the state legislature and onto the governor's desk. But the PRA results confused Owen; he had expected Hemlock executives to have poured money into Ramos' campaign coffers by the tens of thousands. These individuals were listed, but their contributions were relatively low: a few hundred dollars here, a few there. If Ramos was getting paid off for being the drug company's cheerleader in the state capitol, it was not through his campaign. Owen immediately drafted another PRA request, this one delving into a few political action committees that had publicly supported Ramos, but out of an abundance of caution, he dropped the form in his filing cabinet and forgot about it. In one sense, the bad guy—whoever he was—had already won. By making wordless threats that Owen could only interpret as sincere, they had tied his hands, intimidated him from pursuing possible leads and, consequently, remained hidden in shadow.

"This must be why terrorism works so well," he told Al one day. "They scare you into doing nothing. It feels debilitating, like the opposite of freedom."

"What I wouldn't give to have the freedom to debilitate them," the editor retorted angrily.

The young reporter smiled on the inside, pleased that he and his boss felt similarly about the unseen object of their fear and hate.

The last disclosure came on a rainy morning in late December. J.R. drove to the newspaper office and called Owen.

"Hey, I'm downstairs. You got a minute?"

The young man hurried to the lobby, where he saw J.R. watching the downpour from under the outdoor awning. He exited the double doors and joined his friend in the cold.

"Man, it's really coming down," Owen observed. "I much prefer dry and hot to wet and cold."

"Yeah," J.R. said pensively, "but I enjoy the sound of drops pounding around me. Rain is amazing if you think about it. It falls, cycles back to the sky and repeats again and again. It follows a pattern we come to expect, even plan around. Not too much, not too little—just enough to make life possible. Do you ever think how lucky we are?"

"Uh, not really."

"I do … on days like this. I think about the patterns I take for granted, the ones that don't involve me: seasons, orbits, tides, life in general. I wonder if those patterns mean there is a pattern-maker."

Owen's initial confusion turned to shock. J.R. took no notice. He faced the deluge and continued ruminating.

"In my job, if I see a clear pattern of evidence, I conclude that it was purposeful, that somebody planned it that way." He looked over his shoulder at his dubious companion. "How could the entire cosmos obey so many rules and follow such perfect patterns without somebody planning it that way?"

Owen's materialistic worldview stood appalled at the suggestion of a higher power ordering the universe. On a normal day, he would reject not only the message but the messenger. But today he did not. The unexpectedness of J.R.'s comments left him with nothing to say, at least momentarily. His eyes darted about uncomfortably, finally resting on his shoes.

"So, did you have something to tell me?"

"Yeah," the officer said, turning to face Owen. "Eighty years old! Alexis called me today and said the pension plan's actuary assumes their retirees die, on average, at age eighty. You know as well as I do that people don't plan their lives— or deaths—around averages. But in this town, apparently they do. They're dying according to a *pattern* that does not occur naturally, regardless of what an autopsy says."

Owen paused, recalling J.R.'s earlier comments.

"Patterns have pattern-makers!"

"Yes, they do," the officer grinned. "And this pattern has been repeated more than fifty times in one year. Nobody in their right mind would call that a coincidence."

"That's enough to make a believer out of me."

Under the pounding rain, the friends relished their discovery, a critical yet non-actionable piece of data that brought them no closer to identifying a motive or suspect in what, from this point forward, they referred to privately as "the murders." But knowing the mortality assumption of county retirees—the age at which someone was expected to die—provided another needed confirmation that the trail they pursued had at its end a conspiracy to commit mass extermination. Owen took a pen from his pocket and began scribbling notes on his hand.

"I'm thinking we need to better understand what the pension plan's actuary does. What he expects to happen in the future is very relevant to our present. What do you say we get acquainted with the Board of Retirement and its actuary?"

"You're in luck. Alexis said there is a meeting next week."

The following Wednesday, the reporter and police officer arrived at the retirement office separately and sat on opposite ends of the public seating area to avoid any appearance of collusion. Fortunately for them, a dozen other visitors filled the seats. The guests fell into one of two camps: the anti-pension crowd, consisting of a few taxpayer advocates, and the union crowd, consisting of local officials whose purple shirts loudly identified the bloc. On the edges of these opposing parties sat J.R. and Owen, each of whom concluded from the groups' pre-meeting glares that the next hour would be entertaining.

After a roll call, the board chairman, a retired civil servant, welcomed everyone in attendance.

"I am flattered you all showed up to see me today," he

announced. "What, not for me? Well, then, you must be here for our actuary. I hope you enjoy the discussion. Just remember, speakers are limited to two minutes only. Don't make me cut you off."

The board approved the consent agenda and opened the meeting to public comment. The leaders of the two factions in attendance hurried toward the podium to be the first to speak. The union president, an energetic, hippie-like woman in her sixties, reached the lectern first, forcing the taxpayer advocate to return to his seat. The woman laid a few pages of text on the podium and a stopwatch, which she clicked. As she began to address the board, several purple shirts stood behind her in a single-file line.

"The public employees' union would like to read prepared remarks encouraging your board to preserve the current benefit levels for county employees and retirees, and not to cut them to appease the senseless cries of pension-hating Chicken Littles here today who would have you believe that pensions will one day blow up local government budgets."

The woman spoke for her two minutes and then stepped aside for the next union member to resume reading their prepared remarks. This continued for ten minutes. Owen tried taking notes on the content of the speech, but its meandering logic left him with a page full of disconnected thoughts. The final union representative concluded triumphantly: "On behalf of our entire membership, we respectfully ask the Board of Retirement to keep the pension promises made to all county workers, past and present, who were willing to accept lower salaries in exchange for added security in retirement. Thank you."

The purple bloc applauded as the last speaker returned to her seat. Owen, whose sympathies strongly favored union

157

causes, felt a fair amount of pride in how the group organized itself. From the looks on their faces, they too were pleased with their orderly performance—that is, until the board chairman responded.

"We appreciate your input, but I think you misunderstand how the pension plan works. Nobody on this board grants benefits to employees. Even if we wanted to, we could not. That's because the agency we oversee simply administers the retirement benefits promised by elected politicians. Your comments are better suited for them. Now, are there any other remarks from the public?"

As the taxpayer advocates' leader walked to the podium, his supporters directed snarky whispers and glances toward the union contingent, which had suddenly fallen silent.

"I want to respect your time," he began, "so I have only two points to make. First, the taxpayers' association asks that you do not reduce the investment rate assumption, as the actuary is recommending on today's agenda, because it will severely impact the county budget and services that the indigent in our community depend on. Second, we ask that you work with county officials to craft state legislation that will permit the county to replace the pension plan with a deferred compensation plan for future new hires."

A bystander might have thought a puppy had just been skinned alive. A plethora of choice words burst from the union members, furious at the outrageous proposal. Some stood, some sat, but all yelled: "Shut up and sit down! Pension envy! We stand together!"

The board chairman banged his gavel and raised his voice toward the disrupters.

"Show some respect. Quiet down. Quiet!" he demanded.

"Pension haters!" a lone voice cried out, followed by

another loud gavel strike.

The chamber assumed an uncomfortable peace. Casting a rueful glance toward the dagger-eyed army behind him, the speaker resumed his comments.

"As I was saying before the rude interruption, by transitioning to a 401(k)-type plan for new workers—*not* existing ones, by the way, just future ones—the county will have enough money to maintain its current services while financing the pension plan for decades to come."

The small taxpayer assembly applauded their spokesman as he returned to his seat while the rancorous union members blasphemed his name to one another. Unwilling to ignore the verbal abuse, the taxpayer group volleyed its own accusations. Like a match to kindling, the entire seating area erupted into a storm of arm-waving, profanity-filled vitriol. This time, the board chairman, despite numerous attempts to regain control, could not contain the situation. Even Owen, sitting near the purple shirts, began to feel unsafe. Finally, a uniformed J.R. walked into the midst of the shouts and stretched out his arms toward the warring sides.

"Enough!" he shouted.

The force of his tremendous presence stunned the angry factions into momentary compliance. Facing the visitor who had started the uproar, he said in a slow, hard voice: "Sit. Down. Now." He cast a warning glance at the other side before taking a new seat in the middle of the now-quieted parties.

The chairman quickly moved to the next item on the agenda.

"Now we will hear a presentation from the pension plan's consulting actuary. Mr. Petri, you have the stage."

The man who approached the podium was tall and

slender, dressed in a stylish blue suit, and bald as a cue ball. He sauntered to his speaking location and placed his notes on the lectern.

"Good morning. My name is Art Petri, and I am the lead actuary at National Pension Advisors, your board's consulting actuarial firm. I'm told there are a few new trustees here today. This presentation should be a helpful overview of actuarial science for them and a good refresher for the rest of you. The subject matter can be complex and nuanced at times, so feel free to ask questions whenever you like."

In just that short introduction, it became clear to Owen that Mr. Petri was physiologically unable to disconnect his words from his hands; they moved in unison. It was like watching a puppeteer without the puppets and strings. Apart from this idiosyncrasy, however, the actuary spoke with such effortless professionalism that one could not help but listen in rapt attention. Owen followed along with his customary diligence, so much so that he did not notice Lily's stolen glances from across the room.

Mr. Petri warned that his presentation would last about an hour but to not worry because he would try to make it interesting.

"I will be presenting a draft actuarial valuation for the last fiscal year. As many of you know, a valuation is intended to provide updated employee and employer retirement contribution rates for the next fiscal year and to show you, the trustees of the pension plan, how far along the plan has come to reaching full funding. There are always going to be differences between what we *assume* will happen and what *actually* happens. We do a valuation every year as a sort of 'course correction' to make sure you are headed in the right direction, so to speak."

160

A red light appeared on one of the board members' microphones, indicating her intent to comment.

"You mentioned full funding. By that, I assume you mean having enough assets to pay for our liabilities. But our funding percentage is in the low sixties—among the lowest of all California pension plans. How do we get that number up?"

"Good question," Mr. Petri said with both arms. "But I'm going to encourage you to not take that number too seriously because it is just a snapshot in time. What's more important is direction."

The questioner gave a puzzled look.

"Which is better," the actuary asked, "a funded ratio of sixty percent or seventy percent?"

Several voices around the board table said, "Seventy." Others nodded in agreement.

"You would think so, but maybe not. Here is why: If your funded ratio is at sixty and headed north, that's better than if it is at seventy and dropping like a rock." His hand fell on the podium to illustrate which direction rocks fall. "So, don't get too nervous about your poor funding right now. Rather, focus on adopting accurate assumptions about the future that will result in adequate contribution rates that will enable you to sufficiently pre-fund your benefits. Because what you *don't* want is to become a pay-as-you-go plan that issues benefit payments as soon as your income rolls in. The goal is to *grow* the plan's assets so that your children and grandchildren are not paying off the debts that county workers are earning today. In pension lingo, we call that intergenerational equity."

Scattered applause sounded from the audience, mostly from the taxpayer group but even some from the union members.

"Let's talk about assumptions," he continued. "There are

two types: demographic and economic. The demographic assumptions include things like how long plan members will work; how much they will be paid; when they will retire, get disabled, quit or die; and how long benefits will be paid. To be accurate, these assumptions must be based on recent experience. By show of hands, who here thinks they know which demographic assumption has the greatest impact on the plan's future liabilities?"

Two board members said higher salaries.

"Ah, you are mistaken. The answer is mortality: how long your members will live *after* they retire. We don't use the average life expectancy for a typical American man or woman. Our mortality tables are more sophisticated than that, but even they have weaknesses. For example, the current tables fail to take into consideration that younger people are more likely to live longer. It's a reality that is not fully priced into your costs yet. So, don't be surprised if we come back to your board next year recommending generational mortality tables that account for future morality improvements among younger workers. Just to forewarn you, these tables are more accurate than your current ones and will definitely increase employer costs."

He left his last comment hanging, waiting for someone to inquire about this game-changing issue. Nobody took the bait. Owen, however, bristling with curiosity, could hardly restrain himself from blurting one question after another about retiree mortality. But the time for public comment had ended, and he had missed his chance.

"Don't draw attention," he reminded himself. "Relax."

It was with no small amount of angst that he scribbled notes quietly, hoping the speaker would explain why the mortality assumption costs the pension plan so much money.

162

The actuary moved on to his next topic. "Unlike demographic assumptions," he began, "economic assumptions are *forward*-looking and focus on how pension plan assets and employee payroll are expected to grow over time. Of the three economic assumptions—rate of inflation, employer payroll growth and investment rate of return—it is the last one that affects your plan (and every plan) most because all future assets and liabilities—decades worth of them—are calculated based on this rate. For those who are unfamiliar with the investment rate assumption, it is what we expect the pension plan to earn on average, every year, over the life of the plan. Currently, your rate is 7.25 percent, meaning that your board expects to earn 7.25 percent each year. Some years, you will exceed it. Other years, like during a recession, you will not. But, on average, you are assuming a 7.25 annual return on your investments. In today's low-return environment, that rate will be very hard to achieve, which is why we are recommending lowering the assumed rate to seven percent."

As if hearing a gunshot to start a race, board members' microphones lit up to comment on this hot-button topic. The actuary performed admirably at addressing their concerns, but a few commenters pushed back on the recommended assumption change, not because stock markets looked promising but because of the significant effect a lower rate would have on employer contributions.

"Look," one board member argued," I realize our investments have underperformed in recent years, but let's look at this pragmatically. Every time we lower that rate a quarter point, the county's pension bill increases by $20 million. That money is *not* budgeted. Where is it going to come from? The reality is, the county will have to lay off scores of workers, which will drastically cut services to the community. I don't want that on my resume or my conscience."

"No disrespect intended," someone shot back, "but you are acting like a pawn of the county's Board of Supervisors. That's not your job here."

"Wrong!" declared the offended party. "My job is to ensure this organization remains solvent. If the county cannot afford to pay its bills, then the pension plan suffers. I'm looking at the big picture here."

"If the county can't pay its bills, maybe it should manage its money better," a new voice added.

The mood in the room grew increasingly tense as the volume and intensity of the argument escalated. Like the opposing audience members, the board appeared split into two camps: those who believed that higher contribution payments would place an undue burden on the county and taxpayers and those who believed in adopting the most accurate assumptions possible, regardless of the consequences. No amount of gesturing by the actuary could calm the unrest around him. Owen looked anxiously at J.R., who squirmed in his seat, ready to take action again to restore the peace. Just then, the retirement agency's legal counsel calmly rose from her seat and faced the dais. The arguing trustees turned toward her and quieted down. She took a seat and leaned into her microphone.

"To clarify an earlier comment, it is true that when you sit at this table, you should *only* represent the retirement board and plan members. You have a fiduciary duty to act in their best interests. However, there are different ways to act in the best interest of members. This is the forum for discussing such matters, but one at a time, please. Now, Mr. Chairman, I suggest we have the actuary continue his presentation."

"Thank you, counsel. Now, folks, let's try to keep this dignified. Mr. Petri, the floor is yours again."

The palpable anxiety filling the chamber slowly dissipated as the actuary made a final reference to demographic and economic assumptions before proceeding to his next topic. This was the first time that Owen had seen adults, many of whom were consummate professionals, debate so passionately in a public setting—and about pensions? What was it about this issue that incited the emotions of normally level-headed individuals? He jotted his thoughts and attended to the presenter, who wasted no time resuming his presentation before another debate erupted.

"One of the functions that we actuaries perform is to project the long-term and short-term costs of the pension plan. We do that by making assumptions about all future events that could affect the amount and timing of the benefits to be paid. To do that, you need assets. So, another function we perform is to calculate how many assets you will need this year and next year and the year after that, and so on. Think of it as adjusting your mortgage payment every year. But in this case, your mortgage—your total liability—is north of $6 billion."

Groans rose from the dais as the incomprehensible size of the plan's expenses weighed heavy on the board members, for it was their collective responsibility to fund the mountain of debt that never seemed to shrink. The actuary trudged on.

"In the valuation of your plan each year, we compare your members' actual experience against the projected—that is, assumed—experience. To the extent there are differences, the county's future contribution rates are adjusted up or down—but usually up. Again, the trick is to align our assumptions as closely as possible with actual experience.

When we change assumptions, whether they are demographic or economic, we are basically changing our thinking
about the future."

He stepped in front of the podium and clasped his normally active hands in front of his waist.

"If I may weigh in on your earlier argument," he began
tentatively, "the goal of making good assumptions is to pro-
duce level costs for the employer—in this case, the county.
Everyone agrees that having steady costs is a good thing for
budget-planning purposes. Nobody debates that, right?"

Heads around the table nodded.

"Good. I'd like to elaborate on that point by introducing
the only actuarial formula you'll ever need to know: $C + I = B + E$. This means that to be fully funded, retirement contributions made to your plan (C) and investment earnings (I)
must equal your benefit payments to members (B) and your
operating expenses (E)."

He stretched his arms into the air as if holding two buck-
ets.

"On one side are your assets: all contributions and investment earnings. On the other side are your costs: all benefit
payments and expenses of administering the pension plan.
Stick with me now. Here's how it works. The factors on either side of the equation work in opposite directions. If your
investment returns decrease because of a recession, then the
pension plan must compensate for the lost assets by requiring
more contributions from the county. In other words, less I
requires more C. That is the essence of your earlier debate.
Here's another common scenario: benefit payments increase
due to higher salaries and longer-living retirees. Therefore,
benefits (B) increase, which must be balanced by more assets
on the other side of the equation. You'll need higher

contributions (C) or investment returns (I) or both."

Owen's hand ached from furiously taking notes, but the feeling of his head exploding distracted him from the cramp. So many moving parts had to align perfectly for a pension plan to be fully funded. This was no easy task to accomplish. If the investment market crashed, assets would drop, not just in the short term but for many years to come, which would require millions more in retirement contributions, which could decrease the number of plan members employed by the county, which would reduce the county's payroll, which might save the plan money but at the expense of someone's future retirement income. Or, if active employees were granted raises, their future pensions would increase, which would require either higher investment returns to cover the higher costs or more contributions from the county, which could result in fewer services to the community. The possible scenarios were virtually endless.

Owen concluded this was basically a zero-sum game: If it gives a little here, it has to take a little there for the sides to balance. But in the world of pensions, "little" represented an enormous financial cost. The only situation he envisioned to resolve the cold, merciless equation was for investments to *always* exceed the already-too-high assumption rate, a prospect that he knew was not possible. If assets did not come from investment returns, the only other source was retirement contributions. That was the grim reality of pension math.

"It is important to remember," Mr. Petri said, "when we talk about contributions, that includes the money paid by county employees *and* employers. For employees, a percentage of every paycheck—ranging from six to fifteen percent—is put in their retirement accounts. In the last fiscal year, plan members contributed a total of $40 million to the pension plan. But the county paid more—much more. Last year's rates were 38.3 percent of payroll for general members and 63.1 percent of payroll for safety members, totaling $250 million. You might say that sum is a lot of money, but keep in mind that your retirement association paid nearly $300 million in benefit payments in the last fiscal year. That means your pension plan had a negative cash flow of about $50 million."

One of the more fiscally minded board members spoke up: "If we were in the hole $50 million, where did that money come from? Or did it just get added to our mountain of debt?"

"That's a great segue to the final subject of my presentation: unfunded liabilities. Let's start by addressing your question. Your pension plan is governed by a state law that requires employers like the county to pay its annual retirement contribution in full. Not all states require a full payment every year—Illinois and New Jersey are two examples. Not surprisingly, their pension plans are dangerously underfunded. But your county contributed exactly what it was supposed to contribute last year. So, why the $50 million deficit? Remember, contributions are just one source of funding. Your investments should have earned the assumed 7.25 percent, which would have simultaneously grown the fund and made up for negative cash flow. Unfortunately, your investments only earned 1.25 percent. In other words, you missed the target by six percent. Let's see, a $4 billion plan that missed its assumed rate of return by six percent ..."

The actuary pulled a calculator from his pocket and began typing. Board members sat on the edge of their seats like patients expecting their doctor to say, "Sorry, you've got terminal cancer. Get your things in order."

"Ew," he muttered to himself. "Well, the kind of under-performance you experienced last year resulted in an actuarial loss to the tune of roughly $240 million."

The jaws of everyone in the room fell in disbelief, particularly the taxpayer advocates. The purple-shirted union members likewise caught their collective breath upon hearing the astronomical sum. Owen could hardly fathom a loss of that magnitude. Worse yet, that was just the loss from a *single* year. The trustee who asked the question offered a follow-up with far greater solemnity.

"That is quite a large amount. But this is a long-term plan, so I assume that loss will be paid off at some point, right?"

"Oh, yes," Mr. Petri replied. "Another function we perform is to set a long-range schedule of expiring your unfunded liabilities. I just used a new word, so let me define that before moving forward. An *unfunded liability* is simply the cost of a future benefit that is not yet matched by assets. Essentially, you are making a promise to pay a retiree one day, but you don't have the money right now—sort of like buying something on credit. Follow along closely now … this can get confusing."

"*More* confusing?" Owen said under his breath.

"Whenever your plan's actuarial assumptions do not match your actual experience, an actuarial gain or loss occurs. For example, if your investments earn less than the assumed 7.25 percent, you have an actuarial loss. Last year, it was $240 million. Or, let's say your working members don't earn as much money as assumed or maybe your retirees die earlier than assumed—then you have an actuarial gain."

Owen and J.R.'s ears perked up.

"At the end of the year," Mr. Petri continued, "we count all the actuarial gains and losses, all the investment earnings and all the contributions made to the plan. If you have more losses than gains that are not covered by incoming money, then you have an unfunded liability. Again, think of it like not having enough money to pay off the monthly credit card bill. That debt rolls over to the next billing cycle, and you decide how quickly to pay it off. Your plan has roughly $4 billion in assets and $6.5 billion in accrued liabilities, leaving you with $2.5 billion of debt that currently lacks funding. Hence, you have a $2.5 billion unfunded liability that needs to be paid off. And with each passing year of missed assumptions, that unfunded liability grows. Are you with me so far?"

The red light on a microphone lit up, and one of the new trustees on the board made his first public comment of the day.

"Sitting on the board of a warm, fuzzy nonprofit would have been so much easier than dealing with this seismic financial problem," he chuckled. "But it is a problem that needs to be fixed. I'd like to know how."

The actuary brought his hands together and pointed at the questioner. "I am glad you feel that way. It *does* need to be fixed. So, then, what are we going to do about your immense unfunded liability? In your annual valuation, we recommend employee and employer contribution rates that pay for all the pension liabilities that are expected to accrue in a particular year. However, the employer's rate also includes an additional amount designed to slowly expire the unfunded liability. It's like cutting a debt pie into many thin slices and eating one at a time until the pie is gone."

"But if additional liability is being added every year, isn't our debt pie getting bigger?" inquired another board member. "Will it ever be paid off?"

"Yes! *But*—and this is a big *but*—it requires our actuarial

170

assumptions to be met ... all of them ... every year ... for decades."

As the actuary's words left his mouth, Owen thought how ridiculous they sounded. The chance of all assumptions being fulfilled in real life was exactly zero.

"I see skeptical looks on your faces and know what you are thinking," Mr. Petri observed. "Such a situation will never happen, right? That is precisely why it is critical that your board adopts the most accurate assumptions possible, even if it costs your county a lot of money in the short term."

Board members looked at one another like helpless sheep lined up to be sheared. In the most important ways, their governing hands were tied, their path largely predetermined. Nobody uttered a word. Finally, the chairman spoke on behalf of the board.

"Nobody relishes the prospect of sending the county a larger pension bill next year, especially when its tax revenues are already suffering. But, as the actuary has described our situation, adopting more accurate assumptions—for investments, salary increases, retirement rates, mortality rates, and so on—is a necessary step toward ensuring the pension plan's solvency. I suppose the question on everyone's mind is whether the *county* can remain solvent in the meantime."

The board grudgingly adopted the actuary's recommendation, and the meeting ended on that sober note. Even the warring factions in the audience offered each other tolerant nods as they exited the room, blanched by the grim facts they had just heard. Owen stayed behind, reviewing his notes, when J.R. relocated beside him.

"I don't know about you, but life feels a lot more complicated now."

"Yeah, it does," the young man agreed. "It makes me

wonder if the killer understood all this pension math."

"Doubtful. I could probably count on one hand the number of people who understand half of what we just learned."

"And that's saying something because you have *huge* hands," Owen laughed.

The two carried on in their empty corner of the board room when Lily appeared from behind the dais and approached them. The men exchanged a quick glance and nodded a farewell to one another. As J.R. stood to leave, his back to Lily, he looked at his young friend and mouthed, "She is gorgeous," before heading for the door. A grin flitted on the corners of Owen's mouth.

Lily stood before him in an attractive, knee-length skirt, the first thing he noticed after her legs. He would have spent more time admiring her features, but her voice interrupted his thoughts.

"Hi, Owen, it's nice to see you again. Do you mind if I join you?"

"Be my guest. Although, technically, I am the guest here."

"I suppose you are," she smiled. "Can I help you better understand anything that might have confused you during the presentation? Don't take that the wrong way, please. It's just that actuarial science is not an easy subject for anyone to figure out the first time through."

Owen lifted an eyebrow doubtfully. "I see. Are you an expert?"

"Not by a long shot. But having heard similar presentations in the past and written about actuarial assumptions in our newsletter, I'm familiar enough with the subject to be dangerous. Honestly, the only people who really grasp this stuff are the actuaries. Once or twice a year, they descend from their towers of knowledge to share their divine

172

dispensations with us common folk."

"That," Owen said in astonishment, "was a beautiful sentence."

Lily smiled and looked down. "Thanks. My job is words. I like them—how they look on a page, how they sound in my ear, how they feel being spoken. I guess that makes me a word nerd."

She smirked at her unintended rhyme and looked up to see Owen grinning, too. In that moment, their eyes met and held one another in silence. Lily suddenly forgot what she was about to say and started fidgeting with a hem on her skirt. Owen's kind, steady countenance melted her confidence. She faced him with mouth open but nothing interesting to say.

He held her gaze, debating whether to talk business or ask her on a date. *Definitely the date*, he decided without a second thought of journalism. He was about to speak when he looked over her shoulder and saw Alexis staring at them. His bravery dissolved to worry—not for himself but for Lily. He wanted to protect her from any accusation of conflicted interest. That would be bad for everyone. Sighing, he opted to talk business.

"I had hoped you could tell me more about ... the pension plan," he said.

Lily's brow furrowed.

"As you probably know, the article I had intended to write about the deaths of your retirees got pulled. But I'm still looking into the issue." He lowered his voice and leaned in slightly, allowing his knee to gently touch hers. "Would you help me think through who might benefit from these deaths? I've sort of hit a dead end."

Disclosing this fact to Lily required of Owen a step of

faith, an implicit trust that she would not betray his confidence or look down on his failure. Although he instinctively viewed people with suspicion, Lily's presence somehow disarmed his natural bent. He watched her expression, wondering how she would respond.

Lily's countenance rose and fell subtly, apparently torn by what she had just experienced with the handsome acquaintance by her side and their inexplicable moment. She looked away from Owen and then back, as if preparing to say something important. Then their eyes met again. Both sat silent, hearts warming, anticipation building. They both felt it deeply. But he caught the watchful eye of Alexis again and shifted awkwardly. Lily observed his distraction, sat upright in her chair and crossed her legs away from him. She squinted ever so slightly.

"Let me make sure I understand," she said coolly. "You're asking *me* to help *you* with your job? I am sorry, I cannot offer you any assistance. In fact, it is time for me to go. Goodbye."

Lily promptly stood, pivoted and walked toward Alexis, who questioned her about the reporter. From the boss' flat response, Owen concluded he had not caused trouble for her and felt relieved. So, still warm at the thought of her, he became intensely confused when she flipped a switch on the wall and exited the room, leaving him alone and completely in the dark.

« 14 »

That night, Owen sat in a booth at his favorite sports bar. The sights and sounds of happiness and life filled the restaurant as families, couples and business associates came and went. Fans congregated under large screens to watch their favorite teams, whose game-time fortunes caused waves of cheers to pierce the low hum of surrounding conversations. Flirtatious waitresses attended to their guests, paying special attention to those who seemed likely to tip well. Owen pensively sipped his beer, observing what normal people do on a normal evening. Since the death of his parents, he regularly forgot what it felt like to be normal. Nights like this helped him remember.

His conversation with Lily that morning and its odd ending made him ache for his dad, whose sound advice had been a balm to Owen during his teen years. He knew that his father, were he still alive, would have patiently listened to his son's story and then offered a morsel of insight that would have brought some measure of clarity and comfort. Those days were now in the past. Although he gained solace from his beloved grandma, who had become a different kind of balm to his orphaned heart, he still felt alone and in the dark.

Near the bottom of his second pint, his thoughts again turned to Lily. How could they not? She was a being of magnificent beauty and poise. He felt compelled to see her again, to ask what he had done to offend her. That was not his intent. Then again, it never was his intention to alienate the young women he liked, although it seemed to happen with every girlfriend. Owen knew the pattern: He got interested in a girl, they went on a few dates, she shared her heart, he struggled to do the same, they grew apart, and she ended it. He realized the commonality was him, not them.

"Why can't I open up?" he asked himself. "Why is it such a struggle?" He finished his drink and stared into the empty vessel. "It just is."

In the newsroom, Owen's busy schedule distracted him from his relationship sorrows. He had carried his two-beat responsibilities to the satisfaction of Al, who would never admit that explicitly but managed to express his appreciation in subtle or indirect ways.

"Not bad," was the usual compliment when Owen submitted a particularly well-written story. He even received a "Huh, interesting" once after the editor read Owen's write-up about a city-county spat over which governmental entity would get to fine a local dairy that spilled a tanker full of milk on a road separating the jurisdictions. To the delight of the publisher, Owen's article fanned the flames of public-sector debate that spawned several follow-up stories.

"Whoever thinks that journalists only try to report the facts fails to appreciate how much we enjoy stirring the pot," he disclosed to Darcie one day.

She also complimented Owen on his work, although her praise was reliably more vocal and frequent: "I really liked your piece about ..." was a refrain she said at least weekly. With the exception of Ruthie, Darcie was his biggest fan. In her daily rounds through the office, she always spent a minute at his cubicle, asking about his day and committing his answers to memory. Even her makeup decisions were influenced by the colors *he* liked most. For his part, Owen enjoyed Darcie's company. But to him, she was just an acquaintance whose unusual appearance and affinities made her strangely endearing.

A week after the board meeting, Owen accidentally slept past his alarm and arrived at work an hour late. Had this occurred last summer, he would have raced to work, sped past Al's window and dodged his judgmental scowls for the remainder of the day. But his comfort level with the boss had improved since the photo threats gave them common ground. So, on this day, he sauntered by Al's office and offered a neighborly wave. After setting his belongings down, he noticed a manila envelope on his keyboard, a sight both familiar and awful that stilled his heart and stole his breath. He spent a long moment imagining its troubling contents: a photo, a message, a threat. He grabbed it with careful fingers, turned it over and read, "Owen Daniels, *Sunset Times*." The words had been typed on a label affixed neatly to the front side with no return address. This was not at all like the last envelope he received, a fact that steadied his pounding chest. Taking a seat, he opened the seal and removed a single sheet of paper containing two lines of typed text:

Why is the pension plan so underfunded?
- E. Nola

"That's it?" he said, flipping the page over and over again in search of more words. Confident that was the only message to be found, he read it aloud: "Why is the pension plan so underfunded?"

"That's a weird question, huh?" said a voice behind him.

Owen turned to see Darcie looking over his shoulder at the piece of paper.

"You would think if someone wanted to give you a tip, it would be more obvious, like, 'Hey, did you know such-and-such?' or, 'You really ought to ask so-and-so about this one thing.' You know, something more obvious."

He nodded and returned his attention to the message. The question was simple enough, but he did not recognize the person's name. His first thought was Lily, who knew his need for information but whose recent behavior made her a doubtful source. He needed to confirm his suspicion but not with an eavesdropping Darcie nearby. He spun around in his chair.

"Would you do me a favor?"

"Sure, whatever you need."

"Would you check our subscriptions database for the last name Nola? It could be a man or a woman."

"I'm on it."

She hurried down the hallway toward the subscriptions department while Owen grabbed his phone and dialed the pension plan office.

"Retirement Department. This is Lily Allen."

"Hi, Lily, this is Owen from the newspaper. Do you have a minute?"

His question hung unanswered for an unusually long moment. "Yes, but only a minute," she replied.

"I just received an envelope containing a question about your pension plan. Did you send it?"

"My loyalty is to the plan alone. That's all you need to know. As a reminder, please don't quote me or Alexis without permission."

This was not the answer he had expected. Worse, it was not the soft, relaxed tone she had used in earlier conversations. It continued to vex him how one person could seem like two.

"Well, thanks for your time anyway. Goodbye."

He set down the phone and stared at it. If not her, then who? He picked up the paper again and examined it for any hint of authorship. Nothing stood out; it was just a blank sheet with two lines of text—not much to go on. At times like this, he was glad to have J.R. on speed dial. The officer listened to Owen's description of the evidence and rattled off several questions that the reporter, who naturally focused only on the words, had overlooked.

"What quality of paper was used?"

"Normal stock."

"Was the message handwritten or typed?"

"Typed."

"Was anything misspelled?"

"No."

"Is there anything meaningful about the sender's name?"

"The answer may be walking toward me. Gotta go."

Owen hung up just as Darcie reappeared at his cubicle, disappointment on her face.

"There's nobody by that name who subscribes to the paper. So, maybe it's just a concerned citizen?"

179

"Possibly," he replied, "but the timing of the tip makes it more likely that someone in-the-know is giving us a lead. That could only be a handful of people."

"Do you have any guesses about who?"

"I thought I did, but I was wrong," he replied, looking at the cryptic name again. "Well, it doesn't look like we are going to identify Mr. or Mrs. Nola today, but maybe there is something in the message to work with. Its meaning is plain enough. When a pension plan's liabilities exceed its assets, an underfunding results: the greater the disparity, the greater the underfunding."

"Uh, you just lost me. Can you say that again—this time in English?"

"Luckily for you, I specialize in English," he grinned. "Based on the actuarial presentation I heard last week, the Sunset Hills' pension plan is very underfunded. Basically, it has promised to pay a lot of plan member and retirees, but it doesn't have enough money in the bank to meet all those obligations. It has roughly sixty-two cents of assets for every pension dollar promised. Unfortunately, I don't have time to research E. Nola's question thoroughly. Al wants two articles from me by day's end."

Darcie bit her lip and picked at the carpet with the tip of her shoe. "Do you think I could help?" she asked quietly. "I mean, I'm not as smart as you, but I can ask questions and take notes."

"That would be great! You have an eye for detail, and I'm sure you will do a good job. But you must promise—and I am serious about this—you must give me your word that you won't tell anybody about this research."

Darcie began to inquire, but Owen lifted his hand in rebuttal. "Just trust me on this. Please."

Her dark painted lips and eye shadow smiled with eagerness as her legs bounced giddily. He jotted some notes on a sticky pad and handed it to her.

"Here's what you can do: Track down articles mentioning the pension plan going back to 1999. You probably won't find more than a couple dozen. Give priority to those containing the word *funding*. Once you have the articles sorted, let's review what you find. Sound good?"

"I won't let you down, I swear. I'll have something for you soon. Real soon."

She started to leave and then turned back to gush several additional assurances. Owen patiently waited until her enthusiasm settled and her verbal tap tightened. She started to step away before turning around a second time.

"You have no idea how much your trust means to me," she said earnestly. "Thank you."

By mid-afternoon, Darcie had copies of twenty articles. They were printed and sorted according to Owen's stated criteria with every instance of the word *funding* highlighted. After finishing his last writing project of the day, the two took the printouts to a conference room and shut the door. She laid the papers side-by-side around the table chronologically. Owen took a preliminary stroll, nodding his head as he scanned the headlines.

"This is good work, Darce. You even color-coordinated key words," he said, pointing to the numerous highlights. She blushed.

The pair started by reading the oldest news item, which announced that in 2000 the Board of Supervisors had adopted a resolution approving a more generous benefit formula—"3% at 50"—for the county's two thousand safety members. In the article, the five county Supervisors contended that the pension plan was "overfunded" at 103 percent and that the new benefit formula would attract the best firefighters and policemen to public service. Owen picked up the page for a closer look.

"The reporter who wrote this story said there were strong opinions on both sides of the debate, but what guaranteed the resolution's passage was when the actuary claimed the benefit enhancement would only 'minimally affect' the plan's overall funding."

Darcie looked at the next article summarizing the pension plan's follow-up actuarial report.

"Well, it didn't turn out that way," she said. "According to this, there was a larger drop in the funded status than the actuary initially thought. I like the headline we gave it: 'Oops!' in big, bold letters. That's pretty funny."

"Funny for everyone except the Board of Supervisors. That had to be embarrassing."

They made their way down the table's edge to a story containing quotes from the retirement agency's former director, who assured the community that any new liabilities would be paid off quickly.

"Were they?" Darcie inquired.

Owen scanned an article from 2002 about the recent recession that had hurt institutional investors across the nation.

"Apparently not. The economic downturn cut into the plan's earnings, which further deepened its funding woes. But then in 2005," he said, previewing another story, "the Board of Supervisors voted to adopt *another* enhanced benefit formula—"3% at 60"—this time for the county's eight thousand general members. The old actuary had been fired, deservedly, but the new consultant made the same argument about 'cost containment' and 'minimal effect on funding.'"

"So much for learning from their first mistake," Darcie said mockingly.

They kept moving along the table until a headline from 2006—"How Low Can It Go?"—caught Owen's attention.

"Listen to this. A year after adopting the newest benefit formula, the pension plan's funded status plummeted to a new low: seventy-five percent."

Owen remembered the actuary's dramatic hand motion at the board meeting. "Like a rock," he repeated.

As the researchers read articles and editorials published in the years following the benefit enhancements, they learned that the significant drop in funding had awakened the sleepy Sunset Hills community to the dire situation developing at the retirement agency. Politicians took to the airwaves to justify their votes; business leaders used their platforms to assail county leaders for their short-sightedness; and citizens wrote op-eds to the paper, some defending public employees and some criticizing their generous retirement packages.

"I'm starting to see a common theme in the articles from this point forward," Owen observed. "We had budget-conscious taxpayers who were very critical of public employee benefits, and we had public employee unions that dismissed the 'scare tactics' of private-sector workers who had 'pension envy.'"

He put the paper down and turned to Darcie.

"I recently heard someone use that term: *pension envy*. They did not define it, but I assumed it meant that private-sector workers wanted generous retirement packages like those promised to their public-sector counterparts."

"Well duh," she said flatly. "Who *wouldn't* want the benefits and perks they get?"

Owen placed both hands on the table and silently read

with a furrowed brow. He felt conflicted. On one hand, he agreed with Darcie—generous pensions for everyone sounded fabulous. But he also understood that these benefits came at a very high cost to taxpayers: his co-workers, his neighbors, Ruthie, himself. His political sensibilities had always led him to view taxpayer groups as whiners who favored big business over the little guy struggling to pay his bills. Retirees, more than anyone else, deserved to draw from the open hand of government, right?

"But should there be limits on this generosity?" he wondered aloud. "Or at least more public debate about all the costs?"

Darcie shrugged as Owen rounded the table to read more articles. She stood looking at one that he had passed over.

"What do you think this means?" she asked. "It says here that the two new benefit formulas grandfathered the past service of current workers."

Owen stepped to her side and read the paragraph, and then the section, and then the rest of the article. Darcie watched his studious face, his intelligent eyes, lost in thought.

"What it means," he said with sudden recognition, "is that the ten thousand public employees who were still working in 2000 and 2005 had their past service upgraded to the better benefit tiers. *All* of it."

"But wasn't their past work done in the lower benefit tier?"

"Yeah, that's what made the new benefits so expensive. Think of it this way. Let's say you worked for thirty years in a job under Benefit Tier A. Then, Benefit Tier B—which is better—takes effect. Now, not only would you have Tier B going forward, your thirty years at Tier A would be treated like Tier B."

"So, it's like I worked thirty years under Tier B? That would be nice."

"Definitely. But imagine how much it cost the county to upgrade the retirements of ten thousand public workers! I recall the actuary saying that he calculated new retirement contribution rates for the coming fiscal year based on projected costs for that year. That means the safety member rates should have risen in 2001 and the general member rates should have risen in 2006, the years immediately *after* the new benefit tiers took effect. That would ensure there would be enough new assets to match the new liabilities going forward. But put that aside for a second. Just think how many years of service *before* 2000 and 2005 were grandfathered into the new tiers. It's mind-boggling."

Darcie looked as if she knew she should be surprised but did not know exactly why. She raised her eyebrows. "Oh, really?" she muttered.

The response failed to convince Owen.

"Let's try a different explanation. The assets of a pension plan are supposed to match its liabilities, which are the long-term costs of keeping the pension promises made to workers. By 2005, there were ten thousand workers with probably two hundred thousand years of total service that *instantly* got upgraded to more generous benefit tiers. *None* of those years of past service was pre-funded. None of it! It became an immediate liability—like ten thousand maxed-out credit cards hitting at once. Could you imagine how big that bill was?"

This time, Darcie replied with a genuine, "Oh my!" that persuaded Owen she understood the significance of the grandfathering rule. The pair scanned the rest of the articles for any reference to the liability—the enormous bill—created by upgrading all the past years of service into the enhanced benefit tiers. They found references to "unrealistic actuarial assumptions" and "underperforming investments" during the 2008-09 recession as reasons for the pension plan's poor funding, but the *Sunset Times* never reported the actual cost of the new retirement benefits. Owen scratched both sides of his head.

"Why did we not ask that question? I just can't believe it. That's journalistic incompetence! The headline alone would have sold papers."

The clock struck five o'clock and newspaper staff began filing out of the building. Owen gathered the articles into a pile. "Do you mind if I hold on to these?"

"Oh, sure, go ahead. It's your project, after all. *Our* project … sort of," she smiled. "So, what comes next?"

"Tomorrow, I will request a copy of the county resolutions approving the 2000 and 2005 benefit formula enhancements. I'm hoping that provides a lead to follow."

Papers in hand, he moved to leave the room, patting his co-laborer's shoulder on the way out.

"I really appreciate your help, Darce. You are a good researcher."

"It was my pleasure," she whispered as a wave of emotional energy tingled through her body.

◊ ◊ ◊

Owen mustered the courage to call Lily the next morning. This time, their conversation felt more normal. He even perceived a slight warmth returning to her voice. She did not rush off the call as she had done earlier but tarried unnecessarily, wandering from topic to topic.

"How's your double duty going? Are you in love with politics yet?"

"Not quite, but I'm staying busy. We may have uncovered a new lead for my dead retirees story that we need to devote some time to. Don't worry, it's nothing that requires a quote from you."

It was not a full disclosure, he knew, but just enough to gauge her level of interest. Would she ask about the lead? The story? Last week's board meeting?

"We?" she inquired. "Do you have an assistant now?"

"Uh, no. Not exactly. She's just a … a … co-worker."

Lily paused momentarily before replying. "Well, I am a tad disappointed in you, Owen."

"For what?"

"For ending your sentence a minute ago with a preposition. Tsk, tsk."

She laughed, and Owen joined in. This was the Lily he remembered: the one who valued good grammar as much as he did, who could tease without offending, who had endeared herself to him at their first meeting, and who made him catch his breath whenever she came into view. He missed this Lily.

Before ending the call, Owen returned to business. "I need to ask for copies of the board resolutions relating to the pension plan's benefit enhancements in 2000 and 2005. Do you have those handy?"

"Will this be a Public Records Act request?"

"Not if I can help it."

"Good. Legal counsel has to review all PRAs, and that slows down everything."

Within an hour, Lily had emailed scans of the resolutions to Owen with a short note: "Nice catching up with you today. Good luck with your research. And remember to mind your prepositional placement!"

He scoured every word of the Board of Supervisors'

resolutions, which were plagued by legal jargon and endless "Whereas such-and-such" statements. As the article he read yesterday had noted, both resolutions mentioned the grandfathering of prior employee service into the new, higher benefit tiers. What interested him more, however, was something he found atop the first page: the last names of the politicians who voted for the enhancements. Conveniently, the same five people were present for both resolutions, with four "yes" votes and one abstention.

Owen left his desk and found Darcie busy helping another reporter across the newsroom. He motioned for her to come see him, and within moments she stood at his cubicle, breathing hard.

"Wow, that was fast."

"Why waste time, you know?" she said between pants.

"Come with me."

She followed him to a quiet corner where he handed her a few papers.

"Here are the two county resolutions approving enhanced benefits for members of the pension plan. I'd like more information about the politicians who voted for them."

She looked at the names. "All of them?"

"Only the ones who voted yes. When you have time, figure out who these people are and what they're doing now. You might need to call the retirement agency to get their first names. While you are doing that, I will reread the articles you pulled to extract any other useful information or leads. Let's meet on Thursday to review what we found."

The pair returned to their work and conducted their respective inquiries between other tasks. Although they differed in nearly every other way, Owen and Darcie were both diligent researchers, albeit for very different reasons. He sought to satisfy a driving desire for truth. And as best as he could tell, she seemed satisfied simply to please him. Thursday came quickly. They met privately to swap information. Owen's research taught him that the recession in 2008 and 2009 not only crushed the local economy but also devastated the pension plan's assets, which dropped by thirty percent that fiscal year. It also led to the plan promptly lowering its assumed investment rate by a quarter percentage point, an actuarial change that immediately added an additional $200 million to the plan's total unfunded liability and an extra $20 million to the county's annual pension bill. As if that was not devastating enough to the county budget, the Board of Retirement adopted new actuarial assumptions that more accurately reflected plan member experience: The average retirement age, final salary and mortality rate rose because county employees were working longer, earning more money and dying at older ages. These assumption changes translated to even higher costs because they applied to all members for the foreseeable future.

"I don't get why that's a big deal," Darcie confessed. "Why do assumptions come with price tags?"

Owen had come to enjoy her honest questions. It gave him the chance to show off his new knowledge.

"It is because even small changes, when extended over many years, lead to drastically different outcomes. Think of it like a ship that veers off course by one degree. A mile out, the ship is still close to where it originally expected to be. But a thousand miles out, the ship is a very long way from its destination. That's what happens when a pension plan makes even a minor change to its assumptions. That new 'expected reality' charts a different course than what was initially planned. In terms of cost, it's not a big deal after one year, but the total extra cost after thirty years is enormous."

"Yeah, I suppose that makes sense," she nodded.

"So, what did you learn about the politicians?"

Darcie retrieved a folded paper from her pocket and began reading.

"I tracked down each of the politicians listed on the resolutions. Two men retired years ago: One died of old age and the other still lives in town. Another politician left Sunset Hills to launch a medical company. The fourth politician resigned shortly after the 2005 vote and ran for state office. He won his first term but was beaten badly two years later. The loss was so humiliating that he left California! And get this, he lost to the fifth politician, the guy who sat on the Board of Supervisors with him, the one who abstained from the two votes. His name is—drum roll—Mike Lancaster."

"Governor Lancaster?" Owen blurted.

"Yep. After serving as our county Supervisor for several years, he became a state assemblyman, then a state senator, and now the governor."

A long-time fan of Lancaster, Owen knew something of the man's career. In fact, except for Ruthie, who accused the politician of being a tax-and-spend liberal, the Daniels family strongly supported Mike Lancaster. Mr. Daniels had served on his election and reelection campaigns, earning praise from the rising political star as someone who could get out the vote. As a boy, Owen joined his father in walking precincts for Lancaster and even shook the politician's hand at a rally. Knowing that the California governor once lived and worked in Sunset Hills only increased Owen's admiration of him.

"Interesting," he said. "What else did you dig up?"

"Well, not too much besides their careers. Not everyone

returned my calls. Did you know it's almost impossible to get a pharmaceutical executive to pick up the phone? But I was able to find the local guy—he had a lot to say—and even the one who left the state."

"What pharmaceutical executive?" Owen asked, his eyes dilating.

Darcie scanned her notes, searching for the name.

"Um, here he is: Dorian Kemp. He works at a drug company in San Francisco called Hemlock. What an odd name: Hemlock. Isn't that the weed that Socrates ..."

Her voice trailed off into the background as Owen felt his heart stop. He inhaled deeply and held it, as if trying to freeze the moment. His world spun, dizzied by scattered thoughts, worries and revelations. He saw Darcie's mouth moving but heard nothing. What had she done?

"Please tell me you didn't call them," he interrupted.

"Why? What was wrong with calling them?"

He placed his elbows on the table and his forehead into the palms of his hands. What had she done? Again, he was faced with the dilemma of saying something that could cause unimaginable fear if he were wrong or possible protection if he were right. Owen grasped the significance of Darcie's connection linking the pension plan to the retiree murders to Hemlock. He feared he might not be the only person who realized it.

As he sat thinking, she repeated, "What was wrong with calling them, Owen?" Her eyes brimmed with concern. "Oh, no. Did I disappoint you? I'm so sorry. I just wanted more information to give you today. Was that wrong? Oh, please say something."

She stood watching him, awaiting an answer. He stared at her distraught expression, full of an innocence unbroken by the knowledge of her transgression. In that moment, he knew her delicate mind would be crushed under the weight of fear if he spoke candidly. He opted for the same course he had taken with Ruthie—silence. He would bear the burden alone.

"It's just that I didn't want you contacting anyone," he said anxiously. "Did you tell them who you were?"

"Well, sure. I had to leave my name and phone number, but the secretary said my message would be delivered as soon as possible. That was yesterday."

Owen swallowed hard. "You told them who you were?"

"Yes, of course, silly. They needed that information to call me. But I still haven't heard from everyone."

"Darcie, you did a good job," he said solemnly. "Now go home to your mom. Stay inside all night, and let's talk again in the morning. Please promise me you will stay at home."

"If you say so. Should I be worried?"

Owen shook his head nonchalantly. His conscience pricked him as she turned and left.

Before leaving work, he called J.R. about the day's discoveries and explained what Darcie had done.

"That was plain foolish," the officer chided. "You guys are not law enforcement, nor do you have the ability to protect yourselves from threats. I suggest you tell your co-worker what's going on so she can be more careful. Better yet, let me do it. I'll drop by your office in the morning."

"All right. Come by around ten o'clock tomorrow."

The darkness of his circumstances notwithstanding, Owen felt more at peace knowing that J.R. was his well-armed advocate. He hoped Darcie would feel the same comfort. He knew it was stupid to involve her. Ruthie had taught him that innocence, wherever it was found, deserved to be preserved for as long as life permitted. He regretted having to taint his friend the following day.

The next morning, Owen arrived at work and, as usual, scheduled the day's writing projects and interviews. He poured a cup of coffee in the break room and walked by Darcie's cubicle; she was not there. He returned to his desk and spent an hour drafting a business article. When he reached a stopping point, he went looking for her again, but she was not in her normal locations. Owen's anxiety increased as he went from desk to desk, department to department, asking co-workers if they had seen Darcie. Nobody had. Their meeting with J.R. was approaching quickly, and he did not want to delay it to Monday. At Owen's request, Darcie's boss left a message on her cell followed by a text, neither of which she returned.

"That's unusual," the supervisor said. "Darcie always tells me when she will be late."

At hearing this, Owen began to worry. He returned to his cubicle and found J.R.'s massive body squeezed into his chair.

"How do you fit into this little thing?" he joked. "I feel like a fat guy in a little coat."

"Not now. Darcie is missing."

J.R. extracted himself from the seat and joined Owen at the desk of her supervisor, who again called Darcie unsuccessfully. The detective requested her home address, and within moments he and Owen sped toward her house in his patrol car. It was the first time Owen had ridden in a police vehicle with the lights and sirens ablaze, but his gut wrenched too severely for him to enjoy the experience. All his thoughts were on Darcie. The car pulled alongside a little house with Darcie's car in the driveway. Her mom, who worked long shifts, was not at home, but apparently Darcie was still inside. They knocked on the front door first, then the street-facing windows and finally on the backdoor, where curtains were drawn tightly shut. Owen's knocking became pounding.

"Darcie! Are you there? It's me, Owen. Open up!"

Nothing stirred inside. J.R. met Owen around back and found an unlocked window. They removed the screen and slid it open enough for the detective to hoist Owen into the living room. He unlocked the sliding door, and J.R. entered.

Stillness and silence filled the house. Owen opened a few curtains to illuminate their dark surroundings. Despite Darcie's penchant for gothic attire, she and her mother kept a remarkably cheerful house: colorful paintings, ruby red couches, fresh flowers, pastel-colored walls, even a bright orange cat. It reminded Owen that it was unwise to judge a book by its cover. But right now, he just wanted to find the book. They searched the house, each entering a different room.

"Clear." "Clear." "Clear."

Their voices echoed through the eerie silence. The last room at the end of the narrow hallway was a bathroom with its door slightly ajar. They moved toward it carefully. The cat darted in front of their legs, through the crack and out of sight. J.R. drew his firearm and pushed the door. Something blocked its movement, so he pushed harder, forcing his large frame through the tight gap and into the room. It snapped back into place. Owen likewise pushed against the heavy door; it hardly budged. He tried again with little success. It was not until J.R. moved the obstruction from behind the door that Owen squeezed in and saw Darcie's body splayed lifeless across the floor, her head lying in a small pool of blood.

« 15 »

A cold, bitter rain greeted the mourners at Darcie's gravesite. Rows of black dresses and suits huddled underneath umbrellas that dripped water like unending tears. Those who gathered to pay their final respects to the young woman gathered around a hole in the muddy earth where her coffin lay. Few in attendance could hear the minister's voice over the sound of rain pounding on the casket below. Even if the day were still, the great sorrow of that place would have muted his words.

Owen stood off from the crowd with no umbrella or raincoat to shield him from the merciless elements. He deserved no mercy—not from nature, not from Darcie's loved ones, not from the Fate he once trusted to administer justice fairly. His shivering and discomfort were acts of penance that, he knew, could never erase his guilt. He stood at a distance, alone in his regret and shame. The pastor closed his Bible, offered a prayer and dismissed the gathering. Darcie's mother lingered over the coffin for some time before being led away by a friend. The sky continued to fall softly. Until now, Owen could not cry, for his guilt felt too great. But as he stepped toward the hole where the outline of his friend would remain forever, tears filled his eyes. He dropped a single white rose into the earth and wept bitterly.

J.R. watched these events from a nearby pavilion. He remained there not to stay dry but to survey the grounds like a sentinel, keeping an eye on the killer's real focus: Owen. The detective had tried explaining this fact to his young friend on the day of the murder—that Darcie's death was a message intended for *him*—but Owen was not in a state of mind to face that reality. From the moment he saw her lifeless body, his personal ambition and pursuit of truth began to die. When J.R. said her autopsy confirmed Hemlox had killed her before her head even hit the floor, he shrugged.

"What does it matter? She's gone."

J.R. attempted to pull Owen from his grief by offering reasons to fight on, but these fell on deaf ears. The reporter showed up for his job, but neither his heart nor his mind was engaged as once before. He lived and worked as a shell of his former self—emptied of hope, filled with fear and desperate for safety.

It was in this condition that, one evening, he revealed to Ruthie the clandestine photos taken of her. He laid them one by one on her dining room table, saying nothing as the images sent ripples of terror through her quivering frame. Just a few moments passed before she begged him, "Put them away, Owen. Please. I've seen enough." The trauma of knowing that their homes were no longer safe places stirred in them a desire to leave Sunset Hills behind. With much discussion and not a few tears, they agreed that night to sell

Ruthie's house and leave California.

"I don't like it either," he told her, "but it's the only way I know to keep us safe. You can live out your days on a beach somewhere in Florida. How's that sound?"

With the decision made to leave their old lives for the sake of each other, they started planning their move well in advance of Ruthie's eightieth birthday, six months away. Owen gave her the task of selecting a town she liked. Every day, she used her "computing machine" to search along Florida's sunny coasts for cities that met her exacting requirements.

"It must face the Atlantic Ocean. It must be within driving distance of an air-conditioned mall. And it must be within walking distance of an ice cream parlor."

"You know we can buy ice cream at any grocery store, right?"

She wagged her finger. "Don't forget, you put *me* in charge on his point. I insist on being near a parlor like I had growing up."

After a month of searching retirement hotspots, she called her grandson at work and could hardly stop talking. "Oh, I found the most charming little community! You're going to love it, too. It's a quaint town at the state's northeastern tip that will be perfect for both of us. I am so excited!"

"Congratulations, Gram. I am happy that you are happy. Now, let's put your house up for sale."

Two months later, someone made an offer on the property. The bid was insultingly low to Owen. "You should reject it," he advised. "They can do better than that."

Ruthie shook her head. "Time is not on my side, remember. This offer is good enough."

"It's your house, so it's your decision. But I still think you should tell the buyer to pound sand. At least counter for a few thousand more. Please? If not for you, then for my in-heritance."

Ruthie gasped. Owen winked.

The parties signed a sales contract with a 45-day escrow, enough time for him to find a job in the new location. To celebrate their good news, Ruthie and Owen walked to a local ice cream shop that evening to share a sundae.

"I can hardly believe I'm leaving California!" she said between bites. "I haven't moved since I was, well, not much older than you. But who's going to pack up the house? There are so many little things that can break, so many papers and photo albums and …"

"We can worry about those details later," Owen said, his mouth full of hot fudge. "In fact, we can stop worrying completely. Tonight, let's just enjoy the moment."

Owen arrived at work at eight o'clock sharp, something he had not done since Darcie's murder. Her death had shocked everyone in the office and cast a months-long pall over their hearts and quality of work. Not until the warmth of spring-time did its effects begin to lift. Darcie's supervisor had finally removed the memorial items placed in her cubicle by heartbroken co-workers. Owen had wanted to contribute something to the collection—the first obituary she had given him—but he could not bring himself to walk past her desk, knowing that he alone was responsible for its vacancy. In fact, he altogether avoided the hallway leading there, for the pain of his guilt was still too near. Leaving the state would serve another purpose, this one just as personal: avoiding the sight of anything that reminded him of Darcie.

"I see a light at the end of the tunnel," he told Al. "My

grandma turns eighty in three months, and that gives us plenty of time to leave this nightmare I created. I'm actually feeling pretty good about life now. The heavy weight I've carried for the last nine months left as soon as we received an offer on her house."

"You do what you must, but I, uh, I ..."

Al looked away and rested his eyes on his favorite coffee mug. Owen watched his boss curiously. The editor appeared to be gathering something to say, but what that could be, he had no clue. The curmudgeon was not exactly known among newsroom staff for expressive self-disclosure, unless a long, dark-blue streak of profanity counted in his favor. He looked up and continued uncomfortably.

"I think you should know you're an above-average reporter, kid. What I mean is, um, you have a future at this paper if you want it. Maybe even an editor's job one day—if you decide to stick around. That is not an opportunity that shows up often, you know."

He paused, surveying the young man's reaction. Owen sat across from Al's desk with a wrinkled forehead. What had begun as a quasi-compliment had ended with the offer of a lifetime: being a newspaper editor, presumably when Al quit or retired. The man was right—such an opportunity may never come to a reporter, even after decades of work. And yet, here he was, being given the chance to fulfill his journalistic dream, to one day shape the editorial future of the paper, to make a name for himself, to make the *L.A. Times* regret not hiring him after college. This was his chance to live his dream. The only condition was to stay in Sunset Hills. But if he did, Ruthie would never consider moving to Florida. And if she stayed, she would become another Hemlox victim. Owen would lose another family member—his last one—and again be solely responsible for another death. His face grew increasingly tight as the logical dominoes fell one by one in his mind.

"I couldn't live with myself," he said quietly.

"What's that? You can't what?"

Owen shook his head faintly. "I am grateful for your offer, Al. I don't know if you said all that because you really think I'd be a good editor or if you're still upset about Edgar returning to the politics desk. Either way—I cannot believe I am saying this—I have to decline. I need to take my grandma away from here."

Al took a gulp of coffee and reclined in his squeaky chair. "I figured you would say that. It's no use arguing with you. You are as stubborn as I am. Besides, if I were you, I'd probably do the same thing."

"Thanks for understanding. And thanks for the opportunity to work two beats. I'm sure Edgar will pick up where I left off and do fine, so don't stress about him."

"Between you and me, I had hoped he would just quit. You're easier to work with."

Owen grinned and turned to leave.

"By the way," Al added, "you're still in charge of the public servant series. I don't want that moron screwing it up."

The young reporter returned to his cubicle feeling content with his decision and amused by Al's unconventional approach to issuing compliments. He opened his list of county employees to feature next and saw "Jim Jensen," a retiree whose name sounded remotely familiar. As he had done many times before, Owen readied his interview questions and called Mr. Jensen. Out of the gate, the old man hardly shut his mouth. He carried on for two full minutes about his morning before Owen abruptly cut him off.

"I'm sorry, sir, I missed a few of those details." He was not really sorry. "Let's restart the conversation, beginning with your work history."

"Oh, sure, I wouldn't mind at all," Mr. Jensen laughed. "I've got what they call the gift of gab. Born with it, according to my mother. She lived to be ninety-nine. If I got her genes, woo-wee, there's a lot more life to live for me, yes indeed. But my wife and I stay busy. We like to travel. In fact, we went to Tijuana last Christmas and nearly didn't come back. You see, we ..."

Few pet peeves irritated Owen as much as someone who used words frivolously. It was not just that journalism required concise communication; his personality demanded it. For some people, cleanliness was next to godliness. For Owen, it was brevity. This being the case, Mr. Jensen had, in less than five minutes, proven himself to be the most ungodly man alive.

"Excuse me, sir, excuse me," Owen interrupted again. "I only have a few minutes to talk to you, so if you could limit your answers to just my questions, I would appreciate it."

"Oh, certainly. I'm sorry. Having a lot to say can get you into trouble. I learned that when I was on the Board of Supervisors."

The reporter sat up in his chair. *Did he say Board of Supervisors?* Owen felt an impulse to deviate from his script, to inquire into the board's history of setting pension benefits, to extract everything he wanted to know about that awful subject. Then again, maybe he did not want to know. Maybe that stone was better left unturned. He swallowed his natural curiosity and continued.

"Let's talk about other career highlights and some of your favorite memories"—cheeseball facts that make a feel-good piece feel good. The retiree provided details in abundance, a fact that Owen appreciated in spite of his aversion to wordiness, because it would give him plenty of fodder to draw from when writing. In one of his long-winded answers, Mr. Jensen referenced "a decision we made affecting the pension plan and county employees." Owen's eyes swelled; he forced them to stay on his list of pre-approved questions. Deep within, he desperately wanted to roll over that stone and see what squirmed underneath. He took a deep breath.

Remember, he told himself, *your future is no longer in Sunset Hills. Keep the past in the past—for your own good.*

He dutifully asked the next question. As Mr. Jensen droned on, Owen felt his mind wandering and blood pressure increasing. No longer could he even hear the interviewee amid the torrent of his own thoughts.

"I don't think you mentioned *when* you served," he interrupted. "And, if you don't mind me asking, how old are you?"

"You probably gathered that I'm not an insecure type, so I don't mind you asking at all. I am eighty-two years young, almost eighty-three. As for being a county Supervisor, I served three terms from 1994 to 2006."

The answer continued, but Owen hardly listened. He instantly recalled where he had seen the name Jensen—on the 2000 and 2005 resolutions approving the two pension benefit enhancements. Mr. Jensen was among the four politicians who voted for the benefit increases, thus beginning the swift erosion of the pension plan's funded status. Owen realized he was speaking to one of the four men Darcie had called just before her murder.

"You voted for the benefit increases, didn't you?" he said slowly.

"If you mean the '3% at 50' and '3% at 60' formulas, yep, I sure did! Those were some great benefits that helped a lot of people, including me. I won't get into numbers 'cuz that doesn't need to be in the paper, so I'll just say that after 2005, my decision to retire was pretty easy. But, boy, did we catch hell for that vote!"

"We?"

"Yeah. Me, Kemp, Davis and Perez—we voted 'yes' both times. The experts told us the costs of the new benefits would be mostly offset by not giving across-the-board raises to county employees, but, well, I guess not. The math was supposed to work out better, but then 2006 rolls around and we find out there's a $1 billion liability! Ouch."

"A billion dollars?" Owen asked incredulously. "Was that the plan's total liability after your votes?"

"Not exactly," he replied tentatively. "That was the *price* of our two votes—meaning the liability grew a billion bucks as soon as we approved the second benefit formula. That's a pretty big number, huh? Honestly—I'm an old man and I can be honest, right?—I couldn't have been elected dogcatcher if that number got published years ago. So, a few of us left the board for greener pastures after 2005. Me—I just retired."

Owen had promised himself at Darcie's funeral to bury his investigation in her grave, not only for self-protection but also as an act of penance for her death. Mr. Jensen's words tested the reporter's resolve to honor that oath. He wanted to ask about Kemp. He wanted to ask why Lancaster abstained. He wanted to ask how the Board of Supervisors had been duped twice. He wanted to ask Jensen how he had lived past age eighty. But more than the satisfaction of having those questions answered, he desperately wanted to feel safe again. The latter compulsion won the day as Owen asked the final question on his notepad and ended the interview.

Pushing aside his conflicting desires, he began drafting his article about Mr. Jensen's public service. As he searched for a nice way to describe the talkative old man and his checkered career, Ruthie called.

"Hey, Gram, what's going on?"

"Hi, sweetie. I just received a message from the realtor that confused me. She said something about a bad inspection report. I didn't understand what she meant. I was hoping you could drop by tonight and make sense of it."

"Sure, but I might require food for my services."

"That goes without saying. You're a growing boy."

After work, he drove to Ruthie's house and found her at the table, haphazardly flipping through a stack of papers.

"What's for dinner?" he said cheerfully.

"I don't know," she replied distractedly. "The realtor dropped off a copy of the inspection report and the sales contract. I'm supposed to look at the highlighted parts, but all the legal gibberish confuses me. She said she would speak to the other agent but not to get my hopes up."

Owen's smile fell away instantly. He took a seat and read the inspection report top to bottom, including the highlighted section of the sales contract that stated: "This conditional agreement is subject to a satisfactory inspection report. If, in the event that an inspection report of the property reveals structural damage, infestation or contamination, whereby corrective action would extend the conditional agreement beyond the agreed-upon closing date, this contract shall be considered breached and invalid." Owen dropped the papers.

"Oh, no," he whispered.

He looked at the report again before turning toward Ruthie. Her anxious eyes followed his.

"Gram, it says here the wood in your house is full of termites."

"Well, can't we kill them?"

"Yes, but the report says your beams are now too weak."

Owen hesitated, considering the dire implications of what he was about to say.

"The wood holding your house up is too unstable to sell. It would have to be replaced. That means you can't sell until it is all fixed."

"How long will that take?"

"I don't know—maybe a few months?" he answered. "There is a lot to replace."

Her countenance crumbled. For the first time ever, Owen thought she looked elderly. She leaned her head into his chest and cried weakly.

"I will be eighty by then. I will be eighty."

The news haunted Owen for days, disrupting his focus at work and shrouding the glimmer of hope that had dawned in the preceding weeks. Ruthie also began to despair, and her health suffered. Time and fate, both of which the Daniels thought they had defeated, had raised a punishing counterattack that, unbeknown to them, would only worsen.

Later that week, Ruthie called Owen in a near panic. "A friend just told me that a former colleague at the county passed away for unknown reasons. I want you to look him up. Please, Owen. I need to know if he was murdered."

"Gram, I don't want to do that anymore. I don't even look at obituaries because of the bad associations."

"Please do it. It's bothering me to not know. If you don't want to, ask your police friend. I was told the man was *my* age and died on his porch. In broad daylight, Owen!"

As she found back tears, his heart broke anew.

"Okay. But this needs to be the last time."

He scanned a week's worth of obituaries for the name she provided, then a second week and then a third—all the while keeping a mental tally of other dead county retirees he spotted. Although he found no death notice for Ruthie's co-worker, something in the other obits caught his attention: the date of births had changed. He opened his spreadsheet listing the decedents that he and Darcie had tracked; their birth years made them eighty years old at their time of death. But the recent obits listed county retirees whose published dates of birth made them seventy-nine when they died. Owen doubted himself. He added a month's worth of recent decedents to his spreadsheet, subtracted their dates of death from their dates of birth, and saw a pattern in the data that made his skin crawl. He immediately called the retirement office.

"Hi, Alexis, this is Owen Daniels at the newspaper. I just have one question. Did the Board of Retirement recently make any changes to its actuarial assumptions?"

"Yes, about a month ago," she replied. "The actuary recommended slightly higher retirement rates, slightly lower disability rates, and—this one was unexpected—mortality rates set forward a year. All in all, the changes largely offset and were not very significant in terms of future cost to the county. The board approved them all. Why do you ask?"

Owen ignored the question. "What do you mean by 'set forward a year' for the mortality assumption?"

"It means a year earlier than the previous assumption."

"So, rather than assuming a retiree will die at age eighty, you now expect it to happen at age seventy-nine?" He held his breath and waited for the other shoe to drop.

"On average, yes."

Owen said nothing for a long time, so long that Alexis

repeated, "Hello? Hello?" until he eventually responded with an abrupt, "Thank you, but I have to go."

What she thought of him and his odd manners, he did not know, nor did he care at the moment. He compared her answer to the ages on his spreadsheet; they matched perfectly. One thing became unmistakably obvious: The Sunset Hills murderer paid closer attention to the Board of Retirement's actions than he did—and took them far more seriously.

But why? In the scheme of things, what difference does a dead eighty-year-old make? He corrected himself: What difference does a dead seventy-nine-year-old make?

Whatever the answer, Owen felt knocked on his heels again. He realized that the timetable of death had moved up, placing Ruthie in the murderer's crosshairs. The only fact that seemed to work in her favor was that the deaths followed a consistent pattern: older to younger. Owen assumed there were still several county retirees older than Ruthie. He needed to see where his grandma fell on the hit list, assuming the killer kept to the chronological rule. Knowing that order would give him a sense of how much time she had left. It could be a couple of months. Maybe a few weeks. He would not let himself think in terms of days. Pinpricks of sweat gathered under his hairline and arms as his breathing quickened. His mind raced from one possible action plan to the next, all the while his churning emotions made clear thinking nearly impossible. The prospect of losing Ruthie terrified him once again. More than that, it stirred his passion, his sense of justice. Months of self-control had kept his adrenaline at bay, but Alexis' revelation had cracked his dam. Owen felt apathetic no longer. His happy-clappy outlook had perished as a surge of concentrated anger enveloped him. His mind burned hot and lucid once again. He knew he had to resume his investigation, not only for Ruthie but also for Darcie, Al and the dozens of lives destroyed by the villain in the darkness.

Owen filed an official records request with the pension plan for a list of retiree names, dates of birth, and statuses as dead or alive. Lily had said PRAs could take ten days to process, so he submitted the request and then turned his attention to Hemlock Pharmaceuticals and its founder, Dorian Kemp. Hemlock's website claimed Kemp founded his drug company in the Bay Area "with the single-minded mission to improve lives and patient outcomes." Owen balked at the ironic branding.

"You expect me to buy that crap when you sell a drug that ends lives?" he told his computer screen. No response.

He continued reading: "Hemlock initially focused on developing medications to relieve chronic pain and to improve anesthesia effects, and only recently expanded into the nascent end-of-life market in California."

• *Blah, blah, blah* is all Owen heard. His Hemlock well had been poisoned, and the young man refused to believe a word he read. He clicked on the company's most recent financial statements, which showed its gross product sales since inception. It was clear from the remarkable revenue growth that Kemp made his fortune rather quickly as sales of core drugs helped his firm take larger and larger bites of market share. If the dollar amounts alone had not convinced him of Kemp's wealth, social media photos of the executive flying his private jet along the California coast would have sufficed.

He turned his attention to collecting more objective narratives of the drug company's meteoric rise. A 2015 article he found in a San Francisco paper reported that Hemlock announced its ground-breaking assisted-suicide cocktail just weeks after the former governor signed the "End-of-Life Option Act," making California the fifth U.S. state to legalize physician-assisted suicide—or, as its advocates called it, "death with dignity." The timing of the drug's release right after the law's passage raised eyebrows among governmental watchdogs, but these criticisms paled in comparison to the outcry when the State of California quickly and quietly approved a single-source contract with Hemlock to provide euthanasia drugs to in-state physicians. A year later, Kemp took his company public with an IPO that the newspaper aptly described as "an immense windfall for the burgeoning pharmaceutical company with close political ties." Those last words caught Owen's attention. He knew that Assemblyman Ramos certainly fell into that infamous category, but another half-hour of reading old articles brought the reporter no closer to identifying other politicians on the Hemlock bandwagon.

Demonstrating a link between Kemp and Mike Lancaster proved even more difficult. Nothing in the papers mentioned the pair in relation to each other. But given how Hemlock's contract sailed through the capitol, Owen felt convinced they must have stayed in touch after leaving the Sunset Hills Board of Supervisors. He flipped open his notepad to a page full of names and relationships he had uncovered thus far, adding the following note: *Kemp tapped Lancaster's political influence to benefit the drug company? How?* This was his working theory, but as with everything else he tried to nail down, evidence was scarce, if it existed at all. Obtaining the facts needed to confirm his suspicions would require making inquiries at Hemlock and Sacramento, both unsafe options.

Darcie's murder had convinced Owen of how little

provocation was needed to invite a lethal response. So, he played it safe and turned his attention to the drug company's initial public offering, recalling a helpful investigative tip J.R. shared many months ago: "Most criminal activity has a pot of gold at the end of its rainbow. Follow the money and find the criminal." He picked up the phone and called the pension plan's investment officer.

"Hi, Peter, this is Owen at the newspaper. We met last summer when you provided some background information about investments. I was hoping to find out who funded an IPO a few years ago. I know, random question. Could you point me in the right direction?"

"I can do you one better," the friendly voice replied. "I will look it up for you."

"Seriously? That would be great. The company I'm re-searching is Hem—"

Owen stopped himself as the rest of Hemlock's name stuck in his throat. He took a breath and considered the possible mistake he was about to make in his rush for answers.

"How rude of me," he said, trying not to make the conversation seem even weirder. "Here I am taking advantage of your kindness, and I haven't bothered to get to know you. I am sorry."

"Oh, don't mention it."

"No, I really should have done this in the proper order. Tell me about your background. Where have you worked? What led you to our town?"

As if in a job interview, Peter rattled off the highlights of his career: stockbroker in Tampa, investment banker in Philly, bond salesman in New York.

"Impressive resume," Owen replied, still trying to gauge the investor's independence from Sunset Hills politics. "So, this is your first job in California, right?"

"Yep. It's been good so far. But I'm not sure yet if the perfect weather here makes up for the ridiculously high taxes. The jury is still out."

Owen was convinced. "I am *very* glad to hear you are new to California and liking it. Anyhow, as I was saying earlier, the IPO I am interested in was for a company called Hemlock Pharmaceuticals. Ever heard of it?"

"No, but I'll dig around and let you know what turns up. Just to warn you, IPO funding sources are notoriously difficult to find, so this may take a few days."

"No worries. That timeframe is perfectly fine. Thanks again for your help."

Owen felt grateful to tap into the expertise of someone like Peter. Like so many other things, this reminded him of his dad. "It's not always *what* you know, son," he used to say. "It's *who* you know. Sometimes your friends are resources, and sometimes your resources become friends."

He could not help but think of J.R. Nearly three months had passed since they last spoke. Shortly after the funeral, when some of his raw emotion had passed, Owen considered calling to say hello. For one reason or another, he kept putting off the contact. Days turned into weeks, weeks turned into months, and growing embarrassment made it increasingly difficult to pick up the phone. *This must be how people grow apart*, he concluded. It was true—the two friends had grown apart, but Owen felt responsible. He stared at his phone, swallowed his pride and texted two words that reflected his present state of mind: "I'm back."

Owen set the phone in front of him and watched it, wondering if his friend could forgive his lengthy silence. He had not known J.R. long enough to guess how such an offense would be taken. A moment later, his phone buzzed and the answer became clear.

"I knew you'd come around," he texted. "I'll call you."

The phone rang and Owen picked up cautiously. "Hello?"

"Whatzuuuup," the deep voice bellowed, followed by the sound of familiar laughter.

The two spent a long while catching up on each other's lives since the funeral. J.R. proudly announced that he would be a father again and expressed certainty about this one being a boy. Owen congratulated him, noting that the NFL would need a new linebacker in two decades.

"My wife and I don't make skinny babies, that's for sure," he chuckled. "Who knows, in twenty years, maybe I'll be coaching my son's football team. Since I told my wife about how my pension worked, she has been hounding me to retire when I'm fifty so we can travel the world."

"How did you respond to that?"

"I said, 'Woman, I *like* to work! I'm not retiring that young.' And then she huffed around for a few hours until I agreed to retire at fifty-three. It's crazy the kind of things women can make us do! You remember that when you get googly-eyed over that Lily girl."

"She and I haven't spoken since Darcie died. Actually, that's not the only disappointing news I've got."

Owen told J.R. about his failed Florida plans, the new mortality assumption and his discovery that county retirees were beginning to die earlier.

"That *is* bad news," he agreed. "So that's why you're back in the game—to save your grandma?"

Owen said nothing.

"Well, while you've been planning your Florida escape, I've been mapping motivation scenarios for our best lead—

that Kemp guy. He is the only link between the pension plan and the murder weapon—or some form of it. The trouble is, the main criminal motivations don't seem to apply."

"What do you mean?"

"In my experience, criminals—from the geniuses to the morons—are motivated by just a few things: money, power or revenge. If their premeditated crime promises riches or influence or a sense of justice, they can rationalize doing it. Unless Kemp is a sociopath, these are the motivations to look for. Unfortunately, none seems to apply to him."

Owen wrote the three options in his notepad, and they began talking through them, one by one. The problem with a financial motivation was that Kemp would profit very little from selling Hemlox to an assassin who only wanted to kill a couple hundred retirees. The risk would definitely not be worth the reward. However, if the deaths proved the effectiveness of the pills to a potential large buyer, money *could* be a motivating factor. But, after discussing that possibility at length, they agreed it fell flat because the feds had already approved the drug; its effectiveness was well known. Owen put a line through "money" in his notes.

Power as a motivation seemed even less probable. What would Kemp or anyone else gain from the death of seniors in just one county? It was possible, albeit not likely, that the killer felt a twisted power trip from offing innocents, but that would put him in the sociopath category. For the average criminal who retained a sliver of rationality, the constant worry of being discovered and losing existing power would serve as a deterrent to taking such risks. This reality especially applied to Kemp and his burgeoning empire. Owen and J.R. agreed that power did not fit his motivation profile.

The last option, revenge, made the least sense of all.

Certainly, Kemp could not have held grudges against each murdered retiree. The methodical order of deaths by age indicated an impersonal death sentence. Revenge killings would not have been age-specific. Besides, at the peak of the county's leadership ladder, Kemp would have had limited interaction with so many county employees. Owen struck "revenge" from his notepad and tapped his pencil in frustration.

"What you are feeling right now, like you just hit a brick wall, is what I've been dealing with for the last two months," J.R. said. "The only mark I found on Kemp was a blackmail conviction many years ago, but the court sealed those records. We need another lead."

As they ended their call, Owen felt good about reconnecting with a lost friend but disappointed with the results of their analysis. All the puzzle pieces were still not on the table, which made the construction of a crime narrative next to impossible. Between missing facts and motivations, and the mere suspicion that Kemp was somehow involved, the reporter had little to work with. Worse, time refused to slow its relenting assault on his nerves.

The next week, however, brought with it some useful information. Owen's phone rang one evening as he pulled into his apartment complex. He recognized the number on his caller ID and grabbed his notepad, which, when not hiding in his office drawer, was on his person. It contained many secrets that he could not risk misplacing or having stolen. He answered the call.

"Hi, this is Peter. Is it too late to talk?"

"You forget my line of work. There is always time for news, particularly if it's good. What did you learn about Hemlock's IPO?"

"As with most public offerings, a lot of investors jumped

in early, which promptly doubled the stock's share price. Much of the money came through brokerages that serve retail investors. That's common. But a sizable portion came from institutional investors, notably the nation's largest pension plan: the $350 billion California Public Employees Retirement System.

"Why is that notable?"

"A better word would be *unusual*. For an agency that guarantees retirement benefits to two million public workers, CalPERS must invest prudently. Like the Sunset Hills fund, CalPERS had a strict policy prohibiting investment in IPOs because they can be so risky."

"How so?"

"Well, Hemlock had no track record, so the stock could have been a big winner or a big loser—it was a risky buy to say the least. Losing one percent on my investments is not much money, but for an agency that invests $500 million at a time, even small losses are huge numbers. That's why CalPERS does not invest in IPOs. Well, until recently."

"I assume somebody was in charge of checking the policy, right?"

"Most pension plans—like ours, for example—hire outside managers to pick stocks for us. The managers have to invest according to the guidelines we approve, but generally, they have wide latitude in their choices. CalPERS is different. It hires dozens of highly paid, intelligent people to pick stocks for them in-house. Those selections are vetted by individuals and committees higher up the food chain before investments are made. My best guess is that the head of the U.S. equities division made the decision."

As Owen listened, a swell of excitement mixed with worry swept through him. He relished having a new angle to follow, but the prospect of calling CalPERS with pointed questions about Hemlock gave him pause. While Owen considered how to make contact without raising red flags, something the investment officer said caught his attention.

"I'm sorry, Peter. Would you repeat that last part?"

"I was saying that I don't know who at CalPERS decided to invest in the IPO, but I read in a trade publication that the California Senate applied pressure."

"Why would state senators get involved in such minutia?"

"The same reason they stick their fingers in everything else," Peter replied. "Because they can."

"You've been incredibly helpful, sir. I really appreciate your research. Uh, if it's not too much to ask, would you mind not telling Alexis we spoke? I'd hate for her to put the kibosh on future interviews with you if she learned of our unsanctioned phone call."

Peter laughed at the thought of his boss throwing a fit. "If she gets wadded up over something so harmless, she is more insecure than I thought. Don't worry, I won't say a word."

At home, as a packet of frozen dinner rotated in his microwave, Owen searched the California Senate's website for a list of its committees. Before the timer sounded, he had found the Senate Public Employment and Retirement Committee, whose jurisdiction included matters related to CalPERS. If the investment officer had quoted his source accurately, this five-member group influenced the nation's largest pension plan to break its policy and send millions to Kemp's coffers in the form of an IPO investment. It was not a smoking gun, but it further confirmed the unholy alliance between the state capitol and Hemlock. For the first time in his investigation, Owen smelled blood in the water.

« 16 »

Each morning when Owen awoke, he opened his eyes and stared at a little framed photo of Ruthie, which he had moved from the living room to the end table by his bed. She was his first thought in the morning and his last thought at night. Every day that passed brought her closer to a certain yet unexpected death, for although he knew the outcome, her murder could happen at any time. This element of uncertainty motivated him to devote every spare moment to piecing together the fragments of evidence he had compiled over the preceding months. He believed he was approaching a point on the periphery of the mystery that, if he truly sought to unravel it, would require him to step into the lion's den. He hoped that when the time came to take that step, he would be selfless. Until then, Owen faithfully showed up at work and wrote articles for the paper. He spent his breaks and lunches thinking through one possible scenario after another in an effort to construct a narrative that made sense of the facts. In spite of Owen's creative mind and J.R.'s rich experience, the pieces refused to fit cohesively. The missing information they needed remained intentionally hidden and would not be discovered easily or safely. Intuitively, he knew this to be true.

One mild spring afternoon, just after Owen had completed his articles for the day and began tidying his desk, his work phone rang.

"Hi, Owen, it's Lily from the pension plan."

"You are the only Lily I know, so you don't have to say, 'from the pension plan,' unless you want to be wordy," he teased.

"It's good to know you haven't forgotten me entirely. I, um, wanted to discuss your PRA. It …" Lily stopped short. "The request you submitted …"

She paused again, fumbled with her words and finally blurted, "You know, I haven't heard from you in a few months. That's a long time for a reporter, don't you think?"

She clenched her teeth as silent seconds ticked between them.

"Yeah, that would be my fault," he replied uncomfortably. "A friend died, and I kinda dropped out of life for a while. I thought about telling you, but to be perfectly honest, I wasn't ready to talk about it."

"Oh, dear. I had no idea. How selfish of me for thinking … I didn't mean to sound ... How are you holding up?"

Owen sniffed on the other end of the line, mumbling something inaudible. The painful memory of Darcie was still too tender to touch. He could not bring himself to reply honestly. What would he even say?

Lily's voice softened. "I'm so sorry, Owen. Were you two close?"

"In a way," he answered, as if standing on weak legs for the first time since an injury. "It's hard to ... I'm not sure how to ... The thing is, I feel respons—."

He stopped himself, stunned by his near admission. His hand holding the phone quivered, and his heart both raced and wept simultaneously. This was not a conversation he cared to have now—not with Lily, not with anyone, ever.

"Uh, sorry about that tangent. What did you call about?"

He heard her quiet breathing and wondered what she thought of him now. He felt like a stuttering fool who could hardly keep his head at the slightest mention of Darcie. He needed to move beyond this episode and stick to business. Lily seemed to take the hint; her voice resumed its normal professionalism.

"I asked to be the one to tell you that your public records request was granted—in part. You see, legal counsel determined that only *some* of the information you sought was public record. Most of it was not."

"What's public and what's not?" Owen could not hide the frustration in his voice.

"Well, you can have the retiree names but, uh—and please understand, the answer would be same regardless of who asked—not their dates of birth or death."

"That's what I need most! You don't understand how important this is, Lily. I *need* that information. People's lives depend on it. People *I* know."

Lily hesitated, her voice revealing something tearing inside her. "I'm—I'm really sorry, Owen. We can't release that information to you."

He worked valiantly to maintain his composure for the remainder of the call, but in truth, he was an unsettled mess of emotion. He now had no hope of knowing where Ruthie's

219

name fell on the kill list. She could be ten people away from death's doorstep or just one. He hung up with Lily and dialed Ruthie's number to make sure she was alright. They made plans for dinner and closed with their customary salutations.

"Love you, dearie."

"Love you, Gram."

Owen had to clear his head. He went to the office break room and made a pot of coffee. As it brewed, he opened several cabinets to see what calorie-laden junk they held. From the layers of dust, he estimated the packaged foods had been there for months, maybe years. He pulled out an old box of fruit snacks, opened a packet and popped a few in his mouth. Surprisingly, they were still delicious. He turned the carton over and saw a two-year-old expiration date, which prompted a gag reflex that left a nearby trashcan stained by partially chewed gummy bears. Before tossing the box, he again looked at the expiration date. Then a thought arose. He slid the dusty box back in the cabinet and hurried to his desk. He searched the California Senate's website again—this time for a list of legislators on the Public Employment and Retirement Committee from prior terms. His earlier research had only identified current-term members, but CalPERS' investment in the Hemlock IPO occurred in a previous legislative session. A few clicks later, he stared curiously at his computer screen. On it were the names of five elected representatives, one being his hometown political hero, former State Senator Mike Lancaster.

His membership on the committee made perfect sense. Party leaders regularly assign good politicians to key committees, and Lancaster obviously had proven himself to be a promising legislator. Besides, his past Board of Retirement service would have made him an ideal addition to the group.

Even so, Owen called J.R. to get a second opinion, not that he needed one in this particular instance.

"Lancaster's role was probably benign," the officer agreed, "but keep an open mind about the possibility that your guy might have participated in the committee's pressure on CalPERS to support Hemlock. There were only a few people on the committee, so he at least knew about it."

"Fine," Owen consented, "but just for the sake of argument."

"Now that we have reasonable suspicion about Kemp's inappropriate relationship with the state capitol, I think it is time we made direct contact. Secrets don't tell themselves; they usually need a little push to come out and play. Somehow, we are going to provide that nudge."

Owen listened quietly, tightness forming in his gut.

The officer continued. "Obviously, this could be dangerous, especially for you. Assuming you are up for it."

"Of course I'm in," the reporter said quickly—too quickly to fully consider what specific action he had committed himself to. It did not matter. He had already counted the cost of this path and accepted it.

"Good. This means all your future contacts with state politicians, Hemlock employees, CalPERS and anyone beyond our city limits needs to be under a pseudonym. You need a fake ID and employer."

"That's cool. I've always wanted to go by the name Danger."

"Uh, that's not a good idea. Too obvious, don't you think?"

"Well, Danger could be my *middle* name."

He waited patiently for J.R. to laugh, but all he heard was awkward silence.

"Sorry, man, I have no idea what you're talking about. You should stick to traditional, easily forgettable names."

"Okay," Owen said in embarrassment. "I'll just think up a better pseudonym with no middle name."

"Yeah, good idea."

"I could also say I work for the *L.A. Times* because I once interned in its newsroom. That has served me well in the past."

"Now you're on the right track, Mr. Danger," J.R. snickered.

◊ ◊ ◊

The next day, Owen received a call from the paper's receptionist. "I've got a gentleman here for his interview."

"Really? I didn't schedule any interviews today."

Owen grabbed his notepad and headed to the lobby, where Jim Jensen stood chatting up a security guard who, by the desperate look on his face, was thankful someone else's ears had come to relieve his own.

"Mr. Jensen, what you are doing here?" Owen inquired.

"Well, I got to thinking," he said, inhaling deeply to ensure a long-winded answer. "Our last interview didn't include all the details I wanted, so I hoped to have a follow-up with you. We didn't cover my ..."

Owen interrupted Mr. Jensen before his monologue picked up steam. "I'm sorry, sir, the article has already been approved and is queued to be published. We can't retract it now."

"Oh, that's a shame. You see, in retrospect, I should have said that I regretted voting for those two benefit increases. Or, better yet, to cut that part altogether. It really was a difficult time period for all of us on the board."

The old man's reference to the Board of Supervisors reminded Owen of the questions he had wanted to ask earlier but decided against. Now he could scratch that itch.

"Mr. Jensen, in the interest of privacy, let's go somewhere you can speak freely."

Owen escorted his guest to an empty conference room and took a seat. "Just to be clear," he reminded, "the article I wrote will be published, but you are welcome to provide additional filler that I can keep on file in case we decide to do another profile one day. How does that sound?"

"That's good enough for me!"

"Okay, to keep us on track, I'm going to limit the conversation to just a few questions. Feel free to elaborate on those as much as you like."

The retiree inhaled deeply. Thirty minutes later, Owen left the room with pages of notes and a fire in his belly. Normally, so many words would have irritated the reporter's impatient ears, but he overlooked the verbosity because of the fascinating details that poured out of Mr. Jensen's relentless mouth. Owen returned to the newsroom and immediately called J.R. to share the highlights of his illuminating conversation.

"I don't know how this guy got elected," he began. "He has no filter! It's just nonstop verbal diarrhea. Get this: Jensen claimed he no more regretted approving the benefit enhancements than eating a cheesecake. 'Totally worth it, despite the heartburn that follows' were his exact words. Then he described the political backlash from taxpayers as swift and severe. That forced him and the three other politicians who voted 'yes' to publicly justify their decision."

"Did you ask him why Lancaster abstained from the vote in 2000?"

"I did, and his answer intrigued me: 'Not only did Mike support the first benefit enhancement up to the day we voted, he was its biggest cheerleader.' If that is true, I am totally confused! Jensen said that county employees and unions loved Lancaster for his big talk, and the Board of Supervisors let him lead the way. But when it came time to cast a vote, according to Jensen, 'The men stood up and Mike sat down.'"

"How did he talk about Lancaster? Was he angry at him for saying one thing and doing another?"

"No, Jensen seemed more disappointed than upset. He talked about his colleague nicely one moment and negatively the next. I asked him about that ambivalence. Jensen closed his eyes, as if gathering memories. Then he said: 'Mike was a good politician. I'll give him that. And he was a people-pleaser. But that guy was as thin-skinned as a jellyfish when it came to the media. He hated bad publicity. I think that's why he abstained the first time.'"

"What about the second vote in 2005?"

"Jensen said that was purely political. The rest of us Supervisors expected his neutral vote again because his eye was on state office, and he wanted to curry favor with the public. 'Remember,' he told me, 'there are a lot more county tax-payers than county employees. Mike played the numbers game and made the best choice for his career. I can't hold that against him.'"

"Did he say anything about Dorian Kemp and his time on the board?"

"Apparently, Kemp and Lancaster were both ambitious, both shrewd, both sharp as tacks. But Kemp was greedy. That was his default."

Owen perused his notes for any other valuable tidbits to

share.

"Oh, one more interesting thing he said. I asked Jensen if they liked *him* back then. You know what he told me? 'Of course! What's not to like?' He, Kemp and Lancaster stayed in touch for a few years, but eventually they got too busy for him and moved on."

J.R. listened carefully to Owen's recounting of the conversation, jotting a few of his own notes along the way. Finally, he spoke.

"Before I tip my hand on all this new material, what's your take?"

"Well, first off, I don't trust everything Jensen said. A man that talks that much is bound to squeeze in an exaggeration or incomplete memory. That's not to say his story doesn't have merit. I agree that Kemp and Lancaster both seemed ambitious. It's hard to get where they are in life without a willingness to step on a few people. But even if Kemp is a greedy executive and Lancaster is a savvy politician, that doesn't make either man a murderer. After all, they already got what they wanted: money and power. Why bother with retirees in Sunset Hills?"

"Your last point is spot on," J.R. agreed, "but don't let anybody off too quickly. Just because you don't see a motive right away doesn't mean it is not there. Now that we have some color on Kemp and Lancaster, we need to think about how to exploit it. Let's discuss over lunch tomorrow."

At last, Owen had caught a break. As challenging as Mr. Jensen had been to interview, J.R. was right about him providing useful information that would never have otherwise been known. Owen resisted the urge to burst into Al's office to brag about his new lead. He would not have even cared if the surly editor cursed him back to his cubicle. Owen felt exuberant. How he wished his parents could see him today—or any day for that matter. One thing theists had going for them, he admitted, was belief in the afterlife—the hope of seeing a loved one again in a better place. Pure rationalism underpinned by a materialistic worldview afforded no such comfort, no real hope. Yet, at times, Owen craved the benefits of faith while rejecting faith itself. Ironically, it was in these moments that his heart ached for something otherworldly to fill a hole that he did not even believe he had. When thoughts like these troubled him, he distracted himself with music or an audio book. Silence, with the emptiness it exposed, was always an enemy to be avoided.

Owen popped in ear buds and started researching a business story. Attending to this task kept his mind from speculating about tomorrow's planning session with J.R. It also made the day speed by. The next time he looked at his watch, it was past five o'clock. He grabbed his notepad, tucked it safely under his arm and headed out of the building. As he exited the lobby, a familiar voice called his name from behind. He turned to see Lily standing by the wall in a spring dress with a bouquet in her hand. For the first time since they had met, Lily wore her dirty-blonde hair past her shoulders. But it was her pleasant smile and solitary dimple he noticed first.

"If you came to thank me for sending you flowers, sorry, it wasn't me," he said wryly. He stepped toward her and admired the beautiful lilies. "What are these for?"

"You said you lost a friend recently, and I thought you could use something to cheer you up."

He squinted skeptically. "The flowers make sense, but the personal delivery service?"

Lily looked away and blushed, as if caught in a poorly

conceived scheme. Seeing her embarrassment, Owen reached for the stems and gently took them from her hand.

"Thank you ... very much. Nobody ever gave me flowers before."

He brought them closer to his face to smell. Unaccustomed to this activity, he sniffed too hard and inhaled a cloud of pollen, causing him to cough uncontrollably.

Horrified, Lily scoured her purse for a tissue to wipe off the yellow blanketing his nose. Not finding anything useful, she stood helpless until Owen's rancorous coughing fit had ended.

"I didn't realize smelling these things could be so hazardous," he joked.

"I should have bought the ones with red pollen. Then you could have joined the circus."

"You know, some days, being a carnie actually sounds like a good profession. Lately, this job has been—well, let's just say it can be stressful."

"You are always on deadline, right?"

"Deadlines I can handle," he said, again wiping his nose. "It's the other stuff—the things I discover—that make me feel like I'm carrying the weight of the world."

His attention wandered to the brick building, concern shadowing his expression. Lily observed the change.

"You know what you need, Owen? A walk to clear your mind. Are you game?"

"Uh, sure. You look awfully nice, though. Are you sure you're up for it?"

"Absolutely. I wore my walking shoes for just such an occasion."

Her inviting gaze and irresistible dimple left Owen with no excuse. After depositing the bouquet in his car, they began walking the long sidewalks lining the quaint downtown streets. They spoke of co-workers and old friends, of favorite wines and good books, of close family and distant memories. For the first time in years, Owen opened his life to someone besides Ruthie.

"You should know," he told her, "I don't really, you know, talk to other people. I mean, I do for work. But not personal stuff. You know what I mean—personal stuff?"

She nodded.

"So, if I'm not being clear or not making sense, it's probably because I don't practice enough. I haven't maintained many friendships since college."

This was an embarrassing statement to make, but oddly, he did not feel like a failure when talking to her. Her sweet manner put him at ease. Lily likewise spoke of her own experiences, thoughts and goals, but these subjects flowed from her with ease. Her words dripped with honesty and grace, not the business-like brevity Owen had grown accustomed to at work. He was not certain, owing to his long absence from peer relationships, but the hour he and Lily spent sharing their stories felt remarkably like friendship. And maybe something else. Their conversation carried on gently, beautifully, like the soft breeze rolling down the lush western hills. As sunset approached, the street lanterns and overhead alley lights flickered alive for their nightly service.

The happy pair walked slowly by downtown shops. As they strolled from one to another, they joked about the terribly worded business names and slogans posted on storefronts. Lily pointed at a store window and cringed.

"Look at that bad grammar! It's burning my eyes!"

"Its all gotta go … Rite Now!" Owen read. "Agreed, it's painful to even look at. You'd think a fifth-grader wrote it."

Lily opened her purse and pulled out a sticky pad and pen. She jotted something on a note and stuck it on the glass. Owen read it aloud: "Proofing advice: 'It all has to go … right now!'"

"That's better," she said proudly. "Now English majors might consider buying something in there. I hear some of them can be snobby."

She moved to the next window while Owen stood examining her note. He looked at her oddly and then reread her words, this time with a rising admiration. He knew that he enjoyed judging others' mistakes and leaving them to their folly, but she cared enough to help the person in error. She cared. Both professional communicators valued their syntax and grammar, but she used her knowledge for the good of a complete stranger. Owen never knew until that moment how incredibly attractive that quality was in a woman.

The two walked on into the soft night and found themselves facing a large, dark window in which they could faintly see their reflections. This was the first time they had seen themselves together, standing side by side. They stopped to look at the image, considering it in silence. Lily stared at the reflection—not at herself or even at Owen, but at *them*. The corners of her lips inclined ever so subtly. She watched as Owen's reflection slowly reached from his side and touched her hand. She moved her fingers to touch his. In a moment, they were holding hands and breaths.

Some time passed before either spoke, not wanting to ruin the moment. Finally, he turned to her.

"I have something important to tell you."

Hand in hand, they stepped to a nearby bench and sat under a string of bulbs strung across the empty portico. He set her hand down and faced her nervously.

"Lily, you need to know that I am in danger ... constantly. I am working on a story—actually, it's more like an investigation—that has upset some powerful people. We don't exactly know who they are, but we do know they have murdered dozens of your retirees using the same weapon: an assisted-suicide drug that somehow got into their bodies and killed them very quickly. I've been tracking the murders for months."

Lily's expression fell, her delicate eyes filling with moisture. Owen felt for her fingers and held them.

"The friend that died a few months ago was my co-worker, a girl named ..."

He paused for a breath and cleared this throat.

"A girl name Darcie. She contacted the politicians who voted for the pension increases in 2000 and 2005. Two days later, we found her body. Nobody knows how the drug got in her—or in anyone else. But they keep dying, one after another after another, when they turn eighty."

Owen's breathing became stuttered. He had not opened up about Darcie since her death, due in part to facing his guilt and in part to feeling the wrenching hurt that would follow—the kind of hurt he now felt so fresh, so potent, so unrelenting. Lily placed her other hand over his.

"You don't have to go on if it's too difficult."

"No, I need to say it. Keeping it inside is torture." He lowered his gaze and said ruefully, "*I* am responsible for Darcie's murder because *I* gave her the task of researching those men. She'd be alive today if it weren't for *me*."

He felt the urge to cry assaulting his chest and then his head. He fought it back but lost. His shoulders shook as tears of shame, regret and self-hate fell on the soft arms that moved to comfort him. Lily held him close while he wept quietly. Time passed slowly as the soul that Owen did not possess broke to pieces. Between sobs, he heard her whisper a prayer for his comfort.

When Owen's mourning faded, Lily placed her hand gently against his face. "You are not responsible. You didn't do it."

He took her hands into his own and, his head still turned downward, shook it side to side.

"Owen, please look at me."

He struggled to raise his shamed, tear-stained eyes to meet hers.

"You didn't do it," she repeated.

This time he nodded, not because he believed it himself but because she believed it for him, and he trusted her. A few minutes passed with little else to say. Owen took a deep breath and rose to his feet with her hand in his. As they navigated through the night back to their cars, they discussed the investigation and his urgency to solve it because of Ruthie.

"I will help in whatever way I can without breaking the law," she promised.

"Thanks, but there is nothing I need from the retirement agency at this point. Our next step is to make contact with the man responsible for the drug."

"No, you can't do that. It's not safe!"

"I know it seems risky, but J.R. has a plan to hide my identity. And besides that, we are short on other options. It is probably a lot to ask at this point, but please trust us."

In the newspaper parking lot, Owen walked Lily to her car and thanked her for her kindness. She looked up at him and smiled affectionately.

"I think I like you."

"I like you, too. It's nice not feeling alone in all this."

The corners of her lips curved again, exposing the dimple that Owen had very recently come to adore. She took another sticky note from her purse and wrote something on it.

"You know what *alone* is backward, right?"

She handed him the paper, containing a single word:

E.Nola

As recognition of his informant's identity dawned on him, Lily leaned in and kissed his cheek.

"You're not alone anymore. Good night."

« 17 »

D o you want the good news or the bad news first?" J.R. asked as he and Owen sat down for lunch in the corner of a little restaurant.

"Hmm, dessert or veggies?" Owen considered. "Let's start with the veggies."

"I spent last night thinking about what we know and what we don't. As someone who investigates bad guys for a living, I believe our evidence against Kemp is circumstantial. He is only tied to these murders by a drug that his company sells—and even then, it's not *really* his drug because it was doctored somehow. Besides that, he has never appeared at a crime scene, nor do we have a single witness claiming he was involved. All that to say, there's not enough evidence to show up and arrest him."

Owen could not hide his disappointment. He clearly did not expect to hear such an unsatisfying answer, particularly when he felt closer than ever to a breakthrough in the case.

But he accepted J.R.'s objective assessment without debate.

"Okay, then, what's the good news?"

"I think we can force his hand by exploiting what he cherishes most: money and prestige. Someone who has reached his level of success—someone with riches and fame and a secure future—is willing to defend what he has earned from any threat and at any cost."

"How are we supposed to do that?"

"By bringing the threat to his doorstep and hoping he makes a mistake."

J.R. spent the next ten minutes detailing his plan. As he spoke, the color in Owen's face grew paler and paler. His palms began to sweat, and on multiple occasions he forgot to breathe. J.R. pressed on, describing what would happen, who would say what, and where he hoped Kemp would slip up. When the officer had finished, Owen sat back in his chair and drained a glass of water like a marathoner. He looked his friend in the eyes for a long moment before speaking.

"You know, this plan of yours does nothing good for my blood pressure. And I can't say I relish meeting the man I believe is responsible for murdering dozens of people. But if you think it's our best shot at flushing him out, I'm all in. For Gram's sake."

"I think we stand a good chance of achieving that objective. There's just one thing you're lacking."

"What's that?"

"You need to buy a suit."

The plan required Dorian Kemp to be in his office the following day. Owen called his secretary at Hemlock pretending to be a postal agent who needed him to personally sign for an important delivery from the state capitol.

"What is in the package?" she asked. "Who sent it?"

"I have no idea what's inside, ma'am. I just schedule the drops. It says here it's from the State Assembly."

"I see. Mr. Kemp will be available most of tomorrow morning, but if he's out for some reason, may I sign for him?"

"Sure thing. The package will arrive by noon."

"And what delivery service are you with? Hello? Sir, are you there?"

Owen hung up and immediately called J.R. "Tomorrow is a go. He will be there all morning."

The next day, Owen called into work sick. J.R. picked him up in his patrol car, and the pair headed to San Francisco. En route, they reviewed the plan, practicing their roles until Owen felt comfortable playing the part of a detective's assistant. He even looked the part with his mall-bought suit, clean-shaven face and decommissioned ID badge that J.R. had borrowed from the station.

"You certainly seem quite taken by your new look," the officer observed when Owen stared at his reflection in the mirror for the third time.

"It's amazing how certain clothes can make you feel like a completely different person. I might be a six-foot white guy on the outside, but on the inside, I feel like a six-foot-six black man."

He glanced over at his companion, who laughed at the ridiculous comparison.

"Funny, that's how I feel every day."

The humor provided a short reprieve from the growing tension they both felt on the long drive north. As Hemlock's sprawling buildings and glass-encased lobby came into sight, a wave of fear rolled down Owen's back and into his toes, causing him to perspire. J.R. saw Owen wipe his clammy hands along his slacks.

"You got to remember that *they* are the ones under the spotlight, not you. We need to walk in like we own the place. This is *our* investigation, and they are going to do what *we* say."

Owen nodded and repeated the words in his mind.

J.R. parked as close to the lobby as possible. Although his pep talk had calmed Owen somewhat, the apprentice carried a ball of stress in the pit of his stomach that would not go away. They exited the car, straightened their ties and began walking toward the building. Before the automatic door slid open, J.R. leaned toward his partner and said in a low voice, "Don't forget, *we* are in charge here."

The two suits strolled into the lobby with an air of authority. They walked directly to the security desk and, reaching into their jacket pockets, flashed Sunset Hills police badges to the guards on duty.

"I'm Officer Little and this is Officer Mitchell," J.R. began. "We are here to ask Mr. Kemp a few questions about a crime committed in our jurisdiction that might involve him."

The guards, unfamiliar with this type of inquiry, excused themselves to discuss the matter privately. One turned toward a distant camera facing them and motioned for assistance. A supervising guard appeared through a side door and headed in their direction.

"Hello, gentlemen. What's your business here?"

J.R. repeated his statement, this time with a hint of annoyance. "Time is not on our side. Make this happen *now*."

The man stepped away to make a phone call that lasted just seconds. He hung up and returned to the assembly,

236

shaking his head. "I just spoke to his secretary. Apparently, Mr. Kemp is not in the office."

That was Owen's cue. He faced the senior guard and said sharply, "With all due respect, sir, you're lying. Our source confirmed that Kemp is here right now. So, how about you make another call?" Owen feigned annoyance and motioned away with his fingers. "Go ahead. We'll wait here."

The guard, hesitating, stepped away and made another call that lasted longer than the first. This time, he returned a changed man. "I'm sorry for our earlier mistake. Mr. Kemp's schedule is so unpredictable. Right this way, officers."

J.R. and Owen nodded respectively to the other guards and followed the supervisor through a hallway at the end of which stood a private elevator. He inserted a belted key into a security pad next to the lift and then typed an access code. The door opened, and the three men entered. The detectives scanned the compartment's interior, noting two small cameras in opposite corners of the ceiling and another security pad by the door.

Owen's curiosity got the best of him. "This is quite an elevator for one man. Doesn't Mr. Kemp's office have another access point?"

"Yes," was the unelaborated reply.

A bell chimed, and the door opened to the fourth floor, revealing a glass-covered hallway overlooking an indoor atrium below and a reflective sun shaft above. The transparent walkway was an impressive sight indeed, one that robbed the officers of their focus as they approached a pair of tall glass doors. The guard typed an access code and slid his badge. After depositing his guests in the executive lobby, he told them to press a button on a nearby wall when they were ready to leave.

"Nobody wanders around unaccompanied," he warned.

With that simple instruction, he turned and left. Owen and J.R. shared a sense of amazement at the incredible security precautions taken to protect Hemlock's chief executive. Here worked a man, Owen reasoned, who did not want to be touched, accessed or bothered. In this well-protected perch, Kemp could keep the ugly world of pathetic little people out of sight while he amassed for himself fame and fortune at the expense of others. Owen felt a loathing for Kemp creep into his heart, a brooding of hate that would have deepened had J.R. not nudged his shoulder.

"This is it," he whispered. "We're up."

Kemp opened a door and stood before the officers like a prince regaled in the splendor his own glory. He wore a custom-designed Italian suit; his midnight hair was slicked perfectly; gold rings glittered on each hand; he stood bold and unapologetically proud. Yet, his first words did not match his appearance.

"Greetings. You must be Officer Little and Officer Mitchell. How can I help you gentlemen today?"

J.R. stepped forward. "This is a delicate matter, sir. Can we speak in private?"

"Of course. Please follow me."

Kemp led the duo to his lavish office. Beyond the large windows lay the back side of the Hemlock campus, a picturesque hillside to the west and a flowing brook called Styx to the east. Owen and J.R. could not help but bask at the beautiful sights. As if reading their thoughts, Kemp described the surrounding landscape and ecology in impressive detail. While he spoke, he poured a glass of sherry from a crystal container.

"Care for one? It's the best money can buy. No? Over

here I have an assortment of Belgian chocolates and organic nuts grown in the neighboring county. They, too, are quite delicious."

Owen's mouth began to salivate.

"Ever had one of these?" Kemp continued, opening a temperature-controlled case of cigars. "Don't tell anyone ... they are Cubans. The best you'll ever smoke, guaranteed."

"No, thank you," J.R. replied. "I don't smoke."

Owen forced the same answer, even though the thick Cuban tempted his will.

"Well, if you think of anything you'd like, just let me know. I like to be of service."

The mood in the office had unexpectedly changed. Kemp's distractions and friendly discourse softened the determination with which the partners had entered the room. Launching into threats now seemed almost inappropriate. J.R. attempted his first rehearsed line, but the words fell flat. He stammered, looked at the floor and tried again.

"What I mean is, people have died in our town, and, um, we discovered something that, uh, ..."

The normally well-spoken detective reached into his pocket and withdrew a few folded sheets of paper, which he stared at unsteadily. Kemp smirked. Owen watched as their finely tuned plan was unraveling before his eyes. It was not his scheduled turn to speak, but J.R.'s fumbling left him no better option.

"Sit down, Mr. Kemp," Owen ordered. "We have an autopsy here that ties a death in Sunset Hills to your drug, Hemlox. Not just one death, mind you. Dozens."

He took the papers from J.R. and slid them across the table. "The identifying information of the victim is blacked out, but you'll see on page two that the cause of death is most certainly a substance made by your firm."

Kemp's eyes fixed on Owen, who had broken the charm offensive and placed the executive on defense. Coldly, he pinched the tips of the pages between his fingers and pulled them into his line of vision. His review of the report took just moments. He smiled benignly at his accuser.

"This report claims nothing about any drug manufactured at this facility. I see similarities with one of our products, but it is definitely *not* the same thing. If you like, I can confirm that with our lead scientist."

"You mean your wife, Michele?" Owen said, using J.R.'s scheduled line. "Given that she is on your payroll, she is hardly an objective source."

The fog in J.R.'s mind had cleared, and he resumed the interrogation where Owen left off.

"Do you really think you can scientifically exonerate your drug before the press gets wind of this story? Just the accusation of foul play would ruin your company. Investors would flee like rats from a sinking ship."

That last statement halted the rejoinder waiting on Kemp's lips. He looked out his broad window for a short time before turning toward his guests with concern blanketing his countenance. He spoke in slow, measured words.

"What you've brought to my attention is news to me. I was unaware that Hemlox was used illegally until this moment. As soon as you leave, I give you my word that I will conduct an investigation into …"

"Not good enough," J.R. interrupted. "You've got to explain how the drugs went missing from your company. *You* know they did. *We* know they did. So let's skip the dog-and-pony show, shall we?"

The feigned concern on Kemp's face faded to a mixture

240

of derision and worry. Owen, as a newspaperman, knew that Kemp risked his empire if news of the deaths hit the papers before he could prove they were not caused by his drug. J.R. was exactly right about investors pulling funds from the company, followed by a media firestorm that would surely threaten Kemp's job and reputation. On the other hand, he would be a fool to confirm the present accusations and risk strengthening the case against him. Owen wondered how Kemp would avoid the dangers of either path. Was there a safe middle ground to be found?

"About a year ago," Kemp said, "one of our shipping employees stole a case of five hundred pills of Hemlox. He was caught and immediately terminated. We recovered the pills, performed an audit of our process from factory to pharmacy, and tightened our internal controls. I'm sure you could tell as you walked here from the lobby that we take security very seriously."

Owen squinted skeptically and leaned in. "What was the name of the employee?"

The executive stared at him long and hard. "I don't have his name on me, but if you give me your business card, I'd be happy to email it to you."

Kemp watched his opponent and waited. Owen had no business card for his Officer Mitchell character. He glanced at J.R., whose dilated eyes communicated his unwillingness to hand his own card to the enemy. Recognizing their plight, Owen looked across the table defiantly.

"No. You can give us the employee's name right now."

He watched the executive's mind turning, analyzing.

"Let me see your badges," Kemp replied. "I have a right to know who is questioning me."

The officers looked at each other and then at him.

"Put them on the table!" Kemp demanded.

J.R. rose to his full height, his face flush with anger and his eyes aflame.

"I don't take orders from you," he thundered. "Owen, let's go."

The young man looked up wide-eyed at the detective, who, in his emotion, had mistakenly uttered his friend's real name. J.R. realized his error and glanced downward apologetically. The sudden discord between the pair was obvious.

"Yes, Owen," Kemp said with amusement. "It's time for you to go."

They hastily showed themselves out of the office, pressed the call button by the elevator and headed to their vehicle without signing out at the security desk in the lobby. Kemp watched the patrol car leave the premises from a fourth-floor window. Closing his office door, he pulled a cigar from its box, smelled its rich aroma and tapped a few numbers on his cell phone. A voice answered on the other line.

"We have a problem," Kemp said.

Adrenaline surged through J.R. and Owen until Hemlock passed out of view behind them. The meeting had not gone as planned, their sequence of interrogative statements got jumbled, and they left without any hard evidence. However, they had succeeded in irritating Kemp. More importantly, they had threatened his idols. If their opinion of the executive was correct, his serpentine reaction would be swift. Owen took little comfort in knowing his identity was partially masked. If Kemp was motivated, it would not take him long to root out the reporter and make a mess of his investigation, job and life.

J.R. broke the anxious air in the car.

"Well, it wasn't pretty, but I think we did what we came to do. Kemp knows he's under the spotlight now. And he doesn't seem like the type of person to enjoy that kind of attention. I'm sorry about botching my lines back there. I don't know what came over me. One minute I'm ready to squish his pompous little head in my hand, and the next I can't put a sentence together. How embarrassing. But you! Man, did you hit a homerun! Seriously, you ripped the cover off the ball. I was fumbling with my words and papers when you stepped in and laid the hammer down. Bam! I was like, *Who is this guy?*"

"Really?" Owen replied, regaining some self-confidence.

"Yeah. It reminded me of what your dad used to do during contract negotiations. The other side would feel like they were winning, and then your old man would flip their argument upside down and spank 'em hard."

Hearing someone speak well of his father brought a broad smile to Owen's flushed face. He began to relax, allowing himself to admire the passing scenery and to think about seeing Lily again. If he arrived home before dinnertime, he determined to ask her on a date that evening. They could go to his favorite Chinese food restaurant, take a walk along the riverfront and then drop by Ruthie's favorite ice cream shop for dessert. Owen was lost in thought when J.R. interrupted his daydream.

"The driver behind me is in a hurry to get to the freeway."

He rolled down his window and motioned to the vehicle.

"Just pass me, buddy ... get it over with," he said impatiently. "I don't like being pressured to speed, especially on winding roads like this."

He again motioned out the window. Owen turned his head

to see a black SUV with tinted windows accelerate until the vehicles were side by side. Without warning, the SUV rammed the driver's side of the patrol car—and then again, forcing it off the road and down a steep embankment, where the vehicle flipped over. Upside down and in shock, J.R. and Owen put their hands on the ceiling to regain a sense of position. A few of the windows had shattered in the crash. Glass lay all around them.

"You okay?" J.R. asked.

"I think so. My head hurts."

J.R. looked over and saw blood trickling down his friend's face.

"I think you hit your head against the window. Don't move. I'll come get you out."

He unbuckled himself and fell a few inches onto the impacted ceiling. His size made it difficult to maneuver in the vehicle. Worse, his door refused to open.

"Well, I'm not getting out this way. Stay where you are. I'm going to crawl to your side and check the door."

As he struggled to turn around and move his large frame through the small space, he heard a door close in the distance followed by heavy footsteps down the embankment that faced Owen.

"Good. Someone's coming to help us. Just hang on."

Their hopes for assistance from a Good Samaritan quickly turned to terror with the sound of a gun being cocked. J.R. peered out the window to see two sets of feet approaching. He looked at Owen hanging indefensibly between floor and ceiling. A second gun cocked. J.R.'s hand felt for Owen's seat belt and followed it up to the buckle. Disengaging it, Owen's body fell like a rock on broken glass, and he cried out in pain. J.R. threw himself over his friend and listened as twelve bullets sped through the surrounding metal, several hitting him in the back and one in the leg. The reverberating air echoed with the shots and smelled of gun powder. Silence pervaded the car, except for a low groan from Owen.

"Are you okay?" he asked weakly. "J.R., are you okay?"

No reply came. Owen could not see the men, but he heard their steps growing nearer.

"Do you see anybody moving inside?" one asked.

"No," said the other man. "Let's check the bodies."

Owen knew if he were discovered, they would promptly kill him. With J.R.'s body pinning his own to the ceiling, he had no way to escape. He heard the sound of guns being reloaded outside. For the first time in his life, the atheist breathed a prayer—"God, help"—before closing his eyes a final time. He squeezed them tightly and waited to die. He did not know which came first: J.R.'s arm moving or the hot blast of bullets whizzing by. Long moments of quiet passed, and Owen grew impatient waiting for death. Opening his eyes, he saw J.R.'s face looking down at his.

"What happened?" he asked. "How are you not dead?"

"Bullet-proof vest," J.R. replied as he returned his sidearm to its holster. "But I caught one in the leg."

The local police soon arrived and extricated the men from their decimated vehicle. J.R. plopped himself on the ground next to the incapacitated shooters and immediately removed his vest to count the number of bullets lodged inside.

"Six!" he declared proudly. "And there's number seven," pointing to a flesh wound in his thigh.

Owen ripped a long piece of fabric from his shirt and tied it around the wound. J.R. grimaced in pain.

"Ahh, that hurts! But thanks."

"I'm the one who should say thanks. I'd be dead if—"

"Don't mention it," J.R. interrupted. "I couldn't forgive myself if anything happened to you."

The friends sat together until an ambulance arrived. With the exception of a cold compress for his sore head, Owen waived off help and instructed the medic to focus on J.R., who refused to be taken to a local hospital.

"I just want to get home to my family," he said. "Can we get a lift?"

The pair collected their belongings from the totaled patrol car and rode to Sunset Hills with a San Francisco officer, who peppered them with questions. Owen just listened while J.R. explained the events surrounding the crash and shootout. Noticeably absent from his answers was the reason for their trip to the area.

"I'm interested in knowing who those shooters were," J.R. told the driver. "When you find out, would you call me?"

"We might already know. Let me check."

The officer picked up his radio and asked dispatch, "Did we get an ID on the two shooters off Highway 24?"

A minute passed before a grainy voice answered. "Yeah, we pulled a business card off the bodies. They both worked for a security company in Oakland. Officers are en route."

"Call them off!" J.R. pleaded. "My team is in the middle of an investigation. If you hit that site without us, it could ruin months of work. Tell them to wait!"

The officer heeded J.R.'s counsel and promptly called in a hold pending further direction from Sunset Hills. With the officer temporarily occupied with his dispatcher, J.R. turned toward the backseat and whispered to Owen: "When those two guys don't show up for work tonight, the pieces on the chessboard are going to move and we might lose our link to Kemp. Tomorrow, we raid."

« 18 »

It took J.R. little effort the next morning to convince his boss of the need to storm the Oakland facility. The fiery police chief held the belief that violence against one of his officers was violence against all of them.

"We rise as one, we fall as one," he declared. "We are a monster with a hundred heads and a thousand arms. And the gates of hell shall not prevail when we come knockin'."

"Really, the gates of hell?" Owen asked incredulously when J.R. called him with the news.

"Yeah, that's what he actually said. The important thing is, he agreed to send a team with me. We will meet the cops who helped us yesterday to coordinate our raid in early afternoon."

"Are you going in with guns drawn?"

"Given all that's happened, I think we should."

"So, could I accompany your team? I could watch from a safe distance if it would make you feel better."

"Absolutely not! Yesterday was a close call. Too close. You don't need to be put in that kind of danger again. Just sit tight. When the hit is over, I'll call you with an update."

"Fine, keep all the fun for yourself. Just promise me you'll stay out of trouble."

"What would be the fun in that? Don't worry, my friend. Remember, the gates of hell don't stand a chance against me and my crew."

Owen's morning hours passed slowly despite having plenty of work to occupy his thoughts. When lunchtime finally arrived, he grabbed a sandwich and took a walk to distract him from worrying about J.R., who he imagined running headlong into danger again. How did someone like him became so brave? Was it a quality endowed at birth? A skill developed in the crucible of life? Owen hoped to find the same courage when it mattered most. In the midst of these ruminations, he found himself on the path that he and Lily had taken nights earlier and replayed their conversation in his mind. He entered the alley where they had held hands and found the grammatically challenged window advertisement, which the business owner had since corrected. He smiled at the recollection of her note on the glass. He warmed at the memory of her soft hand on his face. Sitting on the bench where he had opened his heart to her, he unwrapped his meal.

The Sunset Hills and Oakland police teams met a mile from the target site to plan their entry and lockdown. Schematics showed the security building having an office in the front and a warehouse in the back. Pairs of officers would be positioned at the four perimeter points while separate teams would enter the site from both ends and eventually meet in the middle. Despite pain in his leg due to the bullet graze, J.R. offered to lead the group pushing through the front. The teams received their assignments, suited up and began the short drive.

Their vehicles approached a plain-looking building with black-paned windows and small signage posted far from the road—too far for a passerby to identify the business operating there. Clearly, that was the point. Three police SUVs whirled to their designated locations, dropping off armed officers along the way. J.R. stepped out and hurried to the front door with his team flanking. On his signal, one of them opened the door while the rest rushed into the lobby with hardly a sound. They had expected to see a receptionist, but nobody sat at the desk. J.R. checked the door leading to the main office area; it was locked. He motioned to a different officer, who picked it with incredible speed, and through the door they stormed into a large workspace with dark offices along the perimeter. With guns drawn, the officers moved silently from room to room, checking for signs of life. Nothing. In fact, the offices did not even have phone hookups. Bewildered by his surroundings, J.R. spoke into the radio on his shoulder.

"Blue team leader, we've got empty offices here. What are you seeing?"

"Red leader, there is an empty garage on the backside. No workers are here, either."

After all-clears sounded throughout the building, the teams converged in the cavernous office space to debrief.

"We must have gotten bad info," said one cop, his finger tapping the trigger guard of the handgun he held.

"No, this is the address listed on the business card we pulled from the shooters yesterday," another replied.

"This is the right location," J.R. agreed, "but I think we were meant to find it empty."

"What do you mean?"

"This company doesn't *want* to be found. If one of its hit men ever got compromised, I suspect that card was designed to misdirect an investigation."

He stepped away from the group and paced around the office, trying to see something, anything, that might provide a clue. Even with his keen investigative eyes, there was nothing to see in the empty space. At a loss, he tried putting himself in Kemp's shoes. Here was a successful businessman whose high-class world got threatened yesterday and who sought to deal with the threat violently. Overt murder was unbecoming for a reputable executive, so he would have hired someone to do his dirty work. Payment requires money, and money has a trail. Would he have paid with his personal funds or the untold millions sitting in Hemlock's bank? Most likely, he would funnel money through Hemlock. But assassins do not send invoices, so how would recurring payments be made without tipping off an auditor? A shell company, one with a security façade, was the best explanation J.R. could conceive in those frustrating minutes.

And then a thought dawned on him. He walked back to the senior officers and posed a question: "If you were a common criminal who wanted to throw off an investigation using a shell company, where would you set up that building in relation to you?"

"As far away as possible."

"Right. But if you were a mastermind, someone who knew what he was doing, where would you set it up?"

The blue team leader nodded with understanding. "Listen up, everyone," he shouted to the surrounding officers.

"We're looking for hidden cameras. Check every corner of the facility, every crack, every broken ceiling panel. Go!"

Policemen combed the building, scanning crevices high and low in every room. J.R. spent his time investigating the lobby, believing that the best location for a camera would be one that provided a clear view of incoming traffic. But thirty painstaking minutes later, neither he nor the others found anything. Another dead end. The team leaders called off the search and exited the building.

"That was a huge waste of time," one of the Sunset Hills officers said on the way out.

J.R. hated to admit it, but he agreed. Nothing had been gained. Worse of all, he felt responsible for the failure. Fresh air and blinding sun greeted him as he stepped outside after being in the dusty, poorly lit building for nearly an hour. He blinked and squinted until his eyes adjusted to the daylight. As he followed his team to their SUV, he looked beyond the vehicle to the neighboring building. From the signage, it appeared to be a small bookkeeping shop. Or was it? J.R. had seen several accounting firms in his lifetime, but none with a row of tiny cameras on its roof: one facing the street, one facing the back and one facing the entrance to the security building. J.R. kept the object in his sight and continued walking as the camera shifted slightly, causing the afternoon sun to reflect in his eye. He winced and put on his sunglasses.

In the SUV, he told his officers what he had seen and then radioed to the team on the other side of the lot.

"Hey, something is not right about the building directly east of us. It's a bookkeeping business that has eyes on us. Can we borrow your crew for another perimeter? I'll take the front."

"Sure, we'll follow you out in a minute."

The cameras tracked the police vehicles' movement out of the parking lot, into the street and then quickly onto the new target's property. One SUV sped around the back exit, where officers jumped out with guns drawn. J.R.'s team stopped short of the front door and congregated beside him. When he gave the signal, he and five others burst into the lobby. A man monitoring computer screens saw the incoming force and yelled, "Cops!" as he took flight. The officers fanned out into the open space, pinning the fleeing man and another who tried to escape through a side door. The overhead lights went out, and a shot was fired, sending disoriented cops behind walls and to the floor for safety. J.R. kept moving through the dark, maze-like room, rounding a corner just in time to dimly see a white coat slip behind a large, closing door. He yelled for support, and two of his men ran his direction. Another shot rang out, sending one of J.R.'s teammates to the ground. A third shot, then a fourth, whizzed into police vests. In the commotion and smoke, no one knew who was firing. More shots. The officers still standing took cover and listened. Nothing moved for a full minute. Then, in the stillness, J.R. heard a cartridge being loaded on the other side of his wall. The shooter was right next to him, separated by inches of drywall. He silently stepped back, aimed his weapon at the wall and unloaded it at chest level. After the shots echoed away, J.R. heard something hit the ground with a thud. A team member rushed into the adjoining room.

"Shooter down! Shooter down!" he called.

The Oakland team punched through the back exit, restored the office lighting and attended to the injured men. Once the all-clear sounded, J.R. marched into the office space, his eyes darting around like a prowling cat.

"Where's the white coat? Who saw the white coat?" he

shouted.

Unhelpful stares greeted him throughout the room.

"We didn't see anything like that out back," the other team leader replied.

"No, I saw the white coat disappear through a door in the hallway." He stepped that direction. "There it is," he pointed.

A battering ram made quick work of the locked metal door. To everyone's surprise, it led not to a room but to a basement, an unheard-of feature in California business architecture. Indiscernible whispers echoed up the poorly lit staircase to their ears. Recognizing that the unreliable lighting would make a blind raid foolish if the occupants had weapons, J.R. took a more diplomatic approach.

"This is Officer Little," he shouted downstairs. "We have a dozen armed cops up here. Your entire security detail has been killed or arrested. You have one minute to come out with your hands up before we rain fire on you. Sixty seconds starts now! One! Two! …"

It took no more than five ticks for a pair of white-coated women to run up the stairs and into a circle of officers with guns pointed at their heads.

"No shoot! No shoot!" they begged in broken English.

While medics bandaged the wounded and officers jotted notes for their incident reports, J.R. sat with the two Asian women alone in a room.

"My name is J.R. What are your names?"

They offered blank stares in return.

"What do you do here? Why are you working in the basement?"

Still no answer.

"Okay. You don't like to talk about work. How about family. Do you have family here?"

They again said nothing but leaned toward one another and exchanged words in a foreign language.

"Excuse me a moment."

He poked his head out of the room and yelled, "I need a translator right away. Let's try Mandarin."

Turning back toward the reticent pair, he lifted his gigantic hand and instructed, "Stay there."

Posting a guard at the door, J.R. descended the dark staircase into a well-lit laboratory roughly the size of a conference room, full of test tubes, caged rodents and chemistry equipment. The chamber's underground location kept it naturally cool, ideal for scientific experimentation hidden from the outside world. A few other investigators rummaged through cabinets of paperwork, cataloguing their findings. J.R. flipped through a drawer full of documents that, to his untrained eye, seemed to be test results of some kind. At the bottom of each was a signature. He moved to another cabinet and found dozens of reports, most with Chinese names at the bottom, but another name appeared on some: Henry Bernard. The detective continued through the laboratory until he found a small refrigerator lined with vials marked numerically. Inside each vial was a powdered substance filling half of each small tube. J.R. pocketed one, grabbed a few reports and headed upstairs.

He set the items in front of the jittery women. "My guess is that you are scientists. If so, what's all this?"

Again, no response.

J.R. opened a few reports and pointed to a name at the bottom. "Is that you?" he asked one of them.

She shook her head and looked at her colleague.

"Is that you?" he repeated to the second woman.

She nodded nervously, and J.R. exhaled in relief. "Okay,

now we're getting somewhere."

He opened another report containing a different name. "And is this you?" he asked the first woman.

She nodded and pointed at herself. Lastly, J.R. found a report displaying the name Henry Bernard and laid his finger on it. "Who is this?"

The scientists spoke to each other and then yammered to J.R. indiscernibly. He stared stupidly at them.

"How am I supposed to conduct a proper interview when I don't understand a word you are saying? I don't have time for this."

One of the ladies rolled her eyes. She pointed to her name on a report and laid her palm flat against the table. She pointed to her colleague's name on a different report and laid her other palm on the table. Then she pointed to Henry Bernard's name, balled a fist and jiggled it over the hand underneath.

"This Bernard," she muttered.

"Bernard is over you?" J.R. asked. "Is he your boss?"

To his pleasant surprise, their heads nodded.

"Well, that's interesting. What about this white powder?"

He held the vial in his hand and began to remove its plug when the women, with one accord, shouted, "No, no, no!" with waving hands and wild eyes. J.R. took the hint. He left the plug in its place and set the glass container carefully on the table, looking at it reverently.

"What *is* this?" he asked soberly. "Is it Hemlox?"

A light of recognition crossed the women's faces. They exchanged a few native words, and one of the pair said, "Hemlox."

J.R. excused himself just as a female translator arrived. He introduced himself, briefly explained the situation and escorted her into the interview room. The scientists began speaking to the Chinese interpreter with such haste that J.R. wondered how many months' worth of words they had bottled up for such an occasion. After quite a bit of back and forth with the translator, she summarized their verbal deluge.

"These women met Dr. Bernard two years ago at a scientific conference in Beijing," she began. "After a few days of discussing pharmaceutical-related topics, he asked for their help on an important project in the United States. He secured their visas, and they left their families and medical schools behind to join Dr. Bernard here. Compared to back home, they made very good money and were relatively happy. But they were told not to leave their apartment, except for grocery shopping and work."

"Find out what they were doing with the white powder," J.R. instructed.

The translator asked the question and listened to a long answer.

"It's difficult to explain," she said. "I don't understand all the technical terms they used, but basically, they are trying to potentize an existing medicine—to make it work better and 'quieter,' whatever that means. But they don't know *why* they are doing it."

"That's exactly what I needed to hear! Please prepare written statements of your conversation and give it to the sergeant on site as soon as possible." Turning to the scientists, he said, "Thanks, ladies. I have to run."

He promptly exited the room with papers and vial in hand. In short order, he tracked down the Oakland team leader.

"I need to make one more hit today. It's for the guy who supervised the women back there."

"Sounds easy enough. Do you need any backup?"

"No, thanks. I've got enough guys. It's just one target."

"Suit yourself. I'll wrap up things here and share the reports as soon as they're ready."

The senior officers shook hands and attended to their respective tasks. As soon as J.R. received directions to Dr. Bernard's home in a nearby suburb, he briefed his team on the job and directed them to their vehicles. En route, J.R. considered the brilliance of using two Chinese scientists to perform illegal experimentation on Hemlox. First and most significantly, the pair could hardly speak English, which would keep them from disclosing their secret activity to inquiring Americans like him. Second, they were young women who, at least in their native culture, embraced a strong deference to male authority, especially a boss. And third, they would have felt an enormous debt to Dr. Bernard for the opportunity for a better life in California. The arrangement was perfect, a masterpiece of planning and execution. It also dawned on him that by rescuing the women before their project was completed—and they had outlived their usefulness—he had likely saved their lives.

When his SUV rolled into the semicircle driveway of Dr. Bernard's two-story home, J.R. and his team dispersed around the property. A sixty-year-old man peered through an upper window of the house and, at seeing the surrounding arsenal, rushed out of sight as J.R. approached the front door. The detective's knocks were not returned, nor were his loud calls for the scientist to show himself. Minutes passed as impatient officers meandered at their posts, waiting for something to happen. The sound of rumbling came from the side yard followed by a smoke-filled explosion and shouting at the back of the house. Officers moved instinctively to the backyard, leaving the front of the property protected only by

257

J.R. and his driver. Suddenly, a garage door on the opposite side of the house opened. A sports car emerged and accelerated down the long driveway. J.R. motioned to the police SUV, which bee-lined toward the fleeing vehicle at full speed, sending it and its passenger whirling into a cement wall at the property line. Dr. Bernard stumbled from his crumpled car and attempted to run, but his head injury and broken leg left him with few faculties to manage a successful escape. By the time J.R. reached the bleeding man, he had passed out from his pain.

When Dr. Bernard regained consciousness, he saw a burly policeman sitting in his dining room sipping a tall glass of water. J.R. smiled at him pleasantly.

"Good afternoon, doctor. Nice of you to join us."

The old man sat handcuffed to a chair facing his captor. He felt the severity of his multiple injuries and cried out at the slightest movement of his battered body. His head throbbed as it continued to leak blood—too much blood. While life remained in the scientist, J.R. wanted to make the most of it.

"An ambulance is on its way. But before I let you get treated, I have a few questions. In the interest of time—and your life—let's cut to the chase. What's your relationship with Dorian Kemp?"

The doctor scoffed and looked away. "You can forget it. I'm not talking to you."

J.R. knew his time to extract a confession was running out quickly, whether from the medics arriving or the suspect dying from blood loss. He had to improvise.

"Well, Kemp had plenty to say about *you* yesterday. To save his own skin, he told us that a stolen case of Hemlox fell into your hands and that you've been performing illegal experimentation on samples."

Dr. Bernard's face fell. He flashed an uncertain glance at J.R. "That's a lie! I stole nothing. Besides, he would never betray me. He *needs* me."

"No," J.R. corrected, "he needed a potentized drug, which you already provided. Look, from the way your head is hemorrhaging, if the paramedics don't arrive in the next few minutes, you're going to die. Why not die doing a good deed? Better yet, why not do the right thing and then fight to live? Tell me what you know about Kemp."

The man shook his head. "You don't understand. I'm *already* dead. Whether it happens today or tomorrow or a month from now, I'm damaged goods. They won't let me live."

J.R. dragged his chair closer to the man, whose dilated eyes revealed a growing awareness of his grave situation.

"*Who* won't let you live?"

"I'm dead already," he said quietly to himself. "It won't matter."

The doctor looked at J.R. for a long, conflicted moment before speaking. "Victor oversaw everything. His security guys didn't just keep an eye on outsiders. They watched us, too. I knew they had orders to keep us moving along, even though the idiots understood *nothing* we did! Knuckle-dragging imbeciles. Honestly, I would rather be teaching microbiology again. I had hoped to return to Berkeley by now, but once you are in, he doesn't let you out."

Dr. Bernard lowered his head and moaned. Feeling a touch of sympathy for the doctor whose life was not his own, J.R. asked a nearby officer for a cloth to put on the bleeding head. A dish towel was brought to him, and he held it gently against the cracked skull.

"Doctor, I need to know more about Hemlox. How did you make it more potent?"

"You're not smart enough to understand," was the anguished reply. "In simple terms, we made the active ingredients stronger and less detectable so that death appeared to happen naturally. Cardiopulmonary paralysis was the mechanism of death. It was my idea," he declared weakly, yet proudly. "*My* idea. Ingenious."

His breathing became labored and his eyes rolled back. J.R. dropped the cloth and stood in front of the dying man's pale face, which rocked like a ship as he fell in and out of consciousness. Ambulance sirens grew louder outside.

"Dr. Bernard!" he said, shaking the drooping shoulders. "Can you hear me?"

The man's eyes squinted open once more.

"Dr. Bernard, how is the drug administered? Is it a powder? A pill? What is it?"

The broken scientist wheezed, searching for oxygen. He fought against nature, against his swiftly approaching mortality, to retain the ghost in his frail machine just long enough for a final utterance, an unrepentant boast to usher him into eternity. He inhaled pain and shuttered.

"No," he said faintly. "We aerosolized it."

« 19 »

As the sun began its evening decline toward the Pacific, J.R. stood in Dr. Bernard's front yard and called Owen.

"Well, it's about time! I've been waiting by my phone like an insecure girlfriend," the reporter said. "So, are you okay? Was the raid successful? What did you find?"

"At first, absolutely nothing. But as we were leaving, I noticed that the bookkeeping shop next door had a security camera facing us. After wasting an hour in a hot, dusty building, that was good enough for me. We raided that facility, and I must say, it was a treasure trove of evidence! That led us to Dr. Bernard. This guy helped a pair of scientists potentize Hemlox and then aerosolize it for easier administration. That's our murder weapon. Well, once we figure out how it's getting into people's bodies. Bernard got seriously injured trying to escape, but before he died he gave me a name, Victor, who had something to do with the drug."

"Who is Victor?"

"I don't know much about him yet. The local PD called me to say they found a locked office at the bookkeeping shop belonging to someone named Victor. There's still a lot to weed through in there. Supposedly, he oversaw the shell company, including the Hemlox project. I think this is the guy responsible for the murder of our retirees."

"Really?" Owen blurted. "Can you confirm that?"

"We arrested a couple guys during the raid, but they aren't talking. So, no, it's not confirmed yet. But they did find—" J.R. hesitated. "They found something you're not going to like, Owen. It's a list of our county retirees sorted by date of birth. Many of the names are crossed out, but there are still many who, uh, what I mean to say is …"

"Just spit it out."

"Your grandma is third on the list."

The words hit Owen like an emotional sucker punch. He gasped and held his breath, like children do when they experience a pain so severe that their bodies freeze. Although he was a journalist by trade, someone who would normally lust over a breaking story like this one, he was first and foremost Ruthie's grandson. In that capacity, J.R.'s news set his heart racing. A dozen questions danced through his mind, but one stood apart.

"How long does she have?"

"Nobody knows. Based on payroll records in Victor's office, he and another employee are still at large. It's possible they will go into hiding, or they might stick to the script. We just don't know yet. Dr. Bernard seemed to think Victor had the drug at his disposal, so I think we assume the worst."

Owen struggled to remain objective on the subject. He wanted to ask for all-day surveillance on Ruthie's house, but he understood the police could not commit such resources to a crime that might not occur for days, maybe weeks. Yet, waiting to see the cards that Fate dealt was not an option—not this time. Besides, Owen had committed to no longer stand aside and let injustice march to its own beat. He was about to ask for full-time protection for his grandma when J.R. spoke.

"Tomorrow, I'll ask the chief for surveillance on the next retiree target. I know it's not what you want, but we still have time to nab the killers before they reach Ruthie. Listen, if the need arises one day, I will personal stay by her side and keep her safe—I promise."

It was not an ideal security plan, but having J.R.'s assurance of protection gave Owen as much comfort as could be expected at such a dark moment.

"Rather than worry, let's keep our hand to the plow," J.R. advised. "I will keep tabs on the investigation of the bookkeeping shell company for any connection to Kemp. I think only his arrest will bust this case wide open. Unfortunately, Dr. Bernard's death severed the one promising link that could have put Kemp behind bars. I will keep digging."

"While you do that, I will start writing a series of articles about our investigation and findings over the past year. Obviously, I won't submit these to be published until we can document all the accusations I intend to level—and I assure you, there will be many."

◊ ◊ ◊

Owen brought dinner to Ruthie's house that night and discussed the news of the day. He mentioned J.R. finding her name on the hit list but did not disclose her position on it.

"I'm not worried," she said. "My pastor said on Sunday that God is sovereign, and that means I am invincible until

He calls me home. That's a comforting thought, isn't it?"

Her response—so full of trust in a divine being, so unearthly minded—surprised him. Having had months to fret about her fate, knowing that at any moment life could end, she had made peace with the future. He opened his mouth to say something rational, like, "You can't trust somebody to save you that you can't even see," but the words refused to be spoken. He was not sure why.

"That doesn't mean I will roll over and die easily," she explained to her suddenly pensive grandson. "I just know my future is in God's hands. And yours. He works through people, too, you know."

Owen, who had repented of his near-death prayer two days earlier, found no logic or comfort in theology. Having faced death at the hands of gun-wielding killers, however, he could appreciate how others might. And so, he left Ruthie's comment unchallenged and smiled at her simple faith, which he both judged and envied.

True to his word, J.R. convinced the police chief to assign an officer to watch the next retiree on Victor's list, who had been notified of the threat and welcomed any and all protection. The street-side stakeout of the house proved successful. A week later, the retiree's eightieth birthday came and went without incident. However, facing budget cuts that left his department short-staffed—ironically, due to higher pension contribution requirements—the chief decided to recall the surveillance over J.R.'s objection. Within twenty-four hours, a relative visiting the retiree discovered her body sprawled across the kitchen floor. J.R. heard the news and bolted to the scene, focusing on anything in the house on which the aerosolized Hemlox could have been applied: food, utensils, napkins, clothes, medication, even dust. He collected samples of each and handed them to the police pathologist for analysis.

Rather than return to the station, he dropped by the newspaper office to tell Owen about the murder. The reporter leaned back in his chair and closed his eyes.

"Are you okay?" J.R. asked.

"Yeah, just thinking," Owen replied calmly. "Time is running out, and we only have one more shot at finding the killer before he finds ..."

Owen stopped abruptly, grimaced and turned away. J.R. shifted awkwardly.

"Hey, if you need time to yourself, we don't need to talk about this now."

"No, no, that's not it. I was just thinking about what I had started to say. We need to find the killer. But maybe it's better if we let *him* find *us*."

Concern spread across the officer's face as Owen proposed his idea. J.R. attempted to dissuade his friend because of the dangers involved, noting that they still had time to make less-risky plans. Even to his own ears, though, the warning rang hollow. Not only did they face the unseen enemy of Victor and his associate, they also worked against the merciless enemy of time.

"I can't tell you what to do, but I'll have your back the whole time—literally, the whole time," J.R. said.

He followed Owen to Al's office, where they argued the plan's merits. Owen would not relent as his boss fired one criticism after another, including one that the young man had not anticipated.

"And what will I do if you die, huh? How am I going to replace you? You're the smartest idiot out there!" he said, pointing toward the newsroom.

Far more than the backhanded compliment, Owen felt

touched by the genuine worry in Al's eyes.

"Then I'll try not to die. And I'll make sure my name is all over the article to keep you out of the spotlight."

"It's your funeral, kid. But if this idea is the best you've got, I will make it happen here. Leave the publisher to me."

Having secured Al's tentative approval and J.R.'s assurances, Owen set his plan in motion. The newspaper's popular Sunday edition would include a short, front-page teaser mentioning the Sunset Hills murders and promising a dramatic exposé of the topic on Wednesday. Owen's name would be highlighted as the investigative reporter responsible for the coming article, to be billed as the biggest news story to hit the city in years.

"That gives the killer two days to find me," Owen told Ruthie that evening. "Try not to worry, Gram. J.R. will be with me whenever I step foot outside. And when I'm home, I won't answer the door."

"No! No, no, no!" she objected. "You don't need to do this. There are other ways, other options. We can … we can leave town tonight and not look back. Let's just go to Florida. Come now, let's pack."

She tried to hurry away for a suitcase, but Owen reached for her arm and gently pulled her toward him. As he had done with Al, the young man stood his ground.

"Gram, we only need one more piece of the puzzle to end this ordeal once and for all. This is how we do it. It will work, and I will be okay."

Ruthie, shaking, could not listen or think clearly any longer. "I can't lose another family member," she cried. "Not you. I love you more than life. You can't."

Owen held the distraught old woman until she had no more tears to shed.

The next day, he drafted the teaser for Sunday's paper. It did not mention the Hemlock CEO by name, but it referenced a "deadly drug produced by a California pharmaceutical company with shady government ties." The write-up was deliberately provocative, for the objective was, in Owen's words, "to piss off Kemp."

"I want him to feel me breathing down his neck," he told J.R. "That's the only way I will get to the top of his hit list and lure Victor from the shadows."

"My wife is not going to appreciate this," he chuckled. "I don't get to see her enough as it is. Now you've got me babysitting you for two days. You're definitely getting cut from her Christmas card list."

The night before the newspaper published its Sunday edition, the friends had a final drink at the bar that had become their go-to spot for sharing case information. This time, however, there were no new facts to share, no new theories to weave. They sipped their brews as they reviewed the schedule for the next week, confirming where Owen needed to go each day and at what time. If J.R. was not available as an escort, another officer would fill in temporarily. At no time was Owen to be left alone, except at night, when a deputy would watch the apartment from his patrol car.

"And if a stranger approaches you at any time," J.R. reminded, "you need to immediately stand behind your security detail. If there is a mist in the air, you need to hold your breath and run. And don't forget to only eat packaged food."

"So many rules!" Owen complained. "Don't worry, I will heed them all. Besides you, they are the only things standing between me and death."

"No need to remind me. Just stick to the plan, please."

The Sunday paper featuring Owen's teaser notice hit the

newsstands as planned. This was certainly not the kind of article he had hoped would make him famous, but he knew it was just a means to an end—one of far greater consequence than the fame he once coveted. He spent the morning looking through old photo albums with Ruthie and taking a long walk with Lily in the afternoon. In the park by her office, the pair talked about the tumultuous events of the preceding year. Lily began with a confession.

"I was kind of annoyed with you when you interrupted my retirement workshop. It definitely was not a good first impression. But then I felt so embarrassed when you said you were a reporter, I nearly cried. I thought you'd tell my boss and I would get reprimanded."

Owen looked at his shoes and grew quiet. "I have a confession, too. That bit about me being offended and threatening to get you in trouble was all a farce. I just wanted to see you squirm a little."

Lily furrowed her brow and looked hard at Owen. "If you didn't have such good grammar, I might not be able to forgive that deception." She entwined her fingers into his and flashed a dimpled grin at his worried face. "Besides, you've sort of grown on me."

"Is my writing the *only* thing you like about me?"

Lily's eyes sparkled. She smiled at him flirtatiously but did not answer.

"I see how it's going to be," he said lightheartedly. "You can ask *me* hard questions, but I can't ask them of you. Maybe if I sent you an email replete with misspelled words and horrific syntax, you'd be forced to reply—just to edit me."

"Oh, that *would* be desperate!" she laughed. "Well, let's just say I think you are special. And brave. And kind."

She placed their hands against her heart. Owen breathed deeply of the affection and freedom he felt in that moment, knowing that the next two days would deny him both. As the sun began to set and coolness swept down from the hills, he placed his arm around Lily's shoulder and held her close to his side as they meandered along the park path.

"If I'm still alive after all this is over," he said, "I need to introduce you to my grandma. I think she would like you, though not nearly as much as I do."

He stopped walking and turned to face her, his heart beating through his chest. With trembling hands, he lightly touched her flushed cheeks and looked tenderly at the delicate face staring back at his.

"I'd like to kiss you."

She smiled and parted her lips.

"Go ahead," she whispered.

◊ ◊ ◊

Owen greeted his Monday morning alarm with a sense of dread at what the day would hold. He shaved, made breakfast and readied himself for work. Before opening the door of his apartment, he looked through its peephole and saw J.R. standing outside. The officer greeted him with a broad, knowing grin. Owen stood there looking confused.

"Somebody kissed a pretty girl last night," he smirked.

Owen rolled his eyes. "Were you spying on me at the park? The surveillance wasn't supposed to start until today."

"Yeah, I thought I'd keep an eye on you until you got home. So, how was it?"

"How was what?"

"The kiss."

Owen shook his head, locked the door and started

descending the stairs with J.R. at his heels. The officer needled him en route to the parking lot until the exasperated young man finally stopped and faced him.

"If you must know, it was great. And if you can keep me alive until the weekend, I plan on doing it again."

"See, that wasn't so hard," J.R. replied innocently. "My curiosity is now satisfied. And you've got something to look forward to. With what lays ahead in the coming days, we will need all the simple pleasures we can get."

Owen groaned.

J.R. followed the reporter to the newspaper building and stayed by his side until he entered. For his safety, Owen remained inside throughout the day, not leaving for lunch or off-site interviews. In fact, the day proceeded like any other, except for local news station requests to interview him about Wednesday's tell-all, which he obviously declined. At five o'clock, he found J.R. sitting in the lobby. The officer escorted his friend to his car and then to his apartment. Owen unlocked the door, but J.R. entered first, checking every room for signs of intrusion or danger.

"Looks good to me," he said. "Remember to stay here with the door locked all night."

He turned to leave and then removed something from his pocket and held it out.

"I almost forgot your dinner: the best frozen burrito money can buy." J.R. swallowed a laugh. "That's an oxymoron if there ever was one."

"Thanks. I think my microwave is going to see a lot of action this week." He cast an uncertain glance around him. "I think I will, too."

"Try not to worry. We will have eyes on you all night. If you think you see a threat, call me. I can be here in a flash."

That evening, Owen watched a boring documentary and nursed a bottle of wine until his nervousness subsided. Sufficiently at ease, he prepared for an early bedtime. Before locking the door to his bedroom, he walked into the living room, grabbed the empty bottle and tipped it against the front door. If someone tried to enter in the middle of the night, it would fall over and wake him. He got the idea from a paranoid schizophrenic he met in college, and it struck him as quite clever.

Thankfully, the precaution served no purpose that night; he found it in the same position the next morning. He poured two glasses of orange juice. Taking a swig of one, he walked to the front door with the other. Through the peephole he saw J.R.'s profile. Owen opened the door and extended the juice.

"This could be the day. You ready?"

"I am if you are," the deep voice replied. "You look terrible, by the way. Go wash up."

"Beauty takes time," he said groggily. "Give me ten minutes."

The pair followed the same routine as the day before, almost to the minute. Owen's day at the office proceeded uneventfully, although he received a mid-morning call that ended abruptly when he answered. He thought little of the hang-up, his mind more occupied by having to eat another bland, packaged sandwich for lunch. "*These* will be the death of me," he muttered to himself. As five o'clock approached, he texted Ruthie and Lily to assure them that all was well. Having gathered his belongings, he proceeded to the lobby, where J.R. was nowhere to be found. In his place stood another officer with his thumbs atop his utility belt, scanning all foot traffic until his charge arrived.

"Hi, I'm Officer Bell. J.R. asked me to escort you home

today," the uniformed man said.

Owen had no reason to distrust Bell, but the change in plans worried him. He excused himself to the restroom and texted J.R. to confirm the legitimacy of the assignment switch. Moments later, an "OK" appeared on his phone. Owen followed the officer to the parking lot, his eyes darting from side to side for any sign of danger. Safely in his car—and somewhat surprised, even disappointed, by the uneventful two days so far—he wondered if he had misjudged Kemp's commitment to protect his empire using whatever means necessary. He hated being wrong, so if nothing came of his plan, he would feel doubly responsible for wasting people's time and resources. This thought plagued him as they drove to his apartment complex. Officer Bell walked Owen to his residence without a single threat in sight. The deputy, standing on the ground floor looking up, pointed at his patrol car in the adjacent parking lot.

"I'll be out there all night, if you need me."

"Thanks," replied Owen. "I'm counting on it."

Upstairs, he changed his clothes and readied himself for the evening. Drawing the blinds, he sat on his couch and ate dinner: instant oatmeal and a bottled fruit smoothie. As the sun set, he opened his blinds and noticed the police car was absent from its earlier location.

Maybe he left to pick up food, Owen thought. But, fifteen minutes later, the officer was still nowhere in sight. Feeling a lump form in his gut, Owen contacted J.R. about the development.

"No worries, bud. All is well. Just sit tight."

Low-hanging storm clouds shrouded the crescent moonlight as Owen settled in for the night. The blinds in his second-floor living room were slightly slanted, revealing the flickering blue light of his television. Suddenly, Owen heard a glass break outside. He stepped to the window and peered into the parking lot, but nothing there was visible because the area had gone completely dark. Now he had no hope of seeing the officer when—or if—he returned from his unexpected absence. To break the rising tension, Owen turned up the volume on the television, turned off the room lights, locked the door and reclaimed his seat.

As the show approached its climax, Owen's heart raced, his attention fixed on the rising drama. Entranced, he did not hear someone picking the lock of his apartment door or the unfamiliar steps at the edge of his living room. He did not feel the presence of a stranger behind him. Nor did he feel the hot sting of three bullets entering his back. The stranger moved toward the body hunched on the couch, looking for any signs of life that required further treatment. He peered down quizzically, but his attention was diverted by the sound of several weapons being cocked and shouts of, "Hands up!" ringing in his ears. The apartment suddenly filled with light as J.R. and his team descended on the shooter, who turned toward the body on the couch and invested another round of steel in it. This was the last thing the man remembered before being knocked unconscious by the hilt of J.R.'s sidearm.

The assassin awoke minutes later with a spectacular headache and his hands handcuffed to his ankles. When his mind cleared of enough fog to utter a few words, he mocked the officers who stood over him.

"Too late, he's dead!"

J.R. cocked his head curiously, walked to the couch, lifted the limp body and set it on the floor in front of the defiant man.

"I'd like you to meet Charlie, our test dummy," J.R.

mocked. "Congratulations on killing a slab of rubber."

Jaw wide open, the man stared at the object dressed in Owen's clothes. The real Owen emerged from his bedroom and glared coldly at the fiend who sought to end his life that evening. He stepped over Charlie and joined J.R., who sat on a stool facing the stranger.

"I'm sure you are very confused," J.R. began. "And why wouldn't you be? You're a dumb thug. So, I'll make this simple and use small words. We knew you were coming and have been waiting for you all day. See, that's where we were hiding," pointing to a hidden nook beside the kitchen. "I must compliment you for playing your part perfectly. And now it's time for you to talk."

He turned to his fellow officers. "Guys, go take a walk."

The policemen filed out of the apartment and closed the door behind them.

J.R. removed his vest and stretched his long, muscular arms in plain view of the handcuffed interviewee.

"This guy here is my friend," he said, glancing at Owen. "Nobody messes with my friends."

His eyes narrowed like an attacking lion. The hulk took two steps and, with one powerful blow, dropped the man's face to the tile floor. J.R. breathed hot words into the assassin's ringing ear.

"You're going to tell me who you are and where Victor is."

The man squirmed but refused to answer. J.R. pressed against the man's soft temple. The deep, dull ache quickly became a sharp, radiating pain that make his brain feel weak.

"Okay, okay, stop," he stammered. "I just work for Victor. He tells me what to do."

"Where is Victor?" he growled. "Where!"

The man's eyes began to roll as he flirted with unconsciousness.

"He's … making … a hit … now."

J.R. rose to his feet, grabbed a radio and promptly dispatched a unit to the house of the second retiree on the hit list. Few words filled the intervening minutes while he and Owen waited. The pair exchanged nervous glances until J.R.'s cell phone finally rang.

"This is Little. What's going on there? … I see … One or both? … Any sign of struggle? … Okay, start without me."

By the time J.R. hung up, Owen wore terror on his face.

"What happened? How did it happen?"

It was pointless to ask. He already knew the answers. His breathing grew short and fast as J.R. looked down and shook his head.

"An officer at the scene confirmed the deaths of the retiree and his spouse. It happened within the last thirty minutes. He said both deaths appeared natural."

Owen stared at his bullet-ridden couch and the assassin slumped beside it.

"One thing is certain—there is nothing natural about it. And now we are out of time."

« 20 »

Owen's highly anticipated article ran in Wednesday's paper, but he was not in the office to enjoy the notoriety and interest it generated among co-workers and readers. These successes, once the beat of his ambitious heart, meant nothing to him now. From the moment he learned that Ruthie was next on Victor's hit list, his single-minded focus was to keep her safe. As soon as J.R. confirmed the second retiree's death the night before, Owen packed a bag of clothes and sped through the lonely Sunset Hills streets to her sleeping house. Using his spare key to enter, he quietly checked on her in bed and then sat on her couch listening intently to the darkness.

Ruthie found him the next morning curled up with goose bumps along his arms. She placed a light blanket over his chilled body and made a pot of coffee for them to share. Weary from a long night of worrying and planning, Owen slept through the sound of the percolating brew, the clanging of silverware and the low notes of Ruthie humming her favorite hymn. It was only the familiar buzz of his phone that awakened the young man from his slumber. He felt for his backpack, pulled out the device and blinked at it until Lily's words came into focus.

"Are you alive? If so, call me."

Her text brought a smile to his overslept face. He pushed himself to a sitting position and looked around. Ruthie peeked out from the kitchen. Seeing his wobbly head, she grabbed a cup of coffee and a plate of scrambled eggs.

"Good morning, dearie," she said, setting the items in front of him. "What brings you here?"

"Oh, last night I got shot in my apartment a few times. I just needed a change of scenery." He winked at her horrified face.

"That is *not* funny, Owen. I was worried sick about you all night. What kind of plan is it to use yourself as bait? That's crazy. And your big police friend was crazy for agreeing to it!" She huffed a bit more and then asked curiously, "So, did it work?"

He did his best to answer without causing his grandma further anxiety. As long as he was safe and the bad guy got caught, she did not need to know every detail of the encounter. This reminded him to check with J.R. on whether the shooter gave up any other useful information. But the first order of business was to disclose to Ruthie the real reason for his unexpected visit.

"Gram," he said softly, "there is one more killer on the loose. His name is Victor, and you are next on his hit list. Until he is in custody, I am going to stay with you. I won't leave your side. Wherever you go, I go. When you take a walk, I take a walk. I am going to be your shadow until this nightmare ends. It has all been worked out with my boss, so don't worry about my job."

"I don't know what to say. I hate being someone's target again, but at least I'll have you as my protector. I appreciate what you are doing, my sweet boy. I'll be sure to bake your favorite pies. Oh, but I'll need to pick up some extra groceries first."

"*We* will pick up some extra groceries," Owen reminded. "We."

After breakfast, he texted Lily to provide proof of life and then called J.R.

"While you were counting sheep on your grandma's couch, I oversaw a crime-scene cleanup that lasted to three o'clock in the morning. Man, I'm tired! We really need to plan this stuff earlier in the day."

"Hopefully, we never need to do this again. Did our would-be assassin have anything interesting to say after I left?"

"Yeah. When he wasn't unconscious, he was actually very helpful. He referred to himself as Victor's right-hand man and claimed to have been assigned most of the retiree hits in town. He referred to his boss as the chief of security, but he did not say who they secured. My assumption is Kemp, but I think we will need Victor to establish a clear link."

"All this points to Victor as Kemp's hatchet man. He does the dirty work while that sociopath sits in his castle blowing cigar smoke over people's graves."

"I happen to agree, but we need a paper trail or testimony confirming that relationship before marching into Hemlock with handcuffs."

"I just want this ordeal to be over," Owen sighed. "I want

the bad guys to go to prison, and I want to write a good story about it. I want Gram to live a long, happy life without fear of tomorrow. And I want to kiss Lily again. Really, all I want is to go back to normal, even if it means I'm an unknown reporter working at a mediocre paper in a quiet town. I'm tired of all this drama and death."

As good friends do, J.R. just listened.

"And here's something else that annoys me. Just when you or I win some victory, even something significant like last night, its sweetness is short-lived. We still have *no idea* how the killers got the drug from an aerosol bottle into their victims. That fact alone places us at an enormous disadvantage to Victor, whose record of stealth murders, mind you, is flawless. Standing against a faceless enemy who uses a hidden weapon that never misses its mark is incredibly daunting and scary." He paused to catch his breath. "But what choice do I have? The game must be played out. I have no good alternative but to see it through, to let it come to Gram. But first through me."

The next few days passed slowly for Owen, who shadowed his grandma night and day. Together, they walked to the mailbox, bought food, visited friends and ate meals. Owen answered her phone calls and her front door. He sanitized her utensils and replaced her toothbrush. He observed the smallest details of her daily life and made adjustments accordingly.

"Oh, is that really necessary?" she asked repeatedly.

"Yes, but it's only temporary," he replied each time.

J.R. often dropped by to check on Ruthie. She thanked him for his kindness with pieces of pie, which he never refused. On the fourth day of this routine, Owen's nervous energy grew intolerable. He itched to leave the confines of the small house and do something else. That afternoon, he took his laptop to Ruthie's front porch, sat in her old wicker chair and emailed Al.

"Got a writing project I can work on during my leave of absence? Research? Phone interview? Anything?"

"No, we're managing fine," the editor replied.

Owen closed the computer and tried to enjoy the serenity of children playing and cars passing along the street. With Ruthie's eightieth birthday less than a month away, he wondered how long this false respite would endure. When would Kemp's henchman show? If he showed at all. With the exception of Victor, J.R. had eviscerated the crew of assassins. Recruiting another kill squad would take time, if that is what Kemp decided to do. Or, he could instruct his security chief to stick to his murderous assignments without backup. Owen remained in the unfortunate position of having to wait to find out.

A week later, J.R. drove up to Ruthie's house for a late-afternoon visit and was surprised to find several cars in the driveway and along the curb. Heeding the new rule she made just for him—to knock on the front door and enter at his leisure—he rapped a few times and stepped inside. Owen saw his friend enter and excitedly headed that direction holding the hand of a beautiful young lady.

"You must be the lovely Lily that Owen has told me so much about. I'm glad he finally got around to introducing us."

"Actually," Owen replied, "Gram invited her over because she hadn't met Lily, either."

Lily extended her hand toward the officer and shook it warmly.

"Owen was not exaggerating when he described you as

Hercules with a badge. It's nice to finally make your acquaintance."

"The pleasure is all mine," he said with a gentlemanly bow.

His deep voice and sheer size had drawn the attention of other guests in the room, including a few elderly women who stopped their chatter to stare at him.

"Nice to meet you all, too," J.R. said. "Mrs. Daniels, I must have missed the memo. Isn't your birthday party in a few weeks?"

"Indeed, it is. I felt like playing bridge, but Owen didn't know the game. So I invited a few friends over to watch me win—again!"

Cackles, boos and laughter sounded around the table. Ruthie stood to introduce her guests one by one. When she got to Lily, she said, "And this is the young lady who has turned Owen's head." Feigning a whisper behind her hand, she added, "I think they're a good match."

The group giggled while Owen and Lily stole glances at one another from the corners of their eyes. The friends and family spent the next half-hour playing cards, eating pie, retelling old stories and enjoying each other's humanity. These precious moments were a needed reprieve for both Ruthie and Owen, who, having remained faithful to their self-imposed safety precautions, felt ready to end their lockdown and resume a normal life of freedom.

J.R.'s phone buzzed.

"Ah, the wife needs me to pick up dinner on the way home. I should get going."

He returned his dessert plate to the kitchen, thanked Ruthie for her hospitality and headed to the front door. Before he could leave, she gave him a hug and kissed his arm because his cheek was so far away.

"Besides my grandson, you are my favorite protector, Officer Little."

"That means a lot to me, Mrs. Daniels. You are in good hands."

She opened the front door, and J.R., not watching his feet, nearly kicked over a bouquet of flowers left on the doorstep.

"How clumsy of me. My momma used to say my feet were too big. I guess she was right. Here you go," he smiled, handing her the vase.

"Oh, how sweet. I have just the place for them."

As Ruthie closed the door and looked at the beautiful floral arrangement, Owen felt grateful that his grandma had so many people who cared about her. It really would have been a shame to leave Sunset Hills and her wonderful friends. Even at their old age, some of them still remembered her birthday, like the kind person who sent this gift three weeks early.

Ruthie carried the glass vase in her hands, the flowers dangling just beneath her chin. Owen looked on with a smile. Then uncertainty. Then recognition. And finally, with breathless terror. As if watching a movie, his mind recalled images it had seen before—a crime scene photo, an autopsy report, Darcie's table, yellow pollen on his nose. In that moment, he knew. Another piece of the puzzle had become suddenly clear. Owen sprang from his chair and yelled, "Gram, no!" as he darted toward the woman whose unsuspecting nose dipped into the flowers to smell.

"Stop!" he cried.

In full sprint, he lunged at the vase, knocking it to the floor in one tremendous crash. Glass and water lay everywhere. He stood up immediately and stared at her stunned expression. Fine white powder and film covered her nostrils. It was too late! Owen grabbed her nose and held it with all his might.

"Don't inhale, Gram! Whatever you do, don't breathe!"

The guests watched in helpless silence as he rushed her to the kitchen sink and turned on the water.

"You must not breathe! Do you understand? Don't breathe! Now close your mouth."

She followed his instructions as he dowsed her face with handfuls of water. Ruthie began to squirm from lack of oxygen. He continued to squeeze her nose.

"Now take a breath through your mouth. Only your mouth!"

She inhaled frantically, heaving deep breaths of life. Owen surveyed her wet face and saw pasty white residue within the nostrils that he pinched between his quivering fingers. He had held the poison in place but unintentionally pressed it deeper into the soft lining of her nose.

"Get me a tissue, now!" he yelled into the other room.

Lily rushed in with a napkin.

"Gram, listen. I'm going to let go of your nose, and you need to blow it with all your might. But take a deep breath through your mouth first. Do you understand?"

With tears filling her eyes, she nodded and inhaled. Owen slowly released his grip, and the woman blew like her life depended on it. Because it did. Lily brought more napkins. Ruthie blew her nose until it bled. Out of air, she stopped, looked into Owen's desperate eyes and passed out. He caught her as she fell to the floor.

"God, no," he whispered. "Please."

At his vehicle, J.R. heard Owen's screams and rushed back into the house just as Ruthie fell unconscious.

"What happened?" he asked.

"The flowers," were the only words Owen could muster.

J.R. understood. He rushed to her side, checked her faint pulse and cast an uncertain look at Owen.

"I have to go after Victor. Keep her breathing."

With an athleticism he had not used in years, J.R. burst through the living room, out the door and to his patrol car. He tore down the street after the nearest moving vehicle in sight, a florist truck that had a full minute's lead. Eyes fixated on it blocks ahead, he accelerated wildly, ripping past stop signs and dodging cross traffic. In his side mirror, Victor saw the police car racing toward him and forced the truck into high gear. It took seconds for J.R. to catch up, but the vehicles' size difference made a forced tailspin unfeasible on city streets. He hoped to direct Victor into the countryside where he would have more room to work. But Victor had different plans. He slammed on his breaks, causing the officer to crash into the truck's back bumper, giving him a push and, more importantly, additional distance from his pursuer.

J.R. picked up his radio and barked orders. "I need backup units to converge at the bridge on the north side of town. Pursuit in progress. Suspect is assumed to be armed. Hurry!"

Both vehicles screeched through neighborhoods as residents watched the car chase from their homes and yards. Victor began veering away from the bridge toward the highway, where rush-hour traffic would make an arrest a danger to more than just himself. To keep the truck on course, J.R. sped to Victor's right side to block the intended turn. The maneuver succeeded but sent the police car plowing through a fire hydrant that left a geyser shooting into the air. The officer fell well behind as Victor increased his speed toward the country roads. J.R. saw the long, narrow bridge in the distance, but his backup had not arrived there yet. Without a barrier on the other side of the waterway, the truck would continue its unimpeded flight. J.R. settled behind Victor as the vehicles raced into the final turn before the overpass. Just then, he heard sirens in the distance and saw lights gathering a half-mile away.

"You're trapped, fool," he said. "Now slow down. C'mon, let up."

Second after second passed, but the truck did not lessen its speed on the tight, two-lane bridge. Instead, Victor accelerated.

"He's going to ram you!" J.R. shouted in vain. "Move!" He picked up his radio. "Tell them to move!"

The waiting officers could not see J.R. waving his arms from behind the approaching truck. In another few moments, it would plow into their vehicles and likely kill one of his colleagues. J.R. feared shooting the truck's tires from behind, as a stray bullet might hit an officer on the other side. Out of time, he took the first evasive action that entered his mind. Speeding alongside the truck, he aimed his gun out his passenger-side window and shot the truck's back tire. The top-heavy vehicle screeched terribly, tilting to one side and then the other like a drunken teeter-totter. The uneven weight traveling at such a great speed caused the truck to tip onto the driver's side and skid wildly before coming to a stop in front of a wall of police cars.

J.R. stepped from his vehicle, drew his sidearm and walked slowly toward Victor, whose bloodied face he could barely see through the cracked windshield. For the sake of his investigation and to guarantee a solid link back to Kemp, he had to take Victor alive. The assassin unbuckled himself. Falling onto broken glass, he cried out in pain. J.R. stepped sideways, craning his neck to better see Victor through the windshield.

"Come out with your hands up!" he yelled at the truck.

Victor moved through the cab, climbing to the passenger-side door above him.

"I only see one of your hands! I want to see both in the air!" J.R. bellowed.

Victor's head emerged from the door, looking in all directions.

"You can't escape. You are surrounded."

Victor lifted his body from the vehicle and lowered himself to the asphalt road, where he stood with a gun in one hand and a cell phone in the other. Hearing the rattle of officers approaching, he tossed his phone on the ground and shot it, sending it spinning to the side of the bridge.

"Drop it!" J.R. demanded. "Now!"

Victor scowled at his pursuer as officers ran around the truck to J.R.'s flank. They saw the gun in the stranger's hand and aimed theirs in his direction. Dropping to his knees, he lowered his gun to the ground but kept his finger on the trigger. His posture of surrender brought officers toward him. With one act of violence left in his cold heart, Victor deftly rolled onto his side and shot a deputy in the abdomen before turning the gun on himself. Two men lay bleeding on the bridge—one clinging to life, the other beyond its reach.

J.R. stood in silent shock, his arms dangling by his sides. With the last assassin neutralized, he should have felt relief, but the satisfaction of victory never crossed his mind. With a single bullet, Victor had ended his own ruinous life and stolen any hope of securing an open-and-shut case against

Kemp.

Over the next hour, police removed damaged vehicles and marked evidence at the scene. J.R. leaned against the bridge railing, staring at the river below. He took stock of the situation, trying to find some good in an otherwise unfortunate, unexpected outcome. The silver lining was that the murderers had been stopped and retirees in town, particularly Ruthie, would sleep better tonight. So many questions remained, though, and he knew these unknowns would relentlessly gnaw at his desire for closure. He consoled himself with the hope that the Oakland investigation would turn up more useful information or that Kemp would provide enough reasonable suspicion to arrest him. But what occupied his mind most was what to tell Owen.

J.R. left the railing and walked toward an officer who had offered to take him back to the station. Then he heard someone call his name.

"Little, come look at this."

J.R. turned to see an investigator stooping at the edge of the bridge, holding out a plastic bag containing Victor's damaged cell phone. He took the bag and looked it over carefully.

"The camera has been blown out, but the rest appears to be intact."

"Do you think the stuff inside is still working?" J.R. inquired.

"Haven't a clue. That's a question for the tech guys."

J.R. pocketed the bag and found his ride back to town. He had been so occupied with the chase and Victor's death that he had forgotten all about Ruthie lying unconscious on the floor.

"Hey, I need to make a stop on the way," he told his driver. "It can't wait."

They pulled up to Ruthie's house and he let himself in. Several worried faces hovered around the old woman, who sat feebly on her couch, breathing cautiously. Owen held her weathered hands in his. J.R. knelt down and gave them both a giant hug.

"It's over, Mrs. Daniels. You are safe now."

She began to cry. Then smile. Then cry some more. A hint of color rose on her pale cheeks as she wiped her eyes and looked up at J.R.

"Oh, don't you worry. These are not tears of sadness. They are tears of relief. And gratitude. And excitement for having my life back. I cry because I'm so happy."

She smiled at the officer and gently patted his hand.

"I promise to make your favorite pie when I feel better."

"No hurry, ma'am. You just rest now, okay?"

J.R. motioned to Owen, who followed the officer to the flowers scattered across the living room floor.

"Has anybody touched these?"

"No, I told everyone to keep their distance."

"Good, I'll need to take them to the station for analysis."

Owen grabbed a clean trash bag. Without breathing, he picked up the flowers and set them inside. J.R. promptly tied a knot in the bag and held the evidence carefully in his arm.

"Just to be safe, let's double bag it."

As they worked the second liner, Owen asked about Victor's arrest. J.R.'s face tightened. He knew this question was coming.

"Uh, he wasn't arrested because he is dead. He shot himself."

The news visibly bothered Owen, but then he shrugged. "When you left earlier, I figured he would end up dead. But my money would have been on you beating him senseless."

"Yeah, it was tempting. But he was more valuable to us alive. Honestly, I'm still upset because he was our primary link to Kemp." J.R. stopped talking and looked at Owen's calm demeanor. "You are not as annoyed as I thought you'd be."

"No, I'm not upset. I got what I wanted: my grandma, safe and sound. That's all that really mattered to me. Just her. For as many days as Fate …" He checked himself. "For as many days as her God gives her."

"Hmm," J.R. muttered. "It's a day full of surprises. Which reminds me, how is that woman still alive? Didn't she inhale the drug?"

Owen shook his head. He stopped, however, as doubt overtook his face.

"I suppose I don't know for sure. She had residue in and around her nose. I can't imagine she didn't breathe some of it. The blood vessels in her nostrils are still inflamed. So, well, I guess she did."

The men faced each other, puzzled. J.R. spoke first.

"I guess we can add that to our list of unsolved mysteries. One more thing before I go. How did you know the Hemlox was on the flowers?"

Owen looked at the wet, glass-covered floor, as if gathering memories from those horrifying moments.

"As soon as I saw her about to smell the petals, I remembered seeing flowers at different crime scenes. The first time was in a photo you showed me last summer. Darcie had a fresh bouquet on her kitchen table, too. Then it dawned on me: what an unassuming way to have someone inhale a deadly drug. You spray it on flowers, leave them at a doorstep and let the victim do the rest. You put the gun in their hand, and they willingly pull the trigger without even knowing it."

"It's wicked. But in terms of strategy …" J.R. hesitated.

"Kind of brilliant," Owen finished sheepishly. "That's an awful thing to say, huh?"

"Yeah, you're a terrible human being."

The pair smiled at each other because they understood, as only friends do.

"We accomplished something significant today, my young friend. Your dad would have been proud."

"Thanks. None of this would have happened without you. Gram and I are indebted forever."

"Don't mention it."

Trash bags in hand, the officer said goodbye to Ruthie and walked out the front door.

◊ ◊ ◊

To celebrate the day, Owen took Ruthie and Lily out to dinner. All their hearts were light, as grandma and grandson enjoyed a sense of liberation from the fears that had enslaved them for far too long. Brimming with undiminished contentment, he was in a story-telling mood. He reminisced about pleasant memories of his parents. Ruthie listened with a broad grin. When it was her turn, she yarned about her early life and the joys of dating Owen's grandpa.

"We were both poor as dirt," she recalled, "so he used to whittle little figurines for me out of wood he found in the Sequoias. One Valentine's Day, he presented me with a perfectly formed engagement ring made from birch. He told me, 'Ruthie, I love you and want to make you my wife. By our wedding day, I will have saved enough to replace this carved ring with a gold one.' And sure enough, he kept his word."

"That is sooo sweet," Lily crooned.

She felt for Owen's hand under the table; their fingers interlocked. She told Ruthie about her first impression of Owen: that he looked like a high-school kid who showed up late to class. The ladies laughed at his expense until he blushed. Not wanting to leave his girlfriend out of the fun, he told about Lily misinterpreting his comment at the retirement office—one intended to protect her from her boss—that caused her to leave him alone in a room with the lights out. Her cheeks turned a darker shade of red.

"I still regret that," she confessed.

The trio carried on until their waiter asked a third time if they wanted dessert. Ruthie declined and looked at her watch.

"After almost being murdered today, I think I've earned a good night's rest. Can you take me home now, Owen?"

On the drive back, he had talk radio turned on softly while his passengers chatted. At a pause in their conversation, Ruthie heard a news reporter mention Governor Lancaster's name.

"I don't like that man, even if he is from our town," she huffed.

In spite of her disapproval, she turned up the volume to hear a clip of his interview earlier in the day. The newscaster described the scene in the rotunda of the capitol building in Sacramento, where a crowd of supporters stood around the governor chanting, "Run, Mike, Run!" while he answered questions about expanding an existing entitlement program in the next fiscal year. The commentator continued, but Ruthie had heard enough. She turned off the radio and crossed her arms.

"Does he think money grows on trees? That man is going to tax us to death."

"You know, Gram, Oliver Wendell Holmes once said that taxes are the price we pay for civilization. Without them, ..."

Owen ended his rebuttal mid-sentence. He did not want to engage in a political debate in front of Lily, particularly after such a felicitous evening. Pulling up to his grandma's house, he walked her to the front door and kissed her uplifted forehead. Once he heard her deadbolt the lock, he returned to his car. Lily stared affectionately at him.

"You're a good man," she said in the stillness.

"Nah. I'm no better than anyone else. I just had great parents. If there *is* any good in me, it's because of them." He looked at Ruthie's house. "And especially because of her."

"Well, I respectfully disagree. I believe you are a good man because you have a good heart that is full of kindness toward those you love. It's a lovable quality."

Owen blushed and diverted his eyes from hers.

"I don't know about you, but I'm in the mood for coffee and a rousing game of Scrabble. But be forewarned: I never lose."

"Neither do I," she countered. "May the best woman win."

They found the coffee shop nearly empty with no one at the game tables, so they claimed a space and picked their tiles.

"I don't want to scare you," she said as she arranged her first word on the board, "but I've made grown men beg for mercy."

"I won't need your mercy," he grinned. "Only your forgiveness after I crush you."

The playful banter continued for some time, but eventually, the soft jazz music in the background and the leisurely pace of the game settled them both. Lily sipped her latte and stared thoughtfully at Owen.

"Do you think we would have met were it not for your investigation?"

"I certainly didn't start it expecting to get a crash course in pensions. But that's what it took to figure out this mystery." He paused. "Now that I think about it, I still haven't figured it out."

He placed a few letters, tallied his score and reclined in thought. Lily watched his mind work as his eyes shifted swiftly, as if moving pieces of scattered information into place. His eyebrows suddenly bent inward.

"What's the matter?" she asked.

Owen grabbed a pen and began writing on a napkin. Lily leaned over to see his notes, but his scribbles made it impossible to read from her vantage point. She tilted her head from side to side to gain a more legible view.

"Your handwriting could use some improvement. What does that say?"

"It's a list of questions that still need to be answered. The first one is obvious: What was the goal of the murders? Why kill dozens of retirees when the only beneficiary is the pension plan? Well, I suppose taxpayers might benefit to some extent, but these murders are too sophisticated for locals. That raises the question of how Hemlock Pharmaceuticals got involved in this whole thing. What does Dorian Kemp have to gain from potentizing an assisted-suicide drug and then hiring a hit team to administer it?"

Lily shook her head. "Sorry, I'm not going to be any help here. But don't let that stop you. Keep going."

"Second, did the two benefit formula increases in 2000 and 2005 have anything to do with the murders? I think they could have. Those two years were dramatic pivot points in the pension plan that led to massive unfunded liabilities. But—and here is where a possible motive arises—when retirees die on time or early, it can lower the unfunded liability, right?"

"Now that's my wheelhouse," Lily said confidently. "The answer is: sort of. The Board of Retirement must first adopt a new mortality assumption that says the average retiree will die at an earlier age, which means there are fewer benefits to pay later. That saves the plan money in the long term, lowers our liabilities and bumps up our funding ratio. In fact, that happened just recently."

"Yeah, I heard. So, retirees dying at younger ages means a lower mortality assumption, which means a better funded status, which means what?"

Owen asked the question rhetorically, but Lily gave it serious consideration.

"From my years at the pension office, I have distinct memories of a few times when the plan's investments were making a lot of money and our funded status was on the rise. The board felt optimistic. My boss was happy. County leadership and the taxpayers' association did not complain. And the media did not hound us. So, maybe that's it."

Owen laid his tiles and looked up. "What do you mean?"

"There have been a few times at my office when the media and taxpayer groups left us alone. We called that 'the quiet before the storm' because it rarely lasted long. But, on rare occasions when our funding was improving and our investments were outperforming, the media were either quiet or gave us a lot of love."

"Why?"

"Because we appeared to be running the pension plan like geniuses. And, we were not costing taxpayers as much money."

Owen leaned toward Lily's bright, intelligent eyes. The corners of his mouth slowly curved upward.

"Media attention is not something we ever considered. J.R. told me that bad guys typically commit crimes for money, power or passion. We had not thought of good PR as a motive, but when you described your board members feeling like geniuses, something clicked in my head about Kemp."

"Hopefully nothing broke," she teased. "Oh, check out my fifty-point word! That puts me well in the lead. I bet that hurt, huh? Are you ready to surrender to a Scrabble opponent who is clearly your superior?"

Owen turned the board to face him and considered the scorecard. A look of eagerness crept across his face as he fingered the napkin.

"My dear Lily, the game is still on. And now it's my move."

« 21 »

O wen spent the next week working behind the scenes with J.R. to lock down evidence needed for them to make their final move. Of critical importance was determining if aerosolized Hemlox covered the flowers delivered to Ruthie. Despite their watery crash, enough residue remained for the local pathologist to confirm Owen's suspicion that the drug had indeed been applied liberally to the petals. To be absolutely certain, J.R. sent a sample to the Bay Area consultant for an outside opinion. The pathologist provided just that, corroborating the initial conclusion days later.

"Well, I think it's safe to confirm that a modified form of Hemlox is the murder weapon," J.R. said proudly.

"It's a small win, but a win nonetheless," Owen added.

"The next thing we need is to pull whatever data we can from Victor's damaged cell phone. Its camera was blown out, but it turned on for our I.T. guys. Unfortunately, we don't have the four-digit passcode. And, as you know, Sunset

297

Hills is not known for its prolific hacker community. We just don't possess the resources—on either side of the law—to crack the code and extract Victor's emails … and whatever other goodies are hiding in there."

J.R. asked several co-workers at the station, but nobody knew anyone capable of breaking into phones. One young officer overheard J.R.'s inquiries and followed him to his office, closing the door as he entered.

"Officer Little, sir, I heard you asking around about a hacker. I might be able to help."

"I'm listening."

"It's not me," he noted quickly. "I'm not techie like that. But I knew a kid at my high school in L.A. who used to prank people by stealing their phones and changing their passwords. Rumor has it that in college, he hacked into his professor's school account to change a bad grade. He got caught, expelled and charged with a misdemeanor."

"What is his name?"

"Not sure. His buddies called him Cave because he liked being alone."

J.R. grimaced. "There are plenty of reasons to dislike your lead, not the least of which is that this guy is a criminal. However, we lack better options. How do I get hold of him?"

It took an hour of searching public records and making a few calls before the junior officer tracked down Cave's contact information for J.R.

"Is there anything I should know about this guy before I call?" J.R. inquired. "Anything I could use as leverage?"

"Well, he often carried a pack of trick cards with him. Beyond that, I don't know. Like I said, he spent a lot of time alone with his computer."

◊ ◊ ◊

Like any sensible hacker, Cave did not answer calls from unknown sources, and a blocked number from the Sunset Hills area code certainly fell into that category. He let J.R.'s call go to voicemail. The officer's message summarized his technical problem and promised a reward for a successful hack.

"I'll make it worth your while," he ended his message. "Call me as soon as you can."

Five minutes turned into ten, ten into twenty, twenty into thirty. J.R. grew impatient, but he feared calling a second time would come across as desperate. Finally, the phone rang.

"Who's this?" said a young, high-pitched voice on the other line.

"This is Officer Little with the Sunset Hills Police Department. Who are you?"

"You know who I am, moron. You just called me." The kid paused. "You can call me Cave. I'm not giving you my real name because I'm not an idiot."

"Fine by me. But for the record, I already know your real name. Here is my issue, Cave. I've got a damaged smart phone that's missing a camera. It turns on, so it appears to be somewhat functional. The owner is dead, and we don't have his passcode. We need to get in. Can you do it?"

"Psss. Stop wasting my time. Bye."

"Wait! Wait! I've got something to compensate you for your time."

Silence.

"What is it?"

J.R. drew a long breath. "An all-expense-paid, one-night trip to Las Vegas with a mezzanine-level ticket to the strip's premier magic show. Take it or leave it."

Again, silence.

"My car guzzles gas. How about some travel money?"

"Okay, I'll throw in fifty bucks for fuel."

"You know, you can't see jack from a mezzanine seat. You gotta be close to see the action better. Can you hook me up with an orchestra seat? I'd even take lower-level if it's on an aisle."

J.R. grew annoyed. "Fine. Cave. Lower level it is. Do we have a deal?"

"Yeah, whatever. Sure."

"Good. Just so we're clear, you only get all this *after* you've cracked the code. I'll text you a meeting location and time shortly. Don't be late."

◊ ◊ ◊

The following evening, J.R. returned to Sunset Hills five hundred bucks poorer but holding Victor's unlocked phone.

"That's one expensive bribe," Owen observed when they met for lunch the next day.

"I prefer to think of it as an investment. I got a feeling there's some juicy stuff hiding in there, something damning we can use against Kemp."

"That would seriously make my day. Who do you have working on it?"

"I handed it to a couple of techs at the station last night. They said they would have the data collected and indexed in a few days, but I said I wanted it stat. I'm not that patient."

"I've heard the most dangerous place in the world is between a cop and his donut. But I believe a close second is between you and that data. Oh look," he said, laughing and pointing. "There's a donut right behind you. Watch out, everyone!"

J.R. rose to his full height and glared down. The

mischievous smirk fell from Owen's face.

"Hey, big guy, I was just kidding."

The giant returned to his seat, cracked a wide grin and belly laughed. "Ha, you should have seen your face! Did you wet yourself? You felt the urge, didn't you? Admit it."

The thought of Owen becoming incontinent sent them both into a hyena fit, so much so that J.R. almost missed his phone ringing. He settled himself enough to answer the call with a believable, "Officer Little speaking."

"Good afternoon, sir. We were able to download a lot of information from the phone you gave us yesterday. It is all indexed by emails, reports, logs and miscellaneous. What do you want us to do now?"

"Save it to the network. I'll be there in a few minutes."

J.R. shot a look of anticipation toward his eavesdropping lunchmate. He rubbed the palms of his hands together, excitement brimming in his wide eyes.

"Let's see what Santa brought us."

The records J.R. reviewed revealed that Victor provided monthly updates to Kemp on the progress of the drug experiments and retiree deaths. However, nearly all of the communications contained scant data, usually just a series of letters and numbers. The characters made little sense until J.R. found Victor's cipher: his first message to Kemp shortly after the pharmaceutical company's IPO. In that email, the security chief drafted an elaborate explanation of his initial progress. Kemp replied with a terse reprimand for Victor's excessive detail.

"In the future," he wrote, "I want your reports to contain essential facts only, preferably coded. Nothing more."

Following that exchange, the conspirators used abbreviated words and numbers. After scanning two years of such data, J.R. stepped into a private room and dialed Owen.

"Jackpot!" he bellowed before the reporter could say a word. "I've seen enough emails, status updates and Hemlock docs from Victor's office in Oakland to throw handcuffs on Kemp today! I am going to prepare a memo to the chief and then get to San Francisco to nab our guy. I've got enough reasonable suspicion to arrest him ten times over!"

"You certainly sound giddy. But before you go waving handcuffs, I want to show you something I just compiled. It might change your mind about arresting Kemp, at least for a while. If I can't convince you to wait, then I won't stand between you and your donut."

The next morning, they met for coffee. Owen brought a diagram he had drawn with overlapping circles and connecting lines that showed what he believed to be the relationships—some benign, some criminal—involved in the Sunset Hills murders. Owen weaved his narrative, starting with the first benefit enhancement vote in 2000 and continuing through the years until a practical concern conceived an ambitious idea that gave birth to a murderous conspiracy with Kemp at its hub.

"We missed something important as we tried to make sense of the individual puzzle pieces," Owen admitted. "We couldn't see the motive, the driving purpose behind it all. But after talking to Lily a few nights ago, I think I stumbled upon it. Rather than me explain what I believe to be the motive in my own words, I want you to watch a video I found online."

Owen played the clip on his phone. At first, J.R. was bewildered. But his expression evolved gradually from confusion and suspicion to recognition and revelation. When the video had ended, Owen propped his elbows atop the table with this chin resting on his folded fingers.

"You have to admit, it's at least possible."

J.R. slid both hands over his shaven head and leaned back into his chair. "This is serious," he said quietly. "How sure are you?"

"Fifty, sixty percent. We won't know for sure unless Kemp opens up. That's why I needed to talk to you before you arrest him. If I am right about the ultimate motive, we have to be strategic with how and when we decide to act."

"Yeah, I see what you mean." He looked into Owen's eyes for a long moment and exhaled angst. "Okay. Let's go over this theory of yours again."

An hour later, holding a page full of notes and to-do lists, they left with a plan to bring the fight to the enemy.

"Timing is critical," Owen reminded. "The rumor is that an announcement will happen within three weeks. That gives you time to get your evidence and questions in order. I'll prepare for my part in the meantime."

Over the next several days, J.R. met with his best criminologists and a colleague in the prosecutor's office to construct a water-tight case against Kemp based on the reams of evidence pulled from the Oakland facility and Victor's phone.

"We can't risk giving him an out because we overlooked something," he told his team. "Let's recheck our sources and evidence. We are only going to push Kemp into a corner if our facts are beyond dispute. Let's take another look at every detail with fresh eyes."

"We just finished indexing every page," a member of the team protested. "Can't office staff check our work so we can move on to another project?"

"Trust me, this is the biggest priority. We need to make withholding the truth painful for Kemp, and that only happens if he knows he is cornered. He needs to beg for mercy. Only then will the truth come out. Let's get back to work, everyone."

The Sunset Hills Police Department completed its re-check the following day but held off sending an arresting unit to Hemlock Pharmaceuticals. It was not an easy sell.

"Hold tight," J.R. repeated to impatient co-workers. "I'm just as anxious as you are, but the time isn't right yet."

Grumbling rose from staff to the police chief, who confronted J.R. about the seemingly unnecessary delay. Behind closed doors, J.R. laid out before his boss the full case against Kemp and his supposed end game. After the presentation, the chief gave simple instructions to the officer: "If anyone hassles you again about dragging your feet, send them to me. You strike when you are ready."

With that, J.R. returned to his office, satisfied, waiting for the go-ahead from Owen.

« 22 »

When the morning dew still sparkled on California's luscious Central Valley, when the bells from church steeples rang across miles of countryside, when everything good and true and beautiful seemed capable of conquering all that was darkness, Owen called J.R. with the long-awaited news.

"The campaign is scheduled to announce on Tuesday morning. We need Kemp tomorrow. Is that possible?"

"Ask and you shall receive."

J.R. contacted his team to schedule the arrest the following day. At sunrise on Monday, they met at the station, gathered the necessary supplies and began caravanning to the Bay Area. En route, J.R. read and reread the evidence linking Kemp to the murders. Undoubtedly, the executive would deny every accusation leveled against him. To admit to the charges would be foolish, as he would immediately lose everything he valued. J.R. assumed his strategy would be to

305

deny, deflect and perhaps intimidate his accusers, as was his past practice. The documents in J.R.'s hands would serve to undermine Kemp's efforts and, more importantly, leave him pondering his future incarceration on the long drive back to Sunset Hills.

"I give Kemp sixty minutes before he buckles," he texted to Owen. "Will call you when it's over."

As Hemlock came into sight, J.R. turned to his team in the back rows of the SUV and reminded the agents of their assignments and positions.

"The fourth floor has a second access point, probably a private stairwell leading to another exit. As soon as we reach the administration building, I want two of you to run around the facility to prevent a back-door escape. Stay on coms and notify us if you see the target."

The black vehicle stopped abruptly in front of the lobby entrance. J.R. and three officers walked briskly to the security guards inside.

"We have a warrant for Dorian Kemp's arrest."

One motioned to a camera staring down at them, and a senior guard promptly emerged from a nearby room. As he approached J.R., the man spoke into his radio quickly and quietly before greeting the guests and hearing their business. He escorted them to the private elevator, through the glass corridor and to the locked doors separating Kemp from the outside world.

Warrant in hand, J.R. stepped onto the executive's floor with his team. Their fingers rested nimbly on their belts as the secretary opened a second locked door and escorted them to Kemp's office. Without bothering to knock, they walked in. Kemp sat behind his large mahogany desk smoking a cigar while casually fingering a silver dollar. To his right, wearing a smart dress suit and a don't-mess-with-me expression stood an unknown woman who, like a sentinel on duty, stared at the entrants. J.R. walked to the desk, laid the warrant down and announced: "Dorian Kemp, you are under arrest. You have the right to remain silent."

"Let me stop you there, Little," he said, placing his cigar in an ashtray and exhaling in the officer's direction. "I thought this was taken care of months ago. You could have saved yourself a lot of time by just calling to schedule an appointment to discuss whatever problems you *think* you have with me."

"Anything you say can and will be used against you in a court of law," J.R. continued.

"And I suppose I also have a right to an attorney?" Kemp mocked.

"That's right," J.R. replied coldly.

"How fortuitous! I've got one right here. I'd like to introduce Carolyn, my general counsel and the person who is going to tell you to go screw yourselves. Carolyn, you're up."

He motioned to her to begin talking.

"I request a day to consult with Mr. Kemp regarding this matter. As the chief executive of Hemlock, responsible for hundreds of employees and their livelihoods, he deserves that allowance."

"This is not a corporate matter, ma'am," J.R. replied. "Mr. Kemp is being arrested for conspiracy and first-degree murder. That's *criminal* activity. So, unless you represent him *personally*, I suggest you step aside and let us do our job."

She started to reply when a look of uncertainty flashed in her eyes. J.R. saw it immediately. He wondered if Kemp had informed her of his extracurricular activity or if she was hearing about it for the first time. He suspected the latter.

"Do you have anything to say before we take your boss to jail?"

Again, the woman hesitated. Kemp grew impatient.

"Go on, Carolyn. Tell them what they can do with that warrant."

She mumbled a few indiscernible syllables.

"Now, Carolyn!" he shouted.

The officers moved around the desk and handcuffed him as the attorney stepped aside. "I—I am sorry, Dorian. I represent Hemlock. I'm a corporate attorney, not a criminal law specialist. But I know someone who is. I'll make a call right now."

Before leaving, she knelt beside Kemp, her countenance tinged with disbelief. "Is there any basis to what they're saying?" she whispered in his ear.

His lips said no, but the eyes she had come to know over the preceding years betrayed the truth. She pursed her lips and stood up to face him.

"As general counsel for this firm, I can only advise you to not say or do anything without legal representation."

Carolyn moved swiftly from the executive suite without looking back.

"Well, that just leaves us, Dorian," J.R. grinned. "I bet you didn't wake up this morning thinking you'd be arrested and charged with murder. Once word reaches the media and the firestorm commences, I suspect you'll be looking for a new job, assuming you can do that from a jail cell. Tomorrow, investment analysts will downgrade Hemlock's stock, which will cost you millions. The court might even seize your assets, like that beautiful plane I've heard so much about. The public scrutiny and disgrace that follows will be unimaginable. You will lose your house, your cars, your professional reputation and every political favor you've earned—or bought."

Political favors.

Kemp, whose eyes had fallen to his desk and remained there as the officer poured salt on his wound, looked up, projecting a confidence that J.R. knew to be as false as the man himself.

"I want immunity," he said suddenly. "I'll tell you things you wouldn't believe. Truly, you would *not* believe! But only in exchange for not going to prison."

J.R. shook his head dismissively, but Kemp pressed.

"Trust me, you'll want this information. But I won't give it without something in writing, something to protect me."

"There is no way you are staying out of jail. You directed the murders of dozens of retirees. You can't talk your way out of that."

"Maybe I can," Kemp said. "Send your guys out."

J.R. nodded to his team, and they exited the room. Kemp sat with his hands cuffed behind his back, the edges of his forehead glistening, as a stone-faced J.R. pulled a device from his pocket, set it on the desk and pressed "Record."

"You've got five minutes. Don't waste my time and don't withhold anything."

"Do you think I'm stupid? Write up an agreement and we'll sign it. You're not getting a word from me without it."

"Fine."

The officer found a blank sheet of paper, drafted a statement of immunity—as best as he knew how—and added his signature. Kemp read the write-up but clearly was not satisfied. After being uncuffed, he supplemented J.R.'s words with many of his own and then signed the document.

"Now let's get this over with," Kemp snarled as the cuffs

were reapplied.

"Alright," the officer resumed. "Your five minutes has started. Go."

The executive swallowed hard and began telling his story, starting with the events of 2000 and moving forward chronologically. There were so many details to lay bare in such a short time, he often spoke in generalities, but that was sufficient for the present need. To J.R.'s amusement, Kemp's descriptions resembled the interconnected diagram Owen had drawn up weeks earlier.

The kid is going to be so impressed with himself when he finds out, J.R. thought.

Kemp spoke like a man with no inhibitions. He named names, identified political favors, revealed felony intent and even admitted to creating a shell company for unspecified "security" reasons. By the end of the allotted time, when Kemp's telling of the diabolical scheme and its gritty execution had been laid bare, J.R. caught his breath. Kemp ended his confession with a look of sinister satisfaction.

"See, I was just a pawn in all this. I played my part, and as of today, I'm out. My conscience is clean."

J.R. winced with moral repugnance. Kemp continued.

"I held up my end of the bargain. You got your statement. Now it's your turn to act." His voice rose to a growl. "Get these chains off me!"

J.R. stared at his opponent for a long, silent moment before grabbing the recorder and placing it in his pocket.

"Alright, guys, come get him," he said to the waiting deputies.

"Wait, what about our deal? We agreed to my immunity! Get your hands off me! You have no right to touch me! We have a signed agreement. Look at it."

J.R. folded the paper and placed it in his pocket. "It doesn't say anything in here about avoiding arrest. In fact, it's probably not even a valid agreement. We will let the court decide that. In the meantime, we are taking you on an all-expense-paid trip to the Sunset Hill police station."

The mold of towering self-assurance and power affixed to the executive's face devolved into wordless fear as the officers lifted the man to his unsteady feet and escorted him away. Seated in front of the grand desk, J.R. turned to see Kemp stumbling along like a sheep to slaughter.

"You may not see it this way," he added, "but trust me, Dorian, you just performed a great public service."

Owen woke at five o'clock the next morning, showered and put on his only suit. As he ate breakfast, a healthy one compared to his usual boxed fare, he opened a worn notepad—his trusted confidant over the past year—containing meticulous records of all the events, facts and ideas that had led him to this great and terrible day. Memories—mostly bad ones—filled his mind with each page he fingered. He flipped back to the beginning, spending a long moment staring at the first obituary Darcie had given him. Owen felt the familiar guilt-laden ache return to his heart, but he pushed it aside.

"Your death won't be in vain, Darce."

In a very real sense, today was a day of ultimate penance, a point of no return. But he would not face it alone. Owen gathered his notes and media badge and drove to Lily's apartment across town. She opened her door before he knocked, stepped into his arms and kissed him sweetly.

"Are you ready for your big day?" she asked.

"Only if you are there with me."

They held hands to his car and then began their long journey to the steps of the state capitol.

"The news conference begins at ten," he reminded, "so we've got about four hours to get there and find good seats. Do you really believe this will work? If I think too long about it, I get nervous and my mind goes blank. That can't happen."

"How about I help you keep the facts fresh?"

Owen welcomed the refresher. For the first hour of the trip, she read his notes aloud, start to finish, while quizzing him on key points of the investigation. When he came to a detail that slipped his memory, she patiently repeated the information until he could recite it verbatim, rewarding him with a kiss that left rose-colored lipstick on his cheek. Unfortunately, his retention lapses grew more frequent. Time and again, he would forget key facts that he had already committed to memory and then, suddenly, recall them.

"I'm concerned about your forgetfulness, Owen. You recover quickly *now*, but at the conference, I can't prompt you. You'll need to figure out a ..."

She stopped speaking. He turned to look at her.

"What's the matter?"

"The right side of your face is covered in lipstick. I've caught onto your little scheme, mister. No more kisses for you!"

Owen grinned slyly and laughed. "That's too bad. I was about to crown you Teacher of the Year."

They entered downtown Sacramento and navigated the busy streets to the capitol building, where a small crowd had already gathered. Media crews faced their cameras toward the podium that stood at the top of a set of long marble stairs. Owen saw a handful of purple-shirted union members milling around the area. Lily recognized the organization's name inscribed on their shirts.

"They belong to the largest public employee association in California. We occasionally see local members at our board meetings, as I'm sure you remember."

The couple walked tentatively to the seating area designated for the media. It was the first time either had attended anything like this. They claimed two open seats in the front row and waited for the event to begin. Thirty minutes later, reporters and newscasters from media outlets throughout the state joined Owen and Lily. Union supporters and a smattering of diverse people gathered along the sides of the podium as suited men and women exited the capitol rotunda and joined the congregants. Last of all, Governor Lancaster emerged from the building with his wife by his side. He walked to the podium and smiled at the dozen people standing around him. Phones snapped pictures, cameras rolled and a hush descended on the congregation.

"Good morning, everyone," the governor began. "For twenty years, I have served my community, my city and my state in a variety of roles, all of which have been a joy to me and my family. I have had the privilege of meeting thousands of Californians who have taught me the importance of investing in every person: young and old, rich and poor, native and immigrant, housed and homeless, and everyone in between. My mission as a public servant has been to do just that—to serve. I believe, like President John F. Kennedy, that to make a truly great nation, its citizens must be willing to take up the mantle of service for the common good. Sometimes it's a labor of love, and sometimes it requires a great deal of sacrifice. My dear wife can testify to that as I've spent many early mornings and late nights working to ensure the great state of California can provide for those who need it most.

"In my tenure as governor, we have made significant strides to bring fairness and equity to those whom the Good Book calls 'the least of these.' We have worked tirelessly to boost our economy by increasing funding for schools, alternative energy initiatives and entrepreneurial programs that identify great ideas and then help them to grow. We have used the power of government to support our public safety personnel, who guard the sense of security that we hold dear. And we have brought greater efficiency to government by investing in better technology so that we, as public servants, can work on behalf of taxpayers more effectively.

"I stand before you today humbled by the trust you have placed in me. I believe I have served the people of California well. And now, I seek a higher calling, one that would enable me to serve not only my fellow Californians but also my fellow Americans. Today I am announcing my candidacy for President of the United States."

The crowd beside Lancaster applauded, chanting the refrain, "Run, Mike, Run." Several reporters sitting by Owen also clapped, which would not have annoyed him a year ago but produced an eye roll this day. Lily looked at him nervously and smiled. She placed her hand on his.

"Be brave," she whispered.

Lancaster raised his hands to quiet the group.

"Finally, I'd like to thank my loyal supporters. I wouldn't be here without you all. I promise to make you proud on the national stage, to leave an indelible mark on this country like I've left here. At this time, I'd be happy to answer some questions."

Media hands shot up around Owen. One inquired about his campaign staff, another about his fundraising, a third about his political competition, and on and on. The raised hand of an unknown reporter from Sunset Hills failed to attract the attention of the newly minted presidential candidate. As the scheduled time for the news conference drew to a close, Lancaster started to thank everyone for coming when Owen stood up and said, "May I ask a final question?"

"Certainly, young man. And you are?"

"I am a reporter at a small newspaper in a town located a few hours from here. I've been a fan of yours since I was a kid. I even shook your hand once at a rally when you were running for state office."

"Well, it's nice to meet you again," he replied, smiling broadly.

"I am from Sunset Hills. I believe you are familiar with the place."

With these words, Lancaster's expression tightened before gradually relaxing into another toothy smile. Owen's first question flew at him like a steel-tipped arrow.

"In the last year alone, dozens of people have been murdered in my city, all of them eighty-year-old, retired public employees who received a pension from the same retirement agency. As a county supervisor in Sunset Hills, you sat on its Board of Retirement for several years. Were you aware that many of your old constituents had died so coincidentally?"

"Uh, no, I didn't," Lancaster answered. "This has nothing to do with today's announcement. Let's wrap this up. Thank you all for ..."

Owen interrupted, this time more loudly. "And did you know, governor, that the retirees all died from the same assisted-suicide drug, Hemlox, which was manufactured by a man you worked with on the Board of Supervisors? His name is Dorian Kemp. Do you remember him?"

"Vaguely, it was a long time ago. This has nothing to do

with …"

"That's interesting. Mr. Kemp has a *very* clear memory of you. In fact, he was arrested yesterday for conspiring to murder retirees in Sunset Hills using a modified version of the drug that he manufactured. And he seems to think that *you* told him to do it. Why would he think that?"

Lancaster stood motionless, his fear-filled eyes darting from reporter to reporter. Like a deer in headlights, he gaped wordlessly as media faces directed their curious looks from Owen to his unsuspecting target. Owen continued.

"As a long-time fan of yours, I did not believe you were involved in any way with this conspiracy. But then I looked into the pension plan you used to oversee, and I discovered that when pensioners die early, that reduces the cost of the plan, which improves its funding status. Everybody likes that, right? Why would that be important to someone like you? The explanation I came up with was that you thought a stronger pension plan would gain you votes in your hometown. But I was wrong."

Owen paused to let Lancaster breathe a sigh of relief before crushing the momentary respite.

"Mr. Kemp explained the real reason: You had your sights on the governor's mansion and later the White House. If the pension plan became insolvent due, in part, to your actions, you would never get elected. That is why you directed him to 'fix' the problem in Sunset Hills and left the dirty work to him. In exchange, you would use your influence in the Assembly and Senate to hastily award his company a sweetheart contract to manufacture a drug that only became legal *after* you pushed an assisted-suicide law through the legislature with the help of Assemblyman Ramos. Does any of this ring a bell?"

"This is all ridiculous," Lancaster announced, cheeks flush. He turned on his heels and stepping briskly toward the capitol to escape the spotlight. As he approached the rotunda entrance, the doors opened suddenly and J.R. stepped out with a pair of officers at his side. To the shock of everyone watching, except Owen and Lily, J.R. read the governor his rights and arrested him. Media outlets live-streamed the dramatic spectacle across the nation as the local crowd gasped and fell silent. The purple shirts and suits dispersed quickly while the media pool turned toward Owen, some glaring betrayal and some astonishment. Lily rose to his side as he addressed his peers.

"I'm sorry to have ruined this event, but I think this story will sell more of your newspapers and airtime. My associate has a document containing all the information I just shared and much more. Feel free to use it to write your own articles and show scripts. My contact information is at the bottom."

Lily walked down the aisles and handed fact sheets to everyone present. Meanwhile, reporters peppered Owen with questions: "How did you learn about this?" "What else do you know about Lancaster and Kemp's alliance?" "How can we verify your sources?" "Do you have an ax to grind with the governor?"

Owen deftly handled the inquiries, having all the important facts of the investigation at the forefront of his mind, thanks to Lily. Standing at the back of the seating area, opposite Owen, she smiled proudly at the man who had just brought down a political giant.

« 23 »

The *Sunset Times* celebrated its newfound notoriety, brought about by the publishing of Owen's exposé, with an office party on Friday night. That week, journalists across the nation had bombarded the newspaper with requests for comment. The coverage was largely fair, although certain outlets—the usual suspects—excoriated Owen with *ad hominem* attacks and innuendo. He ignored them. The shallow adoration of his media peers no longer held the mantle of importance it once did for him.

"It might be too soon to say, but I think I've matured through all this," he told Al, who stood at the outer rim of the festivities with a flask of something spirited in his hand. "A year ago, I would have given anything to write for the *L.A. Times*, to be the next Woodward. But I can do that here just as easily. It's true, we don't live in a metropolis, but our little city has its charms. It took me almost losing my grandma to discover that."

A tipsy co-worker bumped into Al while trying to dance. The old editor recoiled and nudged the reveler back to the crowd. He took a step backward toward the safety of his office.

"You sure this is what you want? These folks?"

Owen watched the mass of partygoers eating finger foods, lining up for karaoke and laughing at themselves. He nodded approvingly.

"Yes, Al. These are my people."

Warmth and happiness filled the newsroom as everyone savored the victory earned by Owen for the struggling newspaper. Even the gray publisher left his distant office to join in the fun. He found two women chatting pleasantly and interrupted them with an uplifted finger.

"This reminds me of when I was a young newspaperman, back in the respectable days of professional journalism. Oh, we had fun then. A bully good time!"

He droned on until one of the ladies cut into the old man's musings. "Yeah, but it couldn't have been as good as this."

Owen overheard the remark and smiled appreciatively.

"They never threw a party like this for one of *my* articles," Al commented. "Then again, I never confronted a presidential candidate. I suppose that deserves a bit of recognition. This past year has been hard on both of us. But now, I can finally go to bed without having nightmares of photos of my brother's family. I'd like to get my hands on the punk who took those pictures and left them on my doorstep."

Owen nodded in agreement as Al turned aside and took a surreptitious drink from his metallic container.

"I've been mulling over your story, kid, but something still doesn't make sense. Why would Kemp ever agree to do what Lancaster asked? He must have known it was illegal."

"That issue stumped me, too, until my police buddy let me listen to the recording of Kemp at his arrest. According to him, Lancaster had made a back-room deal with the unions prior to the 2000 and 2005 pension benefit enhancements: He agreed to lobby the other county Supervisors for the higher benefits in exchange for the unions' full support when he ran for state office. Kemp found out about the deal and threatened to expose Lancaster in the middle of his State Assembly campaign. After he won and left Sunset Hills for Sacramento, he sued Kemp for blackmail and won. The case was publicly listed and therefore a political liability, so he used his influence to seal the court records. That action protected both men and their future careers."

"So, years later, they had each other by the short hairs?"

"Yeah, each had something to lose. Lancaster's ambitions were obvious. Kemp also needed to maintain a stellar exterior for his own corporate rise. Both guys kept quiet and used one another to get what they each wanted: money and power. After State Assemblyman Lancaster became State Senator Lancaster, he started looking at the governor's job and, according to Kemp, worried about his chances of winning."

"Why? He was a popular guy at the time."

"The big risk was if the pension plan's funding status continued to decline. That would cost local taxpayers millions more dollars, and you can be sure he knew that fiscal black mark would haunt him in the papers. That alone could sway independent voters."

"But Lancaster didn't vote for either benefit increase, not in 2000 or 2005," Al recalled. "Why would he feel responsible for the pension plan's poor funding? It wasn't his fault, at least not officially."

"True. But remember, he abstained from both votes,

which he thought was smart politically. But that fence-sitting put him in a bind. On the one hand, not voting *for* the new benefits would upset union members, who would rightly claim that he did not stand up for their interests. The last thing a politician wants is to anger the public safety unions. But the other side of the coin was equally problematic. By not voting *against* the new benefits, he could not really claim to care for the tax-paying masses that represented a larger voting bloc."

"What a pansy."

"Several years went by and Lancaster, now looking to re-side at the White House, realized he had a potential public relations problem that needed to go away. Having sat a stint on the Board of Retirement, he understood pensions enough to know that changing the all-important mortality assumption would reduce the plan's long-term liabilities and short-term costs. That could turn bad PR into good PR—and just in time for his presidential campaign. That required retirees to die on time."

"And that's when he hatched the plan?"

"Yep. I've started calling it his 'pension plan.' I thought the double meaning was clever. The really unfortunate thing is that if the governor actually understood how pensions worked, he would never have focused on retiree deaths. There are other ways to keep taxpayer costs from skyrocket-ing."

Al gave a quizzical look. "Really? Like what?"

"Oh, let's just call it my pension reform wish list. The goal would be to strengthen public pension plans while keeping local governments out of bankruptcy. That's a tough nee-dle to thread, by the way." Owen shook his head. "But it will never happen with short-sighted politicians in charge. The longer they wait to make real reforms, the more pain we will *all* feel when the dam breaks. We are one recession away from catastrophe."

"Sounds like a new series you should write," the editor hinted.

Owen patted him on the back. "I'm not ready to make more enemies yet, but I promise to think about it."

◊ ◊ ◊

That weekend, Owen attended another party, this one for his beloved grandma who had safely turned eighty years old. The same people attended as last year with the notable additions of J.R. and Lily, who sat with Ruthie on the couch swapping embarrassing stories about Owen. He listened patiently, knowing that on her birthday, she could do and say whatever she liked and he must bear it tolerantly. Last year, it was a lecture on the impracticality of socialism. This year, it was stories of him as a toddler hiding his dirty diapers around the house.

"Really, Gram, is this necessary? There are so many other interesting topics besides my diapers."

"Oh, just you wait until you're a grandpa," she replied. "You'll do the same thing. And besides, this young lady needs to know what she's getting into with you."

J.R. raised an eyebrow at Owen. "Remember what I told you about a woman taking over your life. Don't say I didn't warn you." He glanced at Lily and grinned knowingly.

Owen turned toward her and tilted his head questioningly. "Is that true, Lily?"

She folded her hands on her knees and looked the picture of innocence. "Shall we find out?"

"You already won my heart. What choice do I have?"

Ruthie, wide eyed, looked at J.R. and rose from her seat. "Officer, would you help me with pies in the kitchen, please?"

"I'd be happy to. It's getting way too serious out here for my liking."

As they passed by, Owen left his chair and sat next to Lily.

"So, what do you think?" he inquired. "I'm in the news business. You're in the pension business. Is there any chance that representatives from two contentious factions could find common ground?"

"Hmm, I suppose it depends. If you quote me in the paper, then I am afraid there is no hope for us. But," she added, placing her arm around his shoulder and leaning in, "if you mind your grammar and your manners, I might stick around for a very long time. What say you to that, newspaperman?"

Owen looked into her bright eyes until he caught a glimpse of a long, happy future by her side. He placed his forehead gently against hers and answered, "I think that's a story worth pursuing."

# # #

Made in the USA
Las Vegas, NV
29 May 2021

23767460R00192